S0-BGV-031

PRAISE FOR *TANTRUM*

"An intense, gripping political thriller, filled with suspense."
—Tony Collins, author of *Games Women Play*

"Provides a realistic account of the often overlooked in society. Graphic imagery and poetic flair fuels fire behind this must read."
—Walter Vickerie, author of *Swordfight*

"Suspenseful prose and vivid imagery makes everything so real. Readers can't help but to look over their shoulders."
—God Math, author of *Ugly/Beautiful: Me*

"A roller-coaster ride of a novel! Fast-paced—the action is vivid."
—L. Raven James, *RawSistaz Book Review*

"Combines political analysis of DuBois, courage of Baldwin, storytelling brilliance of Wright, and passion of Himes."
—Damon "Amin" Meadows, author of *Convict's Candy*

"A political thriller that brings jolts to readers. Changes the way you view politics and news media forever."
—Castillo, author of *Ghost Town Hustlers*

"*TANTRUM* brings you up-close and personal to the dangers Black politicians face in governmental affairs."
—Jay Bey, author of *Club Avenue*

"Ellison has taken us on a journey filled with vivid imagery, dynamic characters and seductive plot twists."
—Blue, author of *Tattooed Tears*

"A cleverly composed, political thriller that leaves you in awe."
—Rall, author of *For The Love Of Honey*

"Brilliantly captures the essence of scorched-earth politics, combining beguiling characters with unpredictable scenarios."

—Craig Thompson, *Profiles with Craig Thompson, UPN 24*

"Mind-spinning fictional story of political schemes and assassination plots among local political and religious figures."

—*Writer Blocks*

"Written with a captivating, fast-paced flair and compelling, conservative style. Grabs your attention."

—Rodney Carmichael, *Rolling Out*

GHETTOHEAT® PRODUCTIONS

GHETTOHEAT®
CONVICT'S CANDY
HARDER
AND GOD CREATED WOMAN
LONDON REIGN
SONZ OF DARKNESS
GHOST TOWN HUSTLERS
SWORDFIGHT
GAMES WOMEN PLAY
DIRTY WINDOWS
TATTOOED TEARS
SKATE ON!
SOME SEXY, ORGASM 1
UGLY/BEAUTIFUL: ME
CLUB AVENUE
FOR THE LOVE OF HONEY

Copyright © 2008 *TANTRUM* by CHARLES D. ELLISON

Excerpts from:
GHETTOHEAT® © 2008 by HICKSON
CONVICT'S CANDY © 2006 by
DAMON "AMIN" MEADOWS and JASON POOLE
HARDER © 2006 by SHA
AND GOD CREATED WOMAN © 2007 by MIKA MILLER
LONDON REIGN © 2007 by A. C. BRITT
SONZ OF DARKNESS © 2008 by DRU NOBLE
GHOST TOWN HUSTLERS © 2008 by CASTILLO
GAMES WOMEN PLAY © 2008 by TONY COLLINS
DIRTY WINDOWS © 2008 by JOI MOORE
TANTRUM 2 © 2008 by CHARLES D. ELLISON
TATTOOED TEARS © 2008 by BLUE
CLUB AVENUE © 2008 by JAY BEY
FOR THE LOVE OF HONEY © 2008 by RALL
SKATE ON! © 2008 by HICKSON
SOME SEXY, ORGASM 1 © 2008 by DRU NOBLE

Published by GHETTOHEAT®, LLC
P.O. BOX 2746, NEW YORK, NY 10027, USA

Library of Congress Control Number: 2008921420
ISBN: 978-0-9742982-5-2
Printed in the USA. First Edition, September 2008

Sale of this book without a front cover may be unauthorized. If this book is without a cover, it may have been reported to the publisher as "unsold or destroyed" and neither the author(s) nor the publisher may have received payment for it.

No part of this book may be reproduced, stored in or introduced into a retrieval system, or transmitted, in any form or by any means (electronic, mechanical, photocopying, recording or otherwise), without prior written permission of both the copyright owner and the publisher of this book; except in the case of brief quotations embodied in critical articles and reviews.

PUBLISHER'S NOTE

This is a work of fiction. Any names to historical events, real people, living and dead, or to real locales are intended only to give the fiction a setting in historic reality. Other names, characters, places, businesses and incidents are either the product of the author's imagination or are used fictitiously, and their resemblance, if any, to real life counterparts is entirely coincidental.

A GHETTOHEAT PRODUCTION

tantrum

WITHDRAWN

CHARLES D. ELLISON

Dedicated to Dian: best friend, partner, wife, relentless love.
And my dearest daughter, Croix—the future.

In loving memory of my late father, Lawrence Ellison

CONTENTS

ACKNOWLEDGMENTS

Great amounts of time, energy, angst, glory and joy go into writing a book. It doesn't matter if it's a hundred pages or a thousand—that being the case, it would not be right to overlook the support of so many.

Infinite thanks to my precious wife, Dian—her love and loyalty keeps the pen steady and the words flowing. I remain in lasting debt to our children Croix, Tkeyah and Khadijah, each providing inspiration and constant backbone.

Writing would be an unbearable chore rather than the fun and fulfilling exercise it is, if it had not been for my grandmother, Mary Robinson.

Streams of appreciation fall upon combined families: Ellisons, Randalls, Johnsons, Allens, Butlers and others. Without them, there would be little purpose in completing these volumes. From grandmom's constitution, grandpa's brilliance, to Aunt Susie's jazz; and from mom's patient wisdom to dad's depth and charm. There are not enough words to express that appreciation.

Another long overdue "thank you" is embedded in the spirit of this work. Abington Friends School, including Carolyn Frieder and her daughter Susan Frieder, who both literally, saved me at the crossroads. Many thanks also go to former AFS Headmaster and outgoing Sidwell Friends head, Bruce Stewart. From Beverly Cumberbatch, to Philadelphia Express, to Gloria Richardson and Operation Understanding.

Last but not least, big up and deep appreciation to HICKSON, CEO of GHETTOHEAT® for taking this project on. In his admirable struggle to completely redefine "urban literature" as we know it, he's supporting creative expression and opportunity, but HICKSON is contributing—on various levels, to the collective good by simply publishing issues, most of us would prefer ignoring.

Many thanks go out to many more. I'm certain I've missed more than a few, but for those reading now, my appreciation for your support and encouragement remains solid.

You know who you are.

AUTHOR'S NOTE

At the completion of this work, my beloved hometown of *Philadelphia* is gripped in a wave of homicidal violence that has surpassed the national average. Philly's violence is so intense that it's a national headline. It occurs at a rate of nearly two killings a day, not to mention the scores of individuals who are wounded, injured, or emotionally scarred from the deaths of sons, daughters, family and friends.

That violence is against the backdrop of a city in political and economic turmoil: there's high unemployment, crumbling schools, abandoned homes, dirty streets and dysfunctional families. There's the perception of a void in political and community leadership. Creative solutions are lacking. It's all rather distressing, sad and heartbreaking.

Much of *TANTRUM* is a reflection on current events and commentary on *what if*. Still, the novel remains a work of fiction. Any similarity to real people is mere coincidence and unintentional. Actual places and events, however, have been used to maintain, in some instances, geographic and historical integrity.

Charles D. Ellison
June 2008

tantrum

act I: blood & paper cuts

Personal, private, solitary pain is more terrifying than what anyone else can inflict.

—Jim Morrison

chapter 1

BROAD & LEHIGH STREETS

DAY 1

Walking past *Broad Street* delusions is the anonymous, homeless and dirty dread-headed dark man of no darkness, but the blackness of bad happenings consuming him. It's not time that weathers the man as much as the distance of many endless avenues, nameless streets and missed beats thrown off by skips, and fits of gambled fate.

The man owns little beyond an empty wallet and a ripped backpack that survives the dogged survivalist terrain of his depressing, urban adventure. This is what he does, how he exists—the day-in, day-out of a vagabond walk that never ends. And so on this day, the man tackles a long stretch of *Broad Street,* tripping over buckled sidewalks when, for no reason because, his life has no reason, worn sneakers from the local shelter, suddenly spring a right turn into a gas station.

There's nothing unique about this particular gas station since it resembles every other gas station in the city that has pumps, broken car vacuums and dingy mini-marts selling junk food, expired condoms and cigarettes behind bulletproof windows.

The man then attempts to add a little personality to it, adjusting into street-beggar mode while sticking his hands out: "Excuse me—do you have a *dollar* for a bite to eat?" He poses a very strategic question, because it somehow cracks the irritated faces, and gritty *Nicetown* dispositions of people passing him by. A polite question, but it's also fast and pointed enough, yet touching in his acclaimed search for food.

Which is bullshit, the man thinks, *because there's a methadone clinic only blocks away where I might be able to grip a bottle of Oxycontin to wash the day's sins away!*

Most ignore his requests for random charity; a few are pretty *damn* nasty about it. But, a good number offer loose change and crumpled dollar bills—a rare few out of compassion; the rest out of guilt or something like that. He despises the occasional smart-*ass* who will test his *"bite to eat"* by offering to buy the food instead. Those walks to the carryout across the street waste time, and he gets vicious heartburn from the *MSG*. But the man has little choice but to play it off.

We will call him "Dread". His identity is unknown because it is filed away in abandoned houses, train yards, warehouses and cardboard boxes under bridges. There are the humiliations, of course: the muggings at night, drunken kids looking for a bum fight; he might score nauseating sex from an infected crack-head, who requires his scarce dollar for the next fix.

At some point, Dread figured *he* was all worth forgetting. Driver's license, Social Security card, and an old photo of a daughter Dread thinks is his—all of that is at the bottom of a brown, polluted *Schuylkill River.* Strangely enough though, he possesses a library card. The books keep a fraction of sanity maintained, and the man always brings them back on time.

While at the gas station, Dread stops for a moment to case the scene. It's morning, and the stressed-out people are moving about their business quickly, moving briskly in an effort to end the day, as soon as they humanly can. They all shower him with petty looks and pitiless stares, as a frigid fall wind blows through *Broad Street.*

The ominous, refitted brick and metal frame of an abandoned clothing factory rises above *Broad* and *Lehigh* like a haunted Scottish castle on an urban landscape. Within two years, Dread expects a multi-million dollar condominium park to replace the old factory halls across the street from the gas station. If he doesn't get harassed by the impending police presence in the wake of yuppie emergence on his corner, then Dread anticipates new revenue streams from wealthier individuals. He argued this point just yesterday with another lost, dingy soul under the *Ben Franklin Bridge,* while on an extended evening drink binge.

"Them yuppies movin' in? That's loot, son! That's guilty, modern professionals tryin' to get a conscience, so they throw money at you!"

Dread was talkative that night, lit and limed on a killer pint of rum he snatched from the corner liquor store. All Dread could see was a blurred crescendo of *Camden's* skyline lights, dimpling the *Jersey* side of *Delaware,* and the distorted, hamburger meat-face of his other homeless friend—who was just as hopeless as Dread.

"Dread—what you talkin' 'bout? That's called gentrification, my friend. And I will bet that it's not as progressive as you make it sound. It's overpriced condos, rising property taxes and poor folks getting pushed out of homes, because of unfair property assessments," his friend piped on about the evils of outsiders moving into blighted neighborhoods, as if he had personal knowledge about it. Perhaps it's the reason behind his present misfortune.

Dread snorted.

Speech slurred.

Back slumped.

Genitals burning from some unknown *STD.*

"Seems like people livin' there should've been takin' better care of the hood," Dread stated, laughing and spitting spittle of rum. *"Now they want to get vexed because 'The Man' then moved in, and figured how to make profit and high life off rundown homes."*

With an unorganized band of raggedy vagrants and addicts crowding around them to listen in, that evening's conversation carried a political talk show tone quality to it.

So, in the meantime, Dread watches his progress arrive: the construction crews banging away, nails hammered, wood split, massive cranes slowly moving unidentifiable objects in mid-air. The noise scrambles the concrete serenity of a *Northtown* morning, transforming it into a cluttered, neo-ghetto symphony.

Contractors and day laborers with scarred fingers and aging faces, bleed the filth of work that flows into puddles of caked drudgery on stubbed chins. They're like a battalion of ants building out a mound of dirt, but it's a louder, stronger, defiant intensity, that rocks cold metallic atmosphere, and stirs stained pigeons into wing-flapping fury.

Angry birds looking for breadcrumbs and cigarette butts flutter about the building's noise in aimless drift. Dread sees glimpses of opportunity in this, but his sanity is long consumed by a defeated, soul-worn rough. The man's life's file is heavy from the weight of unkempt locks bearing on the skull. Pacing asphalt amid the alcoholic ads, lottery billboards, and scent of price-gouging fuel, Dread pokes his soul for new answers.

"How can I find work with the hard hats banging away up there?" he asks while scanning the organized chaos of construction. *My situation*, Dread continues, *is as dry as that salty stretch of burning funk I can't seem to shake. Damn!* he curses inwardly. *That funk of no direction, funk of regression, that odor of no hope, broken promises and exhausted salutations.*

It's here where the *BANG! CLANK! BANG! CLANK!* of a ground excavator is overheard, blasting the bitter silence of the begging man's introspections.

I am in need of a much-needed break from misery, Dread cries. *I am misery. ...A gig sure could reverse it*! he screams back at the excavator, and the GOD Dread thinks will hear him. Dread looks at the building again, contemplating what dirty or worked hand to shake, hammer to pound, and slab of timber to cut.

Suicide is *not* an option.

Total self-destruction holds no meaning for Dread. Long ago, he learned that men made not only livings, but strove to build legacies in life and death. At least Dread had that much right.

Something, he struggles to guarantee himself, *will give*.

Giving did give in the form of a pricey *SUV*, turning a hard left into the mini-mart parking lot. Immediately recognized and registered with affectionate glee, is the face of its celebrity driver. There's momentary excitement around the gas pumps because, everyone seems to know this cat.

It's like a blessing to Dread. Is it final reprieve for the homeless soul in the face of blistering torment?

Or, supposes Dread, *a bowl of soup on a famished day?*

When the driver appears, however, there are no scenes of Roman gladiators on chariots, or tunic-wearing plebes blowing coliseum horns to announce his arrival. It's a muted entrance. The driver is only stopping for gas.

It just so happens that he's an elected official, a rather well known city Councilman with a controversial populist appeal. Light bulbs are blazing in Dread's head, dimmed and near expired like the exposed bulbs burning wires at the housing project. Still, the man's thoughts on this opportunity (for Dread's the eternal opportunist) are of no deliberate speed; nor did he expect the corresponding, almost metaphysical qualities of this meeting of chance.

While eyeing the sophisticated vision of three-piece suited political high life dismounting trendy automobile, Dread is inspired to mental heights that once teased him as unattainable for many years.

Here, flushes Dread into a jubilee of twisted hair locks, *is my chance*.

Councilman, moving in no perceived rush, parks his vehicle to pump number "5", being superstitious. Men of influence duly appreciate the significance of luck, even during moments when they need simple necessities such as gas.

(*We digress for a moment here because the reader is perplexed about detailing insignificant details like gas pump number "5". But, it's not that insignificant because Councilman won his first election against a heavily funded incumbent by a slim, yet respectable margin of only 5 points. Therefore, it's necessary that he pay homage to "5" when the opportunity presents itself.*)

As the premium grade fuel floods the man's vehicle, public official glances at his platinum watch, with faint attention to the warehouse re-emerging like street *Phoenix* in his home district. Only two blinks away comes Dread.

"Councilman, sir," the homeless man approaches.

"Yes, sir," the politician brightly smiles—his vote-grabbing smile; the smile with the handshake and pulling arm. Only this time, he's *not* shaking hands.

Politician prefers distance, rather than exchange with the homeless man before quaint niceties erupt into election-year promises he knows he can't keep. Besides, conversations with the homeless seemed to always stray south into philosophical explosions, jaundiced further by mental illness.

They became forced forays, dominated by the less fortunate one in the discussion. You couldn't impose the good life you lived by fecklessly shattering the interrupted dreams of the other.

"Sir," inserts Dread, "what I need more than a spared quarter is a job. Would you happen to know anyone in search of extra hands at that building across the street?"

The dreaded man is, indeed, bold.

Do I know anyone? Why, of course I do, Councilman silently smirks. *I let the developers bring the damn plans to me, let them plot and snake their way through* City Hall *since I needed the war money in my campaign chest. I wanted that seat bad! Needed to make the gentrifying compromise so I could make a difference, elsewhere.*

Sizing Dread up, the politician notes his slim, formerly athletic frame, and somewhat sturdy straightness in posture. Dread comes off clean on some level, an honest, good work ethic clean. He seems to be a man who tries—at the very least—down, but not all out.

Dread seems fit for this type of work. No harm in an innocent reference steered the foreman's way. And Councilman reserves the oddest feeling of instinctive comfort with this broken soul on *Broad Street.*

Never mind that Dread is homeless, and no mention of that swank body odor permeating the formalities between them. Everyone, according to Councilman, deserves a second chance.

In fact, once this tank is full I'll walk him over there, Councilman thinks. *Not enough good deeds to bless my day so on with it.*

Plus, people are watching. Politician has to do something.

"Certainly, friend. Give me a second and I'll introduce you to the supervisor," the politician lies. Even though he knows the middleman who arranged the campaign contributions, Councilman could care *less* about an obscure construction site foreman. But, everyone recognizes the politician—or should if they don't.

The clout alone should offer a miracle of sorts, a bit of momentary public relations and image boosting for a legislator, once accused of consorting with aggressive, urban developers, at the expense of the poor.

Dread is as stunned as his smile draws long. Out of months, near now going on years, is a wallow of self-pity and inner loathing that has reached its end. What better note, what sweeter taste than Dread's town's most celebrated public son, snapping the vicious cycle into oblivion. That's much unintended joy, and too much to swallow in one chilly fall morning. It isn't the usual "Dread day", hence his signal to absorb the silver lining of daylight and Heaven bestowed, when Hell had frozen over dozens of previous nine lifetimes.

Small talk bursts into an assault of changing subjects as they cross the street. It goes from light conversation, to heavy bit on the homeless man's life. Every detail and inch of Dread's soul pours onto the sidewalk.

As Dread banters on while Councilman winces in quiet desperation, a staring finger seated against the trigger of an automatic rifle goes unnoticed, some several hundred yards away. Its menacing barrel is still on the mark, ready to burst twenty-five sleek rounds into Councilman's back.

The scope on the gun is steady.

An assassin has been following him all day.

The gunman smiles briefly, shining pride at the dented sedan he personally outfitted and rigged for this mission. Every window in the vehicle is covered in a deep black tint, so no one on the outside can see him. The rifle barrel gently fits into a small front windshield hole while propped atop a three-legged stand, gripping the dashboard.

The car itself is barely noticeable. It fits in nicely with the usual long, depressing stretch of old, gas-guzzling *American* sedans—some abandoned, which line any typical *Philadelphia* street.

All that moves are the gunman's drops of sweat, moistening the black steel barrel. The weapon gradually trusts its mark as the targeted politician continues his conversation, unaware of unwanted attention behind him.

There's a devilish, grim reaper quality to the assassin's patience—the iceman will cometh, the smoke of mirrors boasting an evil mystique behind the loaded finger. He has carefully actualized the situation, plotting multiple scenarios in his trained mind: *If I hit him from here, the blood will splatter there, but if I catch him from that angle, he's less likely to die slowly. If I lower the scope another inch, one or two rounds will enter the skull and exit an eye socket or nose, yet if I shoot like this, gauging wind speed, bystanders will be more distracted by the sound than the image of a politician, falling to the ground in a spray of his own blood.*

The assassin imagines himself plotting endlessly through the thick grass of a *South American* jungle, ignoring the bites and nibbles of antagonistic insects, all irritated by his presence and nature's wild.

Back in the real world, he's pressing the gas slowly, moving stealthily past stop signs and crosswalks. The assassin has been moving like this since Councilman left his *City Hall* office, the assassin careful not to blow cover on his marked path, each step driven, and as deliberate as the brain counseled reflex. Concentrating on the plot at hand plows through each gust of wind this cold morning, the target unconscious of the pale hand casing him through tinted windows.

When the shots pop and the bullet rounds push lethal heat from its chamber, few witnesses today can actually say they saw it. If they claim to have watched the whole event unfold, they're lying because it all moves too fast and superhuman for normal consumption.

Yet, instead of hitting the politician, the first few rounds drills right into Dread's unsuspecting head and back, pushing the hot metal's rapturous call for a killing. To his horrible end and hard luck, the homeless man's cheeks explodes into a fierce vinculum of blood and oxygen, propelling a violent clutch for red air; followed by the epileptic crawl on crimson-stained sidewalk.

Dread shakes fast in his last, virtuous, silent probe for vital signs, frantically watching Councilman's eyes dwell on the split orifice in the man's head; a flood of burgundy flesh once recognized as Dread's face. Perforating tissue ruptures a deep canal of veins breaching the temples, and final flashes of consciousness.

The politician falls quickly to the ground for cover and a split-second reaction to break Dread's fall to asphalt. He holds the wounded homeless close in his lap, pressing forward for answers in a lawless stream of thoughts.

It all moves fast—very fast.

Councilman's still dodging a salvo of bullets coming from several different directions, and has managed to pull himself and Dread behind a construction dumpster.

This man took a bullet...for me? Was that for me?

And it is here when life fast reverses before him, politician randomly thinking of the day thus far: the morning shave, splashing his election-ready grill in a hurried throw of cologne; the smiling *Korean* lady at the local cleaners, handing him fresh-smelling, heavily starched shirts. It is here Councilman silently swears to meet the *unholy assailant, the barbaric son-of-a-bitch, the ignoble punk* who housed him, and his newly-found friend, now dying in politician's arms; Councilman's suit and new shirt soaking in a warm spin cycle, of an unfortunate stranger's blood.

Every eye at the corner of *Broad* and *Lehigh* saw politician shoot back. He aligned the rifle pops with their origin, and marked the unmarked car with dark windows. But, besides Councilman, no one else caught eye of "...the other guy", the unknown gunman was too quick.

"Was like...light speed," a kid went "*OOH-OOH*" in debriefs with homicide detectives, struggling to piece the broad daylight shooting together. Witnesses only caught politician's angry hand pull a .45 from a hidden rib holster. As he fired back, Councilman's pops popped louder than the first shots of the invisible gunman. Pinching flashes, loud blasts, and smoke rose from the *Chevy,* as burning tires sped away; the perpetrating weasel with no license plate.

The sting of city wind chill falls upon the open wound in Dread's head, violated by rocky shreds of broken glass, and GOD forbidding whatever else. An unexpected punch of drilling steel transgressed his skull a second within the span of time he saw the rifle, pushing Councilman out of harm's way.

Perhaps this is what Dread's life was all about, what had prepared him all this time—to save this important man's life at the expense of his own. In those seconds, the countless nights staying warm on the steaming subway vents seemed worth it, his homelessness the training ground for this profound moment.

Seconds later in death, Dread's brain finally collapsed into a soup of warm cranium pus, marking the grand opening of a new anatomical outlet.

Broad and *Lehigh* becomes very silent.

chapter 2

5th & DIAMOND STREETS, PHILADELPHIA
REWIND: 3 YEARS AGO

"Nick Scribbles'" columns were anxious plucks and bursts of a political crack addict, his love for *Capitol Hill's* game as intense as a basehead's love for the smoking pipe. He'd evolved into one of the toughest, most merciless, hack political columnists in Washington, D.C., through a mix of eccentricity and knuckled written punches.

Scribbles loved to spit, and when he'd spit, he spat politics. Not that Scribbles wanted to, he'd just felt compelled to let the rabid foam and human juices, flow in dangling bubbles of saliva that hangs from the lip. This is Scribbles today, but it wasn't always that way.

Why?

The Black-Irish boy from *Philly's Fishtown* section was once one of *Ill-town's* most under-rated *Metro* reporters.

So, one day while on his hated crime-story beat for the daily paper, Scribbles lamented his frequent expeditions into that trash-littered coffin known as *North Philly.* This was long before he'd started discussing politics, but it's the drama that tells his story. It was that day when the brutal realities of the young man's misdirected life had become as brutally honest a crass bastard that Scribbles could be.

Change was a foregone conclusion.

He couldn't justify career paths anymore while getting paid to chase armed thugs in wife-beaters, for the *Metro* section's quote-of-the-week. Homicides, drug-deals, drug-busts, and the pertinent challenges of *North Philly* life were of no concern to the general commuting readership of the *Delaware Valley.* They had their picket fences and homeowner associations to attend to.

Thus, Scribbles' painstaking descriptions of riffs between ex-convicts resulting in bloodied sidewalk mess would get conveniently pushed to the bowels of the *Metro* section…which in and of itself—had already played short stop to the home-running front page.

He'd wanted front page.

"I want front page, boss,*"* Scribbles whines to his editor. *"It's rough over there in* North Town. *Some pretty squalid life-and-death stuff worthy of front page placement, don't you think?"*

"People don't wanna *read about hoods on shooting rampages,"* "Old Man Editor", the-potbelly-scratching-snot-dripper says. *"They need the scoop on what you and I would otherwise regard as insignificant. It's the price we pay for a free press, kid."*

At that, "Old Man Editor" closed his office door, and had proceeded to pick his nose when no one was watching.

It was time for a change.

But change will not arrive, Scribbles had thought, *unless a global warming front crashed a mile-wide twister through* Center City, *destroying old-money mansions,* Rittenhouse Square *living rooms and banker watering holes on* Walnut Street. *That's when the "KUMBAYA" moments happen, the privileged class' funky self-realization that they are just as vulnerable as their unemployed Ill-town friends, rotting away in economic sewage.*

In the meantime, Scribbles grew weary and depressed over his meaningless reporter job at the "Daily Bell". The time had arrived where he would soon scrub the crime beat, rubbing his *Black-Irish* ass in the face of *Philadelphia's* fragile fabric. Scribbles would scour those lunchtime journeys to the baseball games where he'd acquired a lifetime of ulcers, watching his home team barely manage playoff muster. How the city frustrated him; poked at and irritated the man.

The punk skaters thrashing public park benches, the piss-pot subway cars sticking to his slacks, the gutters in every oil-slicked back alley, and the crapulent aroma of polluting gas refineries on the way to the airport. The unemployment rate doesn't help it any, mixed in with crumbling schools and hopeless truants loitering the streets. It's a wonder this place functions, Scribbles had thought. And then he decided that it would function without him. Needing change, desperate for change, Scribbles suddenly had bounced.

He disappeared with little announcement or emotional stir. It was a quick detachment from his ugly routine, an urge to shift pace before the nightmares of *North Philly* devoured him. So, Scribbles had left quickly.

A one-way bus ticket to D.C., a backpack of rolled khakis,

denim and T-shirts, with a pocket full of savings stuffed in a money clip.

This was it.

He'd pressed the editor for the vacant *City Hall* correspondent's gig only a day before, and was turned down in a patronizing display of old man's gruff. "Old Man Editor" had swatted at Scribbles as if he were a buzzing gnat, entertaining an audience of other journalists who privately cheered the young reporter's demise. Sadly enough, it was a competitive business, but Scribbles' usual pride had left a trail of bruised ego and broken confidence.

"Street crimes is where your wet ears need to be, where the voice of the people are, young ambitious friend. We want you to write faster than a speeding bullet on Allegheny Avenue, *and find those sources like* Curious George. *Get the quotes when the police can't get snitches. You hear me?* City Hall *ain't your speed, kid. That drug war over in* Southwest *is where your action's at—now go get 'em!"*

And with that, "Old Man Editor" had given Scribbles an uncomfortably affectionate slap on his ass, like a coach on a football field leading his linemen to the slaughter. But, the next day, bothered by his boss' lack of confidence, and what he'd perceived as a closeted burst of alternative lifestyle, Scribbles was calling into work sick.

"Sick? How sick?"

"Real sick, chief," Scribbles puts on his best attempt at a hoarse voice. *"Feels like...I dunno,* West Nile *virus or somethin' like that. It's hitting me hard."*

"Feels like you're jerking my chain, kid. Puh-l-e-a-z-z-e," Old Man Editor puffs, "you don't know the difference between West Nile *and an itch on your scrotum. No time for practical jokes and punk'd routines—we got a murder and small riot erupting in front of that strip joint on* Spring Garden*—"*

"Chief, you don't hear me. I'm sick, like really sick. Like I'm about to get a spinal tap at the hospital sick. You want me to come in like that? You think a source is gonna give information to some raggedy-ass Irish *guy with bad breath and sweaty palms? I don't think so."*

"...It's on you, kid. I can find someone else to do what you do." A phrase that had irritated Scribbles, considering the editor made it seem like he was too indispensable to get the *City Hall*

transfer a day before. Now, Scribbles was so unimportant as to get replaced as fast as that?

"Don't come in here tomorrow looking for sympathy. Go ahead and get your day off. We'll talk about it later, kid."

Don't wait up, Scribbles had thought.

He then bust loose, Scribbles' clean getaway from *Philly,* properly dramatized by a life of *Black-Irish* frustration; his dash from the trap of a dead-end routine of his own making. After the phone had clicked, freshly unemployed Scribbles was on the trolley racing towards the *Greyhound* bus station to another fate.

On the ride to new glory, he'd stared at a business card the entire time, thinking of its owner: a sweet, slick, "tastes-like-butter" chick who worked at a famous, yet stuffy national daily known as "The Washington Trumpet". They'd met several months ago over *Heinekens* at a smoky bar on *South Street.* Scribbles stared hard at the ski cliff dip in the young lady's cleavage, while she'd fancied the way he drank his imported ale.

A few hours later, they were both taking a nightcap at her parents' empty crib. The stunningly seductive, brunette vixen made Scribbles scream almost Biblical scriptures through the night with her bump and grind, he being sapped of all sexual tension by sunrise.

"What do you do?" Scribbles asks.

This seemed odd that he didn't land this information earlier, especially after exchanging bodily fluids. However, in homey, working-class, union-dominated *Philadelphia,* the last thing you asked was what people did for a living. You wanted to know how they were doing and how this impacted your existence at the moment of first greeting.

"Well," she was catching her breath, as sweat had moved like surf swells into the crevices of the young lady's chest, further down into her belly button, *"I'm a reporter."*

"Really? That's all right—me too." Scribbles was feeling this. Like it was destiny. What were the chances? "*Who do you work for?"*

"'The Trumpet'. 'The Washington Trumpet'."

The snotty way the young lady had dropped that response, made Scribbles' manliness limp for a moment. It wasn't as sexy as he'd wanted the sexiness of the post-sex moment to linger. This is why the *Philly* way of meeting people worked best. Because when she'd said "Trumpet", it shattered the erotic nirvana in the air.

It was like the chick had said, in that brief spurt of small-talk: *"Yeah, you mindless prick, I work for the paper that puts politicians in jail and deep throats the* White House, *while you're chasing nappy-headed Black kids in wife-beaters for the Metro section's quote-of-the-week!*

Okay, so Scribbles' internal racist reflexes, born from years of growing up in a working-class *Fishtown Irish* home, added that last bit at the end, but he'd gotten the picture.

"Well, that's all right," was all Scribbles could reply with, because she'd smelled so good that morning lying on top of him. *"Nice outfit. They break some real stories...."* Yet he was still thinking, *So...oh—yeah. This is funny...so, like, what's your name?*

Scribbles had smiled like an embarrassed pre-teen who just discovered the power of masturbation. The young lady smiled back at the idiocy of that statement—still, he'd found her just so damn...surreal. Several hours of fluid exchange twisted in countless *Joy of Sex* positions, and Scribbles had never thought to get a name.

Their fingers pointed at the other for blame in a universe of giddy confusion and casual intercourse. But, then again, that was always Scribbles: Scribbles the Non-Committal, Player Scribbles—Ask Names Later Scribbles. Still, it was taken care of—he'd gotten a name, a business card, and another sweaty morning ride that made porn stars jealous. Scribbles swore that she was feeling him after that.

"You're sweet, tell you what, if you ever think of getting listed in a 202 area code (since there isn't much to do here in rusty "Filthadelphia"), you give me a call. "The Trumpet" *is always looking for talent, and I could use the extra kick between my legs every now and then."*

Snapping out of the daydream during that *El* train ride to the *Gallery Mall,* Scribbles was groping for her name.

What was her name?

SHANNON, YOU SOBERING DORK! the business card was snapping back at him.

Oh yeah, Shannon. Oh...y-e-a-h, he smiles. *Shannon, Shannon,* he thinks.

Shannon at "The Washington Trumpet".

chapter 3

ON I-95

DAY 2

Mobster extraordinaire, Timothy Bigletani's mad evening dash through *Delaware* turns into a spiked, spectacled run, burning freshly laid asphalt on *95 South.* Nearing 110 mph while pressing the gas of his newly purchased *Audi R8,* Bigletani stirs a mix of spurring middle fingers, gawks and laughs from curious onlookers in other cars. He cares little about his need for speed, potentially creating havoc and multi-car pileups on the freeway—the mobster was in *Delaware* now.

And the *First State* always teased its visiting drivers, as "Land of Few Cops" or, if drivers were sighted, they were announced as if a UFO sighting had occurred in some distant *Southwestern* desert. The police were like *Bigfoot* trampling through *Northwestern* redwoods, or the *Loch Ness Monster* shadowing the shores of the grimy, sewage-infested state-named river, that could be seen off to the *Eastern* horizon of the freeway. But, that wasn't exactly true, now was it?

Many often grimly reminisce of *Delaware's* finest as "the men in stomping black boots", or "the tax-funded thugs of the *First State",* who pulled people of color over for the most trivial offenses. Broken taillights, tires low on air, driving only 5 mph over the speed limit, conveniently mistaking trailing cigarette smoke for reefer, and the infamous: "*you look suspicious.*"

Maybe *Delaware's* fuzz cooled down since then. Too many lawsuits, they say, as well as too few wanting the guilt of racist association. Timothy cares less about this assessment, as it doesn't apply to him or his kind.

At that, "Biglet", as he's famously known, cracked his sinus before drawing weeping clouds of cannabis, as taillights zip around him into infinite zigzags of red nocturnal glaze; thousands of headlights explodes into multiple blasts of universe. Vapor trails of marijuana slicing into Biglet's sense, his foot pressing hard into the power of *German* machinery, anything that's something, suddenly turns or blurs into nothings of a highway's missed landmark.

The roads of this small state ruled.

It's land of outlets—the safari of no sales tax.

A pampering thirty-minute excursion of less traffic or little trouble, save the inanimate road-kill tossed viciously to the side of the speed lane and, sometimes, the annoying occasion of orange construction signs signaling suburban sprawl. It's an *Eastern* hook with a *Western* attitude, freshly peppered by pockets of openness where man was left with a little space to outlaw in, if destined.

Smoke continues flowing to Biglet's brain in trails of herbal fume. *Wilmington* is now buried behind him in a dipping crisscross of digital light, a bloom of dulled electricity and diluted urban flow.

Biglet thinks of *Grand Prix* races and *Autobahn* speedways, absent the reckless luxury of being there. The thick, heavy, molten asphalt wad of Interstate slicing through *Delaware's* heart is his fantasy, only as far as the weed-induced high will take him.

Quickly flipping light switches in a useless act of roadway courtesy, the driver persists in a cold and careless malice of his surroundings, moving at buzzing ease, fleeting in fatuous fowl. There's an unsettling easiness in the high rate of Biglet's speed—ease of expression, expression finding an insane path of diagonal lefts and rights, through a maze of hapless motorists.

He's leaning back into the racing leather of his car in a self-absorbed peace, but dozens of other drivers catching the man's dangerous highway gallop are absolutely terrified. Old women scream, elderly men shift their cars into neutral, scrambling along the edges of the highway, letting Biglet's madness pass. Wives scratch windshields for the comfort of transfixed husbands, who silently wish they owned what Biglet drives. Kids jumping in back seats points in awe at the *South Philly* mobster's speed.

Demon of *V8* engine, busting the hundred-mile per hour sprints, needs speed and supplements of hashish to calm the impending rush of nerves.

Biglet's late for an important meeting.

And tardiness is an unwanted attribute that frequently turns on him. Yet, his life struggles to avoid the last minute at eleventh hour—the crash of time spent, and the regret of goal not reached.

This is how Biglet works and functions.

He arrives at his destination, an unrecognizable and muddy lot, clumsily knocks against a colorless, flat slab of concrete off *Route 301.* Biglet's headlights find small ponds of asphalt impeded by an eroding sea of weeds and tall grass. It's somewhere smacked into the wavy detour of a dirt road adjacent to fields and rows of farm-grown cabbage.

Florescent blue headlights cut into the night pitching ultraviolet forks through *Delaware* agriculture. There's no other light out here; no barns, no houses, no fences, or spotty cows bent into pasture can be seen for miles. There is only the eerie dim of river waterline, and hundreds of bugs, gnats, moths and assorted critters of the insect world, all hanging out on this unseasonably warm night. Four, five, six-legged bits of winged crawlers overwhelming the car hood, and ruining the wax on his *Audi's* black paint.

Biglet waits…

Already confused that he now appears as the one on time, since warp-speeding down *I-95*, and knotting *Route 13* in rubber smoke. Sucking on the cali root, he's as high as the kites Biglet once flew long ago, on youthful spring afternoons in *Fairmont Park.*

chapter 4

SOUTH PHILADELPHIA

DAY 2

Councilman's death was neither instantaneous nor immediate as ordered. It just didn't happen at all.

"Where did the collateral come from?" Mysterious employers ask the blindsided assassin. He remains in shock, spiritually broken by the homeless man's twist of misfortune, getting in the way of his perfect shot. The dark council, assuming they'd hired the right guy, aren't so convinced of the basis for that decision.

They frown.

"Thought you said you had a clear shot?"

"I thought I did, too."

The assassin indulges in his own apocalypse of personal delight, covering up the mistake he made. Sure, he missed his target, but the homeless man's death was an aimless homicidal masterpiece. The killer marvels at this, all his senses congregating in religious admiration for the dreadlocked victim's last grabs for life.

Councilman will never find the gunman, thereby forfeiting any hopes of scheduled meetings in the flaming underworld. But, police later found the assassin's untagged sedan, fitting the description from the earlier *Broad* and *Lehigh* incident, lunged forward on a sidewalk near 7th and *Lombard.*

The fender was lopsided on a bent stop.

The engine was idling.

The driver's door wide open.

The assassin's body hung from the driver's seat.

Something horrific and torturous had happened to him.

Biglet didn't die fast.

A point was being made.

Headlights poked into dawn's dew.

Someone wasn't too thrilled with his performance yesterday. The gunman paid dearly for it.

Investigators are troubled at the offensive pluck of the

shooter and the hands of his murderer: the assassin firing in daylight on a crowded *North Philly* corner; the other gunman ditching the assassin's body and vehicle, early in the morning in a *South Philly* enclave.

Nosy neighborhood residents, adventurers familiar with *South Philly's* hard life, walked or hurried past, their fingers pointing. But this had been fairly common throughout the southern edges of the city. The scene of the crime and its onlookers splattered against a backdrop of red brick row homes, and a few housing projects looming.

The police, late to the scene, scratching heads in confusion ask an unanswerable question: "How did the shooter end up dead so soon after the process of speeding away? And why here, on the other side of the city?"

"Messy it is," spit one detective. *"Messy it is."*

Homicide had actually expected the ditching of the body to have ended somewhere outside *Philadelphia,* perhaps way out over city limits, further north, where the stream flows toward *Norristown;* or, perhaps a daring cross into *North Jersey.* They didn't count on a murdered suspect as openly displayed as this sorry cat was.

You typically didn't find the getaway car conspicuously smashed against a stop sign, and you *certainly* didn't find the shooters' throat slit on a busy residential byway. It's just damn funny, the way it was all done. It appears sloppy, but there's some bizarre method to the madness that they can't quite figure out—as though it was deliberately made sloppy, throwing the fuzz noses into disarray.

Scary this is. Scary indeed.

Picking at his *Blackberry*, the senior detective scrolls anxiously through names, and dials into networks of wise guys on his take. Even though the detective's instinct screams the logic of a possible mob hit, he suspects something else at play. But, he has little to move on other than the mobster theory, which feels weak, given the very cliché way it all gels together.

It's like a poorly written script for a badly rated crime show, making it obvious that someone's trying to outwit the investigators piecing it all together.

Thus, there's no starting point other than the bullets being picked out of the homeless man's brain, and this abandoned car with an unidentified body and guns still in it. Clearly, the dead man in the car carried fake identification to throw off the scent of his shady lifestyle. So they think. Who knows, maybe it isn't the shooter, after all. Maybe it's a dead version of the gunman set there by the real shooter, making the corpse look like the assassin.

That's always a possibility.

This guides investigators into a cold case.

But, hope lies in the fingerprints of the lifeless shooter slumped in the used car. Maybe this will provide something of value…maybe not.

Fishy it is.

Fishy indeed.

chapter 5

NEW YORK AVENUE, WASHINGTON, D.C.

REWIND: 3 YEARS AGO

Turns out "The Washington Trumpet" didn't have that *Capitol Hill* gig Scribbles hungered for.

Damn….

Scribbles caught his frustrated head in open hands, as he'd re-examined the logic of this recent move, at the time, down to a few months worth of bones, (money already devalued against the *Euro* amid economic turmoil); sleeping on a squeaky, soiled mattress in a roach-infested, D.C. motel on *New York* and *Pennsylvania Avenue.*

BAP! BAP! BAP!

Mad slaps to the forehead in a passionate frazzle of stupidity: *You stupid son-of-a-bitch! A mid-life crisis in my late twenties, and now I've got nothing! Not a pot to piss in!*

Well, not exactly. Scribbles conveniently forgot about the small options put before him when he'd reached D.C., either not knowing or unwilling to accept that in this town you had to start somewhere or go nowhere.

He'd become a little *damn* picky and difficult.

Shannon—stunned to hear from some one-night stand she'd barely recalled, held pity for the poor, wretched soul, who used to run after drug lords in *North Philly.* She'd begun weaving a story for Scribbles, selling him wolf tickets about *"having a shot at the Metro desk covering surrounding counties."*

"But, you'll need a car," Shannon continues while turning away from Scribbles, fishing in the fridge for a beer she'd offered moments before, her face curled in bitter irritation over his presence. Why did Shannon let Scribbles come over after an abrupt call from out of nowhere? Perhaps it was the lonely affliction of the loneliness bug on this humid afternoon, her longing for something raw and dirty, like that single night the two had shared, back in their hometown.

Maybe something would happen…and then maybe Scribbles would leave in time for Shannon to gather her senses, and get on with the business of career and padded lifestyle.

"I didn't bring a car," Scribbles replies before he thinks: *What am I saying? "I don't own a car,"* Scribbles blurts. *Where am I gonna get cash for a car?*

Looking around Shannon's studio flat, four stories above a local *Washington* yuppie borough known as *Adams Morgan,* Scribbles figured that the young lady could get him the cash he'd needed for a car. Shannon's apartment was a *Crate & Barrel* ad—a perfectly designed confluence of crisp urban refinement meets sophisticated, bohemian tastes.

Scribbles' stirring manhood was already kicking the folds of his pants, as he'd begun scheming of ways to crack her tough nut exterior and move in.

"That's a problem," Shannon says with hands on her hips. *"Well, I don't know what you're going to do. You might want to find a part-time gig flipping burgers or something, 'cause you'll need to buy a car to cover the metro beats."*

"That's all right. I'll just borrow yours till I get myself situated."

"Right," she replies, annoyed. *"Like I'm lending my convertible to some Philly loser I haven't seen since he banged me? You should've called earlier—get real."*

Not only was Shannon annoyed with Scribbles a.k.a. "Johnny-Come-Lately", there were other variables at work. Quickly handing Scribbles his beer, she'd wished for the "Daily Bell" flunky to hurry it up, get to the point of his visit, and finish the ale fast. Shannon was nervous that her law school boyfriend would arrive unannounced at any moment—he glaring back-and-forth between she and Scribbles while making the connection.

Although Shannon's boyfriend didn't quite hit it the way she'd remembered Scribbles going at it that night on the *Mainline,* he had a future, and a wealthy lobbying family, loaded with old *Potomac* money. Choice was between: grungy and unemployed *Black-Irish* idiot writer, living in a *Northeast D.C.* motel, or…the WASP-prepped, all-*American Georgetown* law graduate, who'd taken Shannon to trendy restaurants but, bored her with details about Ivy League fraternity rushes and the Senator he'd interned for last summer.

She'd quickly chosen the latter.

But, Shannon then wanted a sudden pleasure, a need to satisfy the wetness beneath, holding out for temporary sexual tryst with the former.

Maybe Scribbles' unannounced visit wasn't all that bad.

"Hey, hey. Alright," he sighs. *"...It was an idea."* Looking down, pulling for a dramatic spin on it, Scribbles commenced an attempt to crack Shannon's code. *"Listen. I felt vibes that night we spent together. Positive vibes. I dug you—still dig you and...I know the feeling has got to be mutual..."*

Her eyes flung to the back of her head on that comment. Scribbles was making it obvious, and it had turned Shannon off for a moment, which caused him to pause.

"And you were saying? Get to the point."

Defeated, Scribbles switched gears: *"What else you know about?"*

Shannon told him said there wasn't much else beyond the Metro beats that she knew about. She'd have to check further on it, put her ear to the ground and grind the pavement.

Scribbles then had dropped his own dime: *"...Can I stay at your place, Shannon?"*

She was now heated!

That was tacky.

"NO!" Shannon had shot back, managing to fabricate some sorry story about an autistic kid sister whom her parents would occasionally drop off for extended stays with Shannon.

Scribbles laughs.

Vexed earlier, he'd peeped the Shannon/boyfriend photo on a table in the living room while gulping midway through his beer, so Scribbles had known what was up. Resigned, he'd just accepted that, not willing to press any further, adjusting to the fact that he was on his own.

"You can stay tonight, though," Shannon states while sitting down on the sofa before pausing. "*...On the condition we get reacquainted. And then, afterwards,"* she smiles, "*...I'll think some things over."* The smile exposed her legs running slender from the bottom of a denim mini-skirt, late afternoon casual arousal slowly rubbing together with the twitch of fun things ahead.

Even though Scribbles was a bit surprised by the rapid turnaround of hospitality, he'd really wanted to stay. But, to Shannon's dismay, Scribbles was looking for his backpack and waving goodbye, murmuring under his breath about *"Sloppy seconds"*, and a sarcastic: *"Don't want to wake up your autistic kid sister."*

One moment he was kissing Shannon on stunned cheek, and the next, Scribbles was wandering *Washington* in a drunken stupor, struggling to find out what had happened to all the skyscrapers.

Why did all the buildings reach no higher than the white penis on the Mall?

A poorly planned walk into the *Reflecting Pool* got angry looks, and stern warnings from a few *Park Police* on horse. Walking further up *Constitution Avenue,* cleared his senses a bit, but Scribbles was still lost. He'd needed to think this through, a place to crash and space to focus straight.

Hung over and suffering from dry mouth the next day, Scribbles sat in a local cyber hole, struck with surprise to find an e-mail from Shannon. His "uncompassionate whore" at "The Washington Trumpet" had managed to come through.

Call this woman at The Chamber, Shannon writes. *It's a specialty paper—they focus only on the* Hill. Congress. Bills—*misguided staffers and Congressmen messing with college interns.* White House *stuff, too. I don't know how much you know about these things, but they're looking for a reporter. Entry level. I told her you were hungry, but mad skilled. She owes me some favors. Call her. Don't mess it up. Good luck. SJ*

Congress? Bills? White House stuff? These were terms Scribbles only read in the *"Daily Bell"* National section on coffee breaks, or when he had time to scan (in the wake of a hangover on a pre-dawn channel surf) the cable news ticker. But, this was the real thing, *Washington* flavor and inner-*Beltway* style, all mixed into one permanent, professional vacation. It was also, all very new.

So there at *The Chamber* appears Scribbles in a flash. He's somewhat well dressed, barely scraping a few dollars together for a decent shirt and tie, and his khakis seeming a bit wrinkled from the lack of a working iron. Still, Scribbles is struggling—pretty much hungry for a gig, sitting in this old school editor's office, throwing the charm on her as much as he can.

His whip appeal may work, as *The Chamber* editor occasionally flips her straight crop of silver-lined brunette hair back behind her ear, her forty-five-year-old fingers appearing to quiver a little in static frenzy.

Shannon had given advance notice of Scribbles' first

impression. Told the editor that he was "eye candy".

"Cute, but definitely not polished. He needs some grooming—definitely out of Philly. 'Nuff said. But, he's adorable in a cloddish and dusty sort of way."

Feeding a few lies to butter the sauce, Shannon had talked all about Scribbles.

The disillusioned guy who covered the most horrid depictions of human despair while on the *North Philly* crime beat. Cool cat who exposed a major, open-air based drug ring, embedded deep in a city housing project. Adventurous bloke who dodged bullets fired by angry thugs, wanting revenge for their spots being blown on the front page of the daily paper.

Albeit Shannon had taken creative license to embellish the details, she justified it with her guilt from the previous day, a mixed guilt of broken expectations, and half-baked truths. *The Chamber* editor was interested.

"Really?" the editor answers, her voice an inflection higher than normal.

"Yeah," Shannon shoots back, *"and now he's eager to take on* Congress.*"*

"You're not pulling my leg because this guy probably licked yours? You seem oddly buoyant today. It's not you to get worked up on somebody else."

"Come on," Shannon nervously whips back, *"you know me better than that. I am not a slut,"* as if repeating some ancient preamble expected to save her from sinful descent. But it had worked enough for Scribbles to get him an interview.

There he was parked in *The Chamber* editor's office, as slicked to the last thin, pre-balding strand as he could manage, a struggling vision of Shannon's style advice and veiled threats regarding her reputation. The editor's name was Ms. Kenwick.

Again, that working-class, carnal urge kicked in, and Scribbles felt a blinding crave to bang *The Chamber* editor, too.

"Okay—our mutual friend, Shannon had good things to say about you. Big crime reporter out of the City of Brotherly Love *and cream cheese—your resume appears to say it all."* Ms. Kenwick taps her pen on the paper. *"Impressive, yet still a bit green by our standards. You deal with criminals, we deal with politicians."* A quick laugh from the editor—a joke Scribbles doesn't get, he politely smiles. *"You seem to be doing so well up there, why are you so pressed on coming down here? As I*

understand it, you pretty much moved down here without any prospects, is that correct?"

"New horizons, ma'am. In search of new horizons."

Ms. Kenwick clears her throat: *"I guess...I guess I can understand that,"* her eyes getting thin. *"You have references?"*

At the time, the editor would be calling Scribbles' brother, the gregarious, *Corona*-guzzling, *Temple University* senior and trusty *Philadelphia Weekly* intern, who'd owned a fairly reliable and pin-drop clear cell phone on hand. He'd pose as Scribbles' former editor at the newspaper, representing the two years when Scribbles, a lanky and naive kid from the *Northeast* side of the city, did only two months writing music reviews before growing bored, joining a writing workshop; and meeting "Old Man Editor" at the "Daily Bell" who'd slapped his ass.

Since he was, presumably, in cold turkey on Scribbles, then ten-year police veteran, Sergeant Tennick Harvey, would back Scribbles up on a reference, plus a few other favors. Harvey wasn't near as ready to let the reporter accidentally find that hidden videotape where he loosens blue fury and a nightstick on an innocent *Black* kid near *52nd Street.*

Harvey's contention to Scribbles: "*The kid looked as though he was up to no good.* Whereby Scribbles offers: "*You provide me an open line to what's happening downtown, and I'll make certain I don't know where that videotape is.*"

Ms. Kenwick reaches her point fast, no need for subtlety: *"What do you know about* the Hill?"

Scribbles didn't really know much about that, but he'd started getting cocky enough to feel that he could maneuver his way around it. *"Whuh?* Capitol Hill?" Scribbles goofs.

"What other 'hill' is there?" The editor becomes suddenly annoyed and impatient.

"Well," Scribbles shifts uncomfortably into a tight, leg-cross position, *"I watch* Washington Briefing *every morning and read the papers."* His responses were careless, impulsive and unprepared, and Scribbles knew so.

"That doesn't quite cut it," Ms. Kenwick looking at her watch, *"You need to know how to get around."*

Scribbles didn't know that. She glares.

"*Well, we need samples*, the editor indicates. Scribbles began shifting his eyes around, looking much like an embattled bureaucrat, lying before a committee of inquisitive *Senators* smelling for blood.

"All my samples are back in Philly," was all Scribbles could muster back. Ms. Kenwick did a mental back flip to keep from laughing out loud.

"Well, well, well, well...I don't think this is going to work," she states.

So Scribbles had humbled a bit. He was already daydreaming about those heroin junkies back in *Northeast D.C.*, waiting to ransack his dingy room and rummaging through motel trash for nicotine butts. Damn it was *nasty* over there!

Finally, recovering, Scribbles then resolved to slam his charm: *"I can do this. If I can snag drug lords in* West Philly, *I can catch Congressman cutting deals on pork, or giving favors to get some. And I love to write. I'll find you the stories, I know how to dig."*

He'd posed a look of confidence, yet just defeated enough to register short pity. Clearly, there was desperation at play. Oddly enough, it worked itself into a short silence in the office, catching Ms. Kenwick off-guard. The veteran editor then sighed.

"...Listen, let's do this. For some odd and inexplicable reason I hope I don't regret later, there's something I like about you. Maybe it's because our friend, Shannon gave you such high marks—and she doesn't normally give anyone high marks outside of herself. Maybe because you've got this look about you..." Ms. Kenwick pauses, thinking heavily about what she'd say next. *"Okay...I have an internship for three months. The pay ain't nothing to scratch at. But, hang around. Pay some dues, clean and flush a few toilets for me. Who knows? Throw a few stories my way, and we'll see what happens. How's that sound?"*

"Sounds good, as long as I can write. I love to write, you know."

Back then, Scribbles could live on the few dollars he'd already had in that shrinking money clip that stuck to his thigh. The internship stipend would help with that musty *D.C.* motel Scribbles was soon forced to call home.

It could've been worse.

He could've been homeless.

All Scribbles had wanted to do was get back into the game—the writing game, the game of mismatched fortunes and empty shots of luck.

It wasn't the "Daily Bell", and it sure as *hell* wasn't the steadiness of "The Washington Trumpet" he'd wished for, during that sudden move to *D.C.* But, it was the opportunity to, once again, write full-time. Scribbles would live off the words for two months— he'd barely eaten anything as it was.

"I'll find you stories, Ms. Kenwick," was all Scribbles could say. *"I can get you big stories. I can dig."*

"Surprise me," she replies, shuffling papers to signal the end of the interview.

Ms. Kenwick's curiosity, however, had soon paid off, killing a few scandals and taking little prisoners along the way. Six weeks later, *The Chamber* uncovered a *Senate* staffer porn ring in a conservative *Republican's* office; substantiated rumors of money laundering in the office of one previously and once comfortably obscure *Philadelphia* Congressman. Then burned the *D.C.* Mayor for arranging oddly brokered contracts for a gang of wealthy *K Street* lobbyists, known for their generous campaign contributions.

Phones were blazing.

Subscriptions nearly doubled.

Sorely needed ad revenue trickled in quick since *The Chamber* found itself in the larger media spotlight, in which all articles had been written by "Nick Scribbles".

But who was he?

When asked for an interview on the major news outlets, Scribbles graciously declined, favoring anonymity over major fame. Perhaps he'd feared the consequences of outing powerful people, and felt the underground approach proved the most prudent. Perhaps his natural *Philly* paranoia had set in, the cynicism and distrust of government molded after years of growing up in this struggling, blue-collar steel port.

During this time, Scribbles was none other than the guy nobody knew, and no one would find him since, you see, he was never originally "Nick Scribbles" in the first place—not until he'd arrived in *The Chamber* office.

And so it was rude-fast when Scribbles had snagged himself a cozier spot in *Arlington, Virginia* while managing a half-decent wardrobe. A much more respondent Ms. Kenwick, impressed by his unconventional style and ability to grab sources, provided all the necessary perks—from laptop to cell phone to a small bucket of cash worthy enough to consider a sign-up bonus, no one had known about.

Yet firm instructions were followed: *"Never step foot in*

the office again." When Ms. Kenwick called, they'd exchange information over sushi at a non-descript and low key *Korean* spot, over the *Roosevelt Bridge,* down *Route 66*, onto *Little River Turnpike* in *Annandale.* Scribbles would be her secret weapon.

In a town this small…

And with walls so thin…

It didn't hurt to have one.

chapter 6

TEMPLE UNIVERSITY, NORTH PHILADELPHIA

DAY 3

Minister Ankh is an armchair-revolutionary on steel crutches, one who needs to be redefined. Everything about him is half ass; half ass as only Minister knows so well, in a disturbingly organized way. His closest advisors and associates sense this, albeit swiftly dismissing it. Yet, Ankh still manages to beg a mix of curiosity and flabbergast from crowds, who are bedazzled by his ability to placate reason through much sound, call and response.

It's all in the talk, the sermon.

In this day and age, there's still much room for people like him.

Leaders like me, Ankh portends to himself in a cocky daze.

Deft is he at the art of persuasion. Ankh can call bright sunlight when rain pours, convince a bar full of patrons to digest a pint of rum, even though it's from the bottle he pissed in only hours before. This is how Ankh lives, crystallizing hustles of verbs, adjectives and pronouns: a hustler's quest for sanctity through word of his mouth as the absolute authority.

Historians aptly note that prostitution is the oldest profession in the world. However, is that literal interpretation or misguided context? Perhaps both. Do they mean prostitution as in sexually sophisticated individuals, well learned and experienced in the carnal art of orgasmic solicitation? Or does that definition dare to include the defiant, media-whoring adventures of Minister Ankh on his endless quest for glory and camera lenses?

He's quite a boisterous, microphone-kicking, choir preaching dissident, that Ankh. The questions of how much he prostituted himself, still lingers to this day.

Ego is what really fed Ankh's power all these years, not money. Not big houses, or the instant gratification of this or that capitalist ideal, nor a fattened ride with twenty-inch dubs. Despite staging a major *Black Mafia* comeback in the *City of Brotherly*

Love, Ankh wants none of what power is typically defined as in his part of town.

No standing, long-term political assets that makes his hometown Mayor nervous or the state Governor tremble in terror. Minister barely owns the clothes on his back—no, instead, Ankh prefers the absorption of power through decibel and rhetorical force.

Power, to him, arrives in the form of infrequent newspaper headlines. Power—patronizing *Philly* paper clippings by an inexperienced, patronizing *White* liberal searching for *Black* redemption, or the occasional local news cast on its quest for that typecast, and angry *Black* activist face. Minister Ankh only wants the glory of accumulated fifteen-minute segments of fame, all wrapped into a legacy he can call his own.

When the marches crashed through *Center City,* and social antagonists (driven by a dizzying score of issues) hit the streets in camouflage fatigues and picket signs, scorching the sidewalks of *D.C., New York* and *Chicago,* there was Ankh in *Afro*-regalia.

He took cues from *Jimi Hendrix* at *Woodstock,* saving his best for the very last: a ferocious breath of revolutionary fire, throwing balls of spoken rock into crowds of goofy, middleclass kids looking for trouble; so they could brag about their battle wounds and dusty arrest records, twenty years later.

Ankh personifies ideological emaciation transformed into few identifiable scruples. On the surface, he acts as if a demigod blessed with mythical righteousness, but, in reality, all matters are very political with Ankh. He's a man with whom the ends justified the means.

And the women in Minister's life? He beats them, Ankh's anger knowing no bounds during the moments he feels above both law and reproach. To throw off any suspicion of his cunning, ill-tempered self, Ankh always dresses in over-worn knits of *African* motif, smelling heavily of incense, doused deep in *Middle Eastern* street oils. His closely cut fade is always military tight and neatly trimmed.

Demeanor is always intense.

Mood is serious and self-conflicted in paranoia.

Meeting Minister means being drawn into a mysterious universe of plots, conspiracies, wicked world orders and *Freemasons.*

Today, with specific mission, goal and instruction in

mind, Ankh circles *Temple,* the local urban university, in his routine pursuit of raw recruits. There is an endless, naïve pool of talent on college campuses, ripe for the picking by power-hungry activists and demagogues—Ankh is really in search of one.

She's floating somewhere among the dispossessed and jaded youth, walking aimlessly about from one irrelevant class to another. The rest of them are unfamiliar with the rigors of the real world, the cajoling and pitiful ways of their mass-consumer culture. But, this one Minister looks for, knows much about what her peers do not.

He searches…

Chewing on a stick of cinnamon, Ankh leans one foot into a courtyard bench, and squints at a reflection of sunlight, despite graying clouds and rain in the forecast. Curious onlookers gather about: ten heads…twenty…forty…sixty and growing. A sidewalk of shadows shuffles into a sphere of activists-in-training.

Their eyes pronounce a hunger for new beginnings, for something much more different, and sinister than the drudgery of the Top-Ten world around them. A misguided desire for new ideas, and a misplaced sense of what defined "revolution." Colleges are fruit bowls of human resource at the predatory demagogue's disposal.

"Young, raw, fresh recruits!" Minister Ankh speaks and chews on, beckoning the crowd to come closer. If they only could hear the snorts of laughter under his breath, perhaps they'd think twice.

"This is why I present to you, brave brothers and sisters, our plight for an alternate world order!" He now breaks into one of his infamous soapbox sermons, shattering tranquil sound barriers in the university courtyard. Ankh doesn't have a permit for this, but he'll press on with his speech, since the university police are too nervous to attract an embarrassing headline, or an expensive lawsuit.

As Minister lifts his voice, there are scattering claps throughout the audience, which soon transforms into blocks of applause and cheers for four-hundred-year retribution, as the crowd becomes Blacker and Blacker!

"*Caucasians* have their world order, so why can't *we* of *African* descent? They have their institutions, their governments and their armies, so, *why* can't we?"

The mentioning of "armies" throws the more committed

"Afrocentrites" into *roaring* bursts of praise and unified agreement. However, this doesn't particularly please or appeal to the light flaking of curious *White* attendees, who watch with clinical fascination. The climate in the crowd is getting a bit hot, because *"The Blacks"* are watching *"The Whites"* with ice-cold stares, wondering why they're here.

Ankh capitalizes on this, marketing to his core audience in a public setting. If no one can agree on what's being said, then they manage to show silent consensus on one point: Ankh is brilliantly mad. He controls and conveys an insane genius about himself. If one really knew Minister, one would realize his normal human shortcomings, but watching Ankh the Orator, summons impulses of unconditional respect and unwavering humility.

Minister's accompanying entourage of leather-skinned, charcoal-clothed bodyguards: a thick wall of muscled flesh in an endless, effortless state of militaristic attention, show a force field of power through display. They prepare to bite the biggest bullet for their nickel-and-dime eminence in charge.

Most would wonder how insanity, or this particular nut's love of it, manage the impressive phalanx of might—not to mention Ankh's average height, and the potbelly-love handle, bulging behind his "XL" shirts. Ankh really isn't much to look at; his appearance isn't worth the kind of human heat protecting him. Initial instinct, at first glance, wouldn't detect political material, but it's Minister's presence, augmented by the neatly lined row of uniformed Black men.

Perception rules everything, and if books are judged by the timid grace of their cover, then the city's most visible revolutionary is on to something much larger than the crowds he draws.

"Lost, great kings and queens of the *Diaspora*—lost and stricken! Stricken, bent and hurt by the sharp and unjust ills of what they call this great society! Nonsense, brothers and sisters! Absolute nonsense! What they do not say is that their *own* world…their precious AmeriKKKa-h-h-h—"

"Leave!" a distant, irritating voice in the back of the crowd.

"Their own *enormous* pillars of social and economic advancement are crushed under the weight of contemptuous demons, permeating the imperial *American* fabric…"

"Then leave, dude! Leave!"

"Who is that?" Ankh whispers to himself. The sermon continues, seemingly unfazed by the unknown detractor in the audience. "…In these most tempestuous feats of national crime, we live in a darkening mood of fear, and sometimes uncontrollable panic, as we search for answers to unanswerable questions…"

"Why don't you go back?"

Minister's head snaps: "GO BACK TO WHAT, INSOLENT *FOOL?* SHOW YOURSELF—BE COURAGEOUS AND SHOW US WHO YOU ARE. GO BACK TO WHAT? GO BACK TO *AFRICA?*"

The crowd suddenly takes notice of the scrubbed, sling-pack wearing *Caucasian* with heavy eight-o-clock shadow, wearing a food-stained t-shirt, and baggy, ripped bell bottoms, tripping over begrimed suede sneakers.

Emblazoned in white letters on his black cotton shirt is *"FUCK THE WORLD BANK!"* The guy struggles to wiggle into the mass tan and chocolate faces now staring at him ominously—a few of them prepped to unleash fisted onslaught for interrupting Ankh's speech.

"I didn't say that."

Clearly, the young man is confused and bitter.

But he's harmless.

Perhaps stricken and touched in the head.

Otherwise, he poses no real threat to Ankh and his small army. There's no internal realization of his actions or their dangerous consequences.

Ankh fires back, eager to make an example out of the detractor: "That's what you were *about* to say!"

"But I'm not on the record as saying that. I *didn't* say that. I'm talking about you—*you* need to go back to wherever you came from, and leave us all the *hell* alone." This exchange is now rising to the tempo of bizarre college prank.

The crowd starts laughing.

Minister isn't too pleased by this.

"Stand straight, *coward!* We know what's on your mind!"

"Kiss my *ass,* dude! You can *spit* a good speech, but you *can't* read my mind! I'm so *tired* of your *African* sob story, it's time for you to crawl back under that rock you came from."

"You mean 'hut', right?"

"Naw, dude—rock! Rock! If it's that bad here, then *step* the *hell* back to wherever you came from!"

Grumbling escalates into cries of foul play, while nasty looks quickly spurn a series of shoving matches. Quaint college campus courtyard soon transforms into an isolated street uprising. At this stage, one can see the university police streaming in on bicycles and cruisers—soon, the call will go out to the city police department for backup.

Meanwhile, the instigator, possibly high, is wildly flailing his thin arms about, unsuccessfully blocking countless bumps, knocks, punches, jabs and wind-cracking scratches. Ankh fumes to ignore the mid-day college crowd antagonist, cursing him for the interruption, before moving back to his topic over the melee of shouting matches, police sirens, and faces getting pushed in.

Minister roars and rolls on, his speech rising above the brawl, inspiring those surrounding the loco *White* kid with taped glasses, to shove the guy along into the outer periphery of the amassed crowd. Little did any eye notice Ankh motioning two of his suited bodyguards, one traveling a flank faster than the other, swerving into bodies of assorted young politicos swearing for revolution.

"CRUSH THE *CRACKER!*" Ankh drones into their ears. "When you finish, throw him out for the *pigs,* and let them try to figure out what happened!"

"GET *CRACKER!*" they shout. "STRING HIS STRINGY *ASS* UP AND HIDE THE REMAINS!"

chapter 7

1st & G STREETS, NE, D.C.

DAY 4

Babylon on the *Potomac* is where Scribbles' unleashed journalistic duck fits. It's the seedy underbelly of *Washington, D.C.'s* deepest secrets where he draws mudslings of inspiration. This is where it really eclipsed for him—fame never before realized when camping outside drug-infested *North Philly* housing projects for the next great crossfire of automatic weapons.

They, Scribbles' old bosses, never saw the potential back then, the same way readers of his infamous *Chamber* column see it now. It's the turning point in Scribbles' lopsided and spotty writing career. No, forget that—the journalist scribbles. He's "Nick Scribbles": King of the Alphabet, Prince of Word Drop—Master of Written Gab.

For three years now, Scribbles has pummeled through the nation's *Capitol* with a punishing pen in a crooked left hand, with fingers that speeds through laptop keys like a comic book hero. He scribbles hard and fast till the lead cracks; the ink leaks no more, and the paper in his laser jet split.

Scribbles is crazy like that—a weird, insane, bipolar mind-job-of-a-storefront-thug, to the point of no sane return. He doesn't know how to really talk about it, flex it, or express his mental state in any other way but writing.

"Scribbles-to-bits with talk!" "Nick Scribbles" says. "*Talk?* …Bite on this: talk is *cheap!* Talk is noodles-and-spoodles, and stripped O's of laziness." Instead, it all comes together when the columnist writes—when he scribbles.

What's a Nick-to-knack-and-nag-about when the scribbling is so intense? Easy: Scribbles is, at his core, stoned on the lift of politics. He's the poli-sci smoke stack.

Scribbles is high on the ideology and partisan bickering that defines the tone inside *Washington.* He doesn't like to admit it but, Scribbles enjoys his politics in a special way, likes it in the morning sunny side-up, swimming in O.J., and lounging on his milk-less bowl of dry *Frosted Mini-Wheats.* In his new post-*Philly* life, Scribbles is a changed man…a charged man.

Scribbles devours "The Washington Trumpet", nibbles on the *Washington Clock,* gets fly with *Hill Run,* and dreams of full-throttle carnal action with the evening lady network anchors and Sunday morning talk show co-hosts. In his fantasies, ego in overdrive, Scribbles franticly bangs all his favorite *Beltway* insider chicks," turning them round-and-round atop the *Capitol Dome,* pushing the women into helps and howls of sex-blasted hyperbole.

These are the racy, exploited thoughts of manhood unleashed, periodically filling Scribbles' head with the unthinkable and outright unimaginable.

He also hates. At times, Scribbles burns with mad, scribbling, acidic rage, as crabbed and cranky as a pus-popping venereal disease.

"And I suspect," Once noted the journalistic prick of private rage in his daily online blog, *"that the reason why all these people read my piss of ornery nonsense, is because they hate, too. That's right! We're all one, big, happily, hating-ass human family. Aren't we?*

"Doesn't it just make you wanna scream? Your elected officials are wack—you're wack for electing them. They pimp you, campaign and dazzle bullshit *before you, pander your issues into irrelevance and you still vote for them because of what they wear, how well they kiss your baby or drink your liquor. That doesn't bother you?*

"The formulated polls, the press conferences, the State of the Union, *and the red carpet walks through the* Rose Garden? *Guess what? I'm about to burst your bubble and tell all about how wack that is. Tell all about the smoke and public policy pomp that routinely blows smoke up your ass. Wack because they don't want you to know the real: the "corrupticons" who plan and fund the scam in the first place.*

"Those polls the pundits swear by? Wack! Nobody asked you or me for our damned opinion. All they do is survey a mall of loitering, middle-aged, sex-deprived, White *suburban soccer moms, angry that "Charlie" is dipping the office intern, rather than getting an ulcer from staring at his miserable, cellulite-stacked wife.*

"The talking heads are equally wack. You know them—stuffy, empty-suit, tightwad blokes. When the party of choice manages to rent the White House, *the talk shows sound like sloppy*

fiction. Another show on another network flips the format, add town hall flavor to it with no taste, and keeps the same set of sour, cheap and stale lager. Wack! This Week is that wack! Meet the Wack!"

Scribbles blurs with a furious five of fisted fingers at the thought of the pork-belly, earmarking *Hill* staffers fraternizing with lobbyists, and other assorted *K Street* pimps; future dictators posing as gatekeepers of democracy, as they crunch on peanuts, *Sam Adam* pints and apple martinis every Tuesday at happy hour.

Scribbles is worn on what he claims is the wack and foolishness of *Washington*, but he can't get away from it—Scribbles can't escape. The flame has drawn him in, the spiraling smoke seduces Scribbles, and the bong of democracy lures him closer to the ultimate fix.

He lives for this.

Yet, the journalist now has it in his mind to confront his troubled soul—Scribbles wants to let the whole world know what's behind his dreaded scribbles, and what drove his mind off the cliff of the *George Washington Parkway,* into that great, oversized specimen dish of bacterium, known as the *Potomac River.* Scribbles needs to expose his intestinal entrails for everyone to see.

I've discovered this marshland cut of Babylon, made it a home, but now finally see Washington, D.C. for what it really is—bubbling with the fart-in-the-tub ferocity of co-branded decadence and democracy gone awry, Scribbles thinks.

Ah, the stories he will tell.

Cracking his knuckles, lubricating the pen, and dusting that battered keyboard, Scribbles itches to spill some beans. He clutches on to the broomstick of backdoor perdition, telling all what it's about, and why things happen the way you expect or wish it shouldn't happen. All of this brought to you by "Nick Scribbles", because Scribbles needs to spit.

Come back next week and he'll scribble on it: the set-ups, the scandals; the dark realm of lost souls between campaign promises and election guarantees.

Consultant pockets lined, while few politicians are held accountable for the resulting impact on the average Jane and Joe. Scribbles soon shows the blood-money trails and fattened "Hunchbacks" of *Capitol Hill,* pundits playing musical chairs on the conscience of the body politic. The deals, even the wet handshakes and butt slaps after slick, slippery lay-ups on the *Congressional* court.

Scribbles is now worn on that, passed; been-there-done-that, and strung out on D.C. He hasn't even been there as long as most, but Scribbles just can't stomach the taste of it anymore. The pungent odor of his complicity in it overtakes the conflicted columnist. There's a sudden need for a change of pace. Only the weak in soul and limp in wrist grow fond enough of Babylon to stay mired in it.

Scribbles needs a new swing, not a new gig.

I dig the gig, he thinks. *I dig the bi-weekly cheddar, and I'm finally getting my propers and the probability of book deals. Ms. Kenwick and The Chamber are more than generous.*

On certain nights, when the beer is flat, the cable movies are tired, and his hand is fatigued from loneliness, Ms. Kenwick stops through for a little rum and coke, romping her shapely, pre-menopause measurements into a strip-teasing frenzy, that ends up in sweat on the five sides of Scribbles' two-bedroom.

He has no right to complain—Scribbles has it good. But his hometown beckons him once again. Nostalgia, sweet and sour, floats about Scribbles' *Arlington, Virginian* suite, every time he catches his home teams in a losing streak. Scribbles' apartment is studded with sports team collectibles and signed jerseys in gilded frames, the journalist becoming his hometown's biggest fan away from home.

Scribbles publicly chides local restaurant owners for attempting to replicate *Philly* cheese steaks, and somehow manages to find the most remote link of anything close to *Southeastern Pennsylvania.* Yet even he realizes that such behavior is, at best, becoming grossly odd for a man his age.

Perhaps the driving force behind Scribbles' homesick stupor is contained in the desperate anonymity of his profession and condition. Scribbles doesn't really exist; he only appears on paper in letters, with his humanity turned back against the world in hiding.

Scribbles is a figment of *Washington* scorn and legend, gossip, innuendo, jealousy and self-destruction. No one knows him, although many rake the leaves of several *Beltway* yards to find him. Hiding Scribbles proves to be increasingly problematic for *The Chamber,* and its veteran iron maiden of the *Washington* press corps.

Ms. Kenwick: an ambitious, middle-aged woman of inward mega-feminism, who melts into fruit smoothies during occasional sexual bliss with Scribbles. Unbeknownst to Scribbles, she's ready to die before revealing his true identity. Therefore, Ms. Kenwick jumps great lengths to hide him: stuffs envelopes of money from justified petty cash withdrawals, hidden and highly-secured intranet exchanges via chat, shadow Internet service providers set up by blackmailed hackers, and mysterious multiple drop-off points throughout the vast expanse of *Washington's* metropolitan labyrinth.

The heat is on.

Because of Scribbles' uncanny expertise in the art of snooping, Members of *Congress* piss in their tailored trousers while staffers mop up the mess. He strikes fear in *Washington's* elite, causing many of them to think twice before falling into the city's scandalous cesspool. And it's always been this way, journalists knowing more about the politician's pitfalls than the politicians do. But, this particular brand of news hunter is different.

Scribbles investigates, drops hints then exposes with no regard, caring little about the how fast or hard the "big guy" falls. It's the "big guy" who kept his family struggling on meager wage for years, left his hometown neighborhoods in perpetual blight and disrepair, so why should he care? The other reporters rub shoulders with the politician—Scribbles wants none of that.

He eliminates them.

Since Scribbles is this prototypically enigmatic, wiry *White* guy whom anyone could mistake for a tourist, he can go into places unnoticed, and talk to people unknown. His sources are the dispossessed and unsuccessful—chattering *Latino* janitors, uniformed and resentful *Capitol Hill* police who step the *Hill* beat, *sisters* privately admired by whoring men of power, clattering and jingling through the upholstered halls of *Congress* and *K Street,* nosy receptionists, secretaries, clerks and assistants; those both straight and gay, who are in the real, rather than the know—persons who are whisperers, whistlers and tipping points for "Nick Scribbles".

Still, such glory isn't enough for the lonely journalist. Scribbles' affection for the "game" is lost in a burning cynicism of his plight. He can't figure what's his place, what his future holds, or what Scribbles needs to do to get there. Despite the awards received, the accolades showered upon him as invisible policy watchdog, and the envy of editorial scum nationwide, Scribbles holds a heavy emotional load.

The fun is wearing thin. It's thankless and friendless.

The articles he writes become malicious bouts of verbal anarchy. No longer is Scribbles writing for kicks or the compensation that follows, he now scribes in vignettes of scorched papyrus, just for the hell of it. The bitterness of transparent existence leaks through his pores in gallons.

"To answer the sobering questions of several readers," Scribbles recently pens in his daily blog, "*I plead the fifth to explain why my writings may seem too angry to read or handle. If I have offended you, hey, let me know once you've finished the first set, and I'll adjust the volume a bit...then we'll decide which work ends up in the littered halls of which mind. I concede: it can be a trite loud, can't it? Maybe not...I think it could be worse—the language could hit even heavier. But, I have to admit, anger is a friend in comfort, it's something rudely familiar, and these days it is the only comfort I know. If you have been beaten enough, and are powerless to prevent it from happening again, then the anger residing within your soul is a tight vice to hang on to.*

"I have convinced myself that I really don't seem like the angry type. My composure is always so...composed. My disposition seems almost tranquil, sometimes, some say I am in another world of my own creation. ...Anger, even under increasing pressure, can be strangely peaceful for me—yet, I'm aware of the consequences—I know, it shows in the writings. The reason being is that, I usually put tremendous faith in keeping myself cool and even-tempered, though I get a little angry once in a while and bust an uneven, wobbling chip on my shoulder. But, you wouldn't be able to tell where the chip is. It's where the chips fall somewhere beneath the catacombs beyond anger's dungeon. I keep it hidden in a closet, submerged. It does not care too much for an audience.

"I'm not fooling you, though, and if you know me entirely too well, you know I possess this unhealthy and dangerous talent, when emotions are bottled and disrupted into an acidic fizzle, until the blood runs and spills over. Therefore, as therapy, I write. I paint the most plainspoken frustrations one can illustrate on paper. Sooner or later it should be enough to extinguish and forever quell the oppressive waters of this expressive rage I'm

living with.

"In such a state, I am the untested weapon, the loose cannon, loosely searching for the perfect moment when ammunition can be unleashed like a hot whiz of concentrated water, spraying straight from the tip of a rocking tea kettle. This is the most dangerous kind of weapon, since it has no controlling mechanism. It doesn't even have a trigger. It builds energy from within, and struggles against the tendency to idly wait for the fire, or for someone else to start it. An untested weapon makes the fire—the loose cannon spreads it.

"Don't misinterpret me, I'm not really looking for a fight. I don't deserve some unplanned, untamed, irrelevant and rabid rage, so you can point at 'that angry guy over there.' No. I can only write what is, and what is…is on my mind. Here stands a man angrily faced down in the mud of his own convictions, clashing with the intention to deny his humanity. Considering this, one should only assume that anger is but a passing rain cloud, feigning a great storm, while it really teases a drizzle. Anger is therefore 'relative', and merely a simmering precedent to a steaming, consistently tapped and tortured rage.

"Don't you sometimes feel this great, angry storm as the crucial remedy? But, yes, I forgot, we are too angry. Many of us remain in a mental and spiritual stasis while anger has been historically proven, and in certain cases, rightly justified. Yet, we tend to give our anger to the magnificent, omnipotent powers-that-be, in exchange for a dull, constricted, controlled and restricted life. It reflects a sobering effort to dissuade us from conjuring 'theories', and believing that the dangerous reconfiguration of this extraordinary social landscape, is a madness of engineered frontlines, trenches and genocide-driven mechanisms."

As homesick Scribbles oozes out of him, Ms. Kenwick sprays a nervous drizzle of perspiration on her newspaper. Why she once felt that Scribbles seemed ready for perpetual invisibility was mainly based on him between her legs, rather than sound business.

All good things must come to an end, Ms. Kenwick reasons. So now she must find a way to end it with grace: "We'll find you a nice out, Scribbles."

"An *out?* What do you mean?" Scribbles doesn't like the sound of this.

"Write a book…take some time off, perhaps even paid

leave."

* * * * *

"Write a book," is all what Scribbles keeps hearing from Ms. Kenwick, as she kisses his left ear lightly tonight: "I'll find you a publisher."

Poor, faceless and unknown "Nick Scribbles". Ms. Kenwick weeps for him at one point while riding his couch, Scribbles breaking sweat and sperm from behind her like some violent rapist.

The frustration is stunning.

Concerned, she gives her silent approval, permitting the columnist to craft-cutting literary achievements in cyberspace, moving from webzine to webzine, offering a side to Scribbles never before read. The web presents a liberating sanctuary where he can reveal himself… without revealing too much.

A relentless lust for recognition grabs at Scribbles in the worst way: attention and reward.

He thinks: *Isn't this why I left home in the first damn place?* "Damn," Scribbles laments, feeling overworked, unchallenged and under-appreciated. In D.C., the vast sea of pundits, readers and observers widely respect him not for who he is, but what Scribbles puts in paragraphs. This fact tears through him in ways untold, because it isn't Scribbles who receives the countless awards and awes of critics, it's his column.

Scribbles also can't burst his grill onto the scene by sitting on conference panels or parading the talk show circuit. No—only others can do that in defense of, or blunt agitation against him.

His job is to remain invisible.

Only others can ponder, mull and get fame on the toil of Scribbles' work. It's the first time his opportunity isn't really his—it's everybody else's.

Broken and embittered, the invisible journalist then looks northward and sniffs home to *Philly* for answers. Scribbles soon finds them in the spirit of a vibrant, six-foot-two, celebrity city Councilman: a newcomer who appears from total obscurity, suddenly crafting an urban renaissance from blown smoke. Already, people speak of him as many other things: Mayor, Congressman, Governor, Senator…President? Yet, despite the expectations, this dude is different. He's vocal on the issues, but eerily silent on what *his* plans are.

Forget the issues, the Scribbles will muse, tell us about the guy. The journalist, like the rest, wants to know the personality, the fate and fortunes. Speeches, platforms and stumps are irrelevant. Great ideas will pass across the desks of every editor, staff reporter, producer and content manager at the cost of a penny for every thought (or a quarter depending on how fast the dollar drops). But great human beings writing history through public acts are at most times, rare and priceless.

So Scribbles figures it's time to refocus. His columns will periodically postulate on *"...the grassroots whiz kid making the inevitable drive to* Capitol Hill. *Can he make it to the* White House?*"* In his dreams, Scribbles will caution.

Councilman's already an Independent, a pure minus for national stage politics, since voters never really vote Independent, despite polls suggesting they will. It's a partisan world, a universe of two poles: Red and Blue. Americans possess little patience for the Purple, or the shades of grey. They need firm answers and a cut-and-dry they can point to in times of trouble.

Yet, Scribbles continues building on his emotional storms until finally, it all boils over into another column.

"What the hell *is this, Scribbles?"* a crushed Ms. Kenwick scolds her favorite writer in a mix of gall and lover's passion. Political advertisers don't pay for mentally dismembered columnists, going through a geographic identity crisis.

"Just print it," he taps back into the secure online chat lounge, where they meet secretly to discuss column business.

"I don't understand this. There's absolutely nothing in here resembling anything remotely Washington. *I don't want to read about some small-time Councilman in some dirty,* East Coast *jungle. You're not going AWOL on me, now are you, sweetheart?"*

"What? Crazy? No. I'm just a bit exhausted. A bit washed out on this Hill stuff. I need a distraction. I want to go back home. Write about home."

"Home?"

"Yeah. Home: City of Firsts, and old money. Where the smell of politics is antique, but a bit more tolerable, since it's all local shit. I can stomach that."

"What the hell *is back home, Scribbles?"* Ms. Kenwick is vexed. It feels as though Scribbles is leaving her without directly addressing the issue of their relationship.

"It's that Councilman. The new kid everybody says is eyeing Congressman Sandel's seat. I don't think he is, I think Councilman is real. He's beyond and bigger than us—it's like he moves on an idea as though he's never campaigning, giving no thought to the consequences. I want write about him."

Ms. Kenwick now pauses before breathing into her keyboard.

"Plus, someone just tried to kill the guy. How many city legislators do you know with a price on their head? That's some cool shit! *I want to cover that."*

She gives in: *"Okay...take a few months of paid vacation. The catch here is, you give me one D.C. column every month. As for now, pick a paper back home, and I'll see about brokering some sort of contract for you."*

Philly's hometown's *Daily News* obliges. Scribbles is going back home—but *not* as the same person he was when the columnist first left. Scribbles reluctantly concedes to continuing the professional concealment and anonymity. It sucks, but at least he'll be back home.

Below his weekly scribe, the signature photo box won't show the real "Nick Scribbles". It will, instead, show the back of his head. Which is fine by a guy who just spent much of a career telling others to kiss his *ass!*

chapter 8

OFF ROUTE 13

DAY 5

Known simply as "Counselor" to the power brokers he rolls with, Germani is rubbing tired eyes and a chiseled chin. He examines his watch for exact time while fishing an inside pocket for cell phone. As Germani makes a call, Biglet clumsily answers on the other end.

"Mr. G—what can I do you for?"

"We're behind you."

Sitting in his car, Biglet swings around nervously in the four winds, searching for signs or profiles of human silhouette.

"U-h-h-h…I don't see you, man, it's too dark out here. C'mon, Counselor, cut the *spook* shit out—it ain't cool."

"You're late, Biglet."

"Fashionably," Biglet jokes back. "You waited for me, so?"

"*That's* not cool," Germani snips back in a short, crispy monotone that subdues Biglet's herbal-induced high.

"Well…you know how it is, Counselor. I'm a busy guy. Places to be. Things to do—"

"Weed to smoke."

Biglet figures he can't play verbal tap dance on *Broadway* with what he can't see. Pulling on oxygen, Biglet calms slightly, before placing a ready finger on the *Beretta* handgun, jammed between his car seat and the emergency brake.

Doors locked.

Biglet refuses to leave the car.

"You comin' out, Counselor?"

"Why is the Councilman still alive?"

"Is this line secure? You hacked into a backend?"

"We *own* these lines, Mr. Bigletani. We're well within range of our devices."

Biglet expected the questioning and shoots back with practiced response: "Homeless guy got in the way and got got—ruined our man's shot. It seems the unlucky *bastard* may have noticed the shooter and deflected the bullet. On top of that, see, the Councilman was packed…used it on our man. Our guy, like an ass, didn't know how to leave the crime scene without breaking noise."

Germani already knows the details.

"Yes. We took care of your assassin."

"Yeah, Counselor. Yeah, I heard about that. You *didn't* need to do that, I could've taken care of him myself."

"You can barely *piss* straight, Biglet. The last set of moves wasn't smart."

"Well, it wasn't my move."

"But, it was your *people* who left the trail. Good police are sniffing on it as we speak. It makes things complicated, and the people I represent don't *care* for those kinds of complications. Needless to say, we didn't want to authorize a hit on the failing hit man, but we had to do what had to get done. He would've been caught and compromised if we hadn't. You should've arranged his immediate transfer to us."

"I don't work like that. I don't have *time* for the politics—you people make it difficult. This is *very* simple stuff, Counselor, it *ain't* rocket science!" Biglet blows a short cough of laughter to lighten the mood. A stone-faced Germani refuses to acknowledge the humor in it.

"Yes, we can see that now…" Germani responds.

Liabilities become liabilities, as they suddenly acquire an edge of instability. Biglet's arrogance fit the sequence—his inept connections proving little worth.

This is the modern mob at Biglet's service: an ancient, decaying graveyard of crime bosses, young hardheads of mostly *Italian* or *Sicilian* descent, strung on high-end drugs, and gum-snapping, gossipy women.

The gap of silence pitting breathless tension against cold menace, rips through Biglet like a machete blade on flesh.

"Listen, Counselor, my associates continue to assure me and relay to you that our mutual friend's retirement will be swift…and even painless if need be. We're certain this will uphold the good spirit of our…" longer pause, "…contractual arrangement."

Biglet's long pauses and sweaty palms betray inner relapses of guilt and fear. A rapid and cautious analysis is made of Germani's stoned and frozen tones. This is a fruitless endeavor, a shooting comet—a spinning galaxy of uncertainty, past the black depths of coded miscellany. Thus, Biglet's language hobbles along in pauses and haphazard expeditions; sentences become sober ellipses dropping into melancholy.

The mob captain senses what's coming next, but Biglet doesn't reach for his gun fast enough.

It wouldn't have made much of a difference.

Before his last word, speeding flashes of quick light pierces the darkness, and whips through the front windshield, cracking lines of glass. It comes so fast that, Biglet's now bloody mass is pinned to the driver's seat.

Walking across the edge of the mobster's car, Germani carefully peers into the driver's seat, and examines the captain's carcass with reasonable satisfaction.

Biglet's death is certain and acceptable.

"Counselor" now feels comfortable enough to achieve his objective through more negotiable and effective means.

act 2:
politricks

Anyone who makes up their mind before they hear the issue is a fucking fool.

—Chris Rock

chapter 9

CITY HALL SHOESHINE STAND

DAY 6

Every session at *City Hall's* shoeshine stand resembles a vividly uncomfortable recollection of the summer when Councilman lost control.

It was the summer when he realized that he didn't know himself. Spurred by uncomfortable thoughts on his existence and self-worth, Councilman resorted to the devil's workshop of a troubled and, perhaps, idle mind. For some freakish reason, shoeshine stands reminded him of that. Maybe that was because he always recalled that fierce, alcohol-fueled fight at a *D.C.* shoeshine stand the legislator triggered with a young, overpaid smart-ass lobbyist who risked arguing over the latest football standings.

That his team wasn't doing so hot didn't sit well with Councilman, an underpaid policy wonk at the time, who'd just finished loading up on a few flasks of warm sake during an afternoon sushi lunch of "pity me." The dirty-blonde-headed *asshole* in the *Brooks Brothers* suit just happened to remind the low-level analyst of everything that was wrong that summer, and those years leading up.

When it became abundantly clear that the politician was about to lose an otherwise tame tug of sports trash talk, Councilman remembers ripping his half-shined shoe from the hand of the stunned shine man below him, and kicking the *hell* out of the lobbyist's shin in the seat beside him, who responded with a clumsily-violent knuckle smash to the drunk man's left cheek.

A few moments of scuffling found both men being pulled apart by a group of stupefied shoeshine workers, all irritated by the belligerence of the drunken professional picking a fight at their high-volume money pit. Even though Councilman was a frequent customer who tipped fairly well, fights made for bad business, thereby setting good reason for excommunication.

On condition that they wouldn't say a word to the cops about it (as the lobbyist, predictably, limped away in search for the authorities), the politician was never to set foot at that spot again.

Like that moment during the fight, every visit to the stand is a moment of rush, the heart-thumping blood and mucus curl in the throat exhilaration of a distance runner, hitting a hill on a triathlon course.

He takes the hill. Kills the hill.

Councilman quickly guns dirt-cracked legs to the muddy top, before descending the free-fall, free-running gravity sprint to the bottom of the other side.

He's feeling quite a bit of it these days—the run now is like a sixteen-story egg drop on freshly paved street. The memories of that fight are unforgiving.

Shoeshine Man works feverishly: *SWISH-SWISH-SWISH-SWISH-SWISH: WHIP—SMACK!* Old cat who relishes the old school shine. Between each cloth whip, he curses young cats and their use of hairdryers to thicken the final shine.

"They don't know any better," Shoeshine Man resigns.

Each cracking of the cotton cloth represents a broken moment of when. The past has loomed into the way things, people and machines were. The mood of time, lost on the grizzly ugliness of the near present—a time, some time a little after *that* time.

"What was that all about?" Councilman grimaces aloud, and Shoeshine Man while on his shoes, gives a look of coal and crossword puzzles, squinting to figure the strange, young man's angle.

SWISH-SWISH-SWISH-SWISH-SWISH: WHIP—SMACK!

"What's that, sir?" Shoeshine Man quizzes.

"Nothing."

WHIP—SMACK!

"Nuthin'?" *Young cat is touched in the head*, Shoeshine Man thinks to himself.

"Not a thing. I'm straight."

So, cutting off his audience below—our protagonist begins to think of events, only several days behind him. The blood stains from the homeless man's fatal gunshot wounds has long since washed away, but there's a yellow strip of police tape still fluttering violently on the corner of *Broad and Lehigh Streets* in *North Philly*.

Councilman knows the bullets weren't after his dread-locked friend.... Reflections on his life now flash about him, in a powerful soul search: *What was it? What brings me here?*

SWISH-SWISH-SWISH-SWISH-SWISH...

Councilman's drifting on the *"SWISH"*, now comes the *"SNAP"* of the shoeshine rag. All the while, he's staring at a mid-day copy of the *Philadelphia Bell:* the ink a light soot of black on the young legislator's hands, lines of "Times New Roman" dancing information, headlines, dates, stories, columns before Councilman's eyes set on page A12.

He's looking through the newspaper for answers a few others could answer, but newspaper editors and their owners are hardly ever that generous; the answers are within the answers that can't answer the question around every word aroused.

Distracted and withdrawn, Councilman can't restrain himself from the distant strangling of the reporter, who continues a confused divorce from the meat of her story on page A12: *"Suicide Bomber Kills 26 At Popular Jerusalem Nightspot; 5 Israeli Soldiers Among Dead"*.

The reporter's scene descriptions are distressingly horrific, as though she's scripting a box-office horror hit, rather than a news story: *"Feet, hands, heads, intestinal debris, scattered where the club's DJ once stood in the glory of his dance mix"*. An *Associated News* photo to the right underscores the pure evil of the deed.

Oddly enough, Councilman misses or declines to understand the politics of the situation. Absent from this is explanation and technical content. The expressions of terror and sensationalized adjectives he understands as a trademark of the journalist's business, but somewhere along the roasting strings of antennae that carries her editor-bound e-mail through satellite connections, this story loses its curious flavor.

Or maybe it was spilled in the reporter's hotel shower drain with the blood from cuts and marks, caused by shredded glass. Councilman imagines her on the cold floor of a tub, cursing her curiosity and career, crying like a child in a maddening flurry of hands that scrubbed the journalist's naked body, into a frenzied state of mental breakdown. *So much blood*, she'd cry, *so much death and destruction...for what?* the reporter would cry some more, in an aimless search for a god.

So why did she walk into the club? Councilman wonders, thousands of miles away in a comfort zone from it all. *What possessed her to see the aftermath of it?*

Perhaps her reasons flowed into pierced arms and legs during the journalist's intense walk through the club's VIP section, once a hangout for *Jerusalem's* young elite. Now a ripped hole of blasted body parts, thrown cartilage and melted martini glasses, once held by human hands in the midst of a toast, only seconds before chaos was unleashed. Also, she might've passed on pulling her reasons from the puddle of vomit strained and pushed from the inner tubes of her terrified gut.

Flipping back to the front page, Councilman begins to connect with this reporter, surprised to discover that he actually knows her.

What's her name again? Sharon, Shanice, Serena...something like that. Naw, it's...Shannon. Yeah, Shannon. Shannon's in the Middle East? *Damn, unlucky her. Don't really know her, but wouldn't have minded further acquaintance...She was a good piece of ass. Yeah, yeah—I remember this girl....*

Back in D.C., *over five years ago...I remember being on the verge of announcing my candidacy...well—thinking about it. Thinking that I would...I don't know; it was a funny, silent quest that I hadn't yet decided on. But, I wanted to make a run back home, back in the* City of Brotherly Love *and Broke Brothers. Thing was, there was no money to raise in Ill-town, not like the kind of money you could find in D.C.*

It was a veiled think-tank fundraiser for some favor-making Member of Congress. Yeah, it was a typical July night—mosquitoes were biting the shit out of me, and the humidity weighed heavy with a heat index of code red. Global warming is a bitch!

Shannon...Yeah, she was a left-leaning "Washington Trumpet" staff writer at the time covering a right-wing reception. That girl was literally sipping on gin and lit from blazing juice when she stumbled over to me. I don't think Shannon was really even covering the event, probably just hanging out with nothing better to do.... We had conversation.

I recall her being a boisterous, busty, buxom sort with a brain. Shannon's breath that night was mixed with Altoids *and cranberry vodka, she stuttering whispered oddities about the aging Congressman, only ten feet to our right—a frail* Blue Dog *conservative* Democrat, *who once grabbed Shannon's pretty, precious, college-graduate posterior on the elevator, climbing towards the Congressional press gallery. Oh, how she loved politics and how politics loved her back.*

"He's married, you know..." Shannon spits a small rain of

liquor on my suit jacket. I don't care because now, I'm feeling her—I want her, drunk or sober. Judging from Shannon's look it could be either, and I won't feel guilty about the sex—if any, the next morning. She now scans me—a funny, from eye-to-crotch level inspection that suggests there's more to our conversation than just the conversation.

All the while, Shannon speaks of the Congressman's marital indiscretions in an attempt to lure me into some freakish recipe for a hot one-night stand, a contrived effort to impress and seduce me.

"A-n-d?" I drawl on for a few, deliberately corny seconds later. "I take it that's supposed to make a difference?"

"Exactly," she speeds on, "you catch up quick, sport. I heard about you, too."

How does Shannon know me? I'm not doing anything right now. Haven't even announced my run for Council back in Philly. *It's not like I had told anybody about it. How did my name get in this? "Oh, you don't say," I play along. "What about me?"*

"You're the new kid on the block. You act like you don't know, but you do. You play the game...yet you're still kind of green," her fingers manage to pull a string of lint from my arm, "but, you're kind of suave, too—in your own right. A little too good to be true for your own good.... You keep quiet at times, then..." Shannon pushes up close enough for me to smell her scent, "...other times, I hear, you know how to loosen it up...."

A drunken finger manages to poke the middle of my chest, accompanied by a slanted, seductive smile that gains attention, and several growing inches of excitement leaning into my right pocket. But, something in Shannon's delivery doesn't settle too well with me.

It stirs up images of chirpy, sophomoric Capitol Hill *interns, in search of flings with Congressmen and* K Street *lobbyists.*

It's a tempting proposal...

A choice between keeping it real on the outside, or getting reeled into the dank, soiled underworld of the inside. My creamy filling of cesspool espresso has reached a gaffe of a limit.

I'm tired.

Unlike her Jones for me, I don't feel like this is the correct thing to do. It doesn't smell right, smells like the raspberry vodka lingering on her lips, so, I reluctantly pass on it.

Plus, I'm married right now.
Something is trouble about Shannon...
But a girl like her, you don't just do one night.
No.
You tear it up on multiple nights.
And she'll want more than I can provide.

Councilman remembers Shannon and the passed opportunity of repeated one-night stands, wrinkled-pillow escapades, and orgasmic jumping jacks on *Swedish*-made futons.

Easy.

Yet, there was never a connection.

No real chemistry.

No soul.

No love.

No firm stand as the firmness of Shannon's alluring, vanilla frame. She represents what Councilman continues to detest about the game he chose to play—Shannon's politics. Councilman reflects on his past encounter with the young lady and quickly shakes his head, while Shoeshine Man continues his tap dance on leather loafers.

Back then, Shannon was an inquisitive and ambitious slim from *Bryn Mawr,* the *Philly* girl who really wasn't from *Philly* because, you didn't know about *Philly* living in the suburbs.

So don't front with your life holed up and sheltered on the City Line like you know when you don't.

Yet a homegirl—not in the way Councilman knew, but of something distant known as home.

Even though he didn't get a taste, Shannon and the young future legislator still yakked it up for an hour about home. The two joked about the *Sixers,* chilled on the *Flyers,* and got enraged over the *Eagles,* who couldn't win a *Super Bowl.* Then, naturally, a dialogue on the schools they went to, and the schools their friends went to.

"Damn! How bad are the schools now?"

Councilman and Shannon connected six degrees of hometown separation, seeing whose friend knew whose friend that ultimately knew your friend. D.C. was full of them and that—improving innovative methods of mindless small talk. It bored him, but it was a small price to pay for a reporter's quiet endorsement. Councilman didn't need a headline about the arrogant, city Council candidate who didn't give average people the time of day, but spent his time schmoozing interest groups and political action committees for campaign money.

Despite the daydreams, effervescent smile and perfect waist size, the young legislator concluded that this wasn't the right maiden, time or place: Lily-*White Bryn Mawr* suburban honey-pot, hooked with hood candidate from the gravel *Black Logan* section of Philly. Councilman imagined how that would look to voters back home.

He'd lose the campaign, but would end up becoming Shannon's urban conquest, her "Lord of the Concrete Jungle" for the closet skank's mantle. Shannon's job at "The Trumpet" had been as stale as the life she staged, hence, the young lady was driven that night by a drill of jungle fever, and "*Illadelphia*" taboo, as Shannon desperately sought to shatter the cycle within.

"Cheap ass 'Trumpet'," Councilman remembers her huffing that night. *"I'm still humping these* Hill *beats and shoving recorders in these old farts' faces for the next best quote-of-the-week. I don't get paid enough!"*

"You work for 'The Trumpet', though," he counters. *"That's got to say something. Are you bored?"*

"Bored? Hell yes!" Shannon belches, *"This* Hill *hotty has about had it with the penetrating stares of these wrinkled statesmen, and the drone and whine of committee hearings, running from press conference to press conference, and hearing to hearing. After a minute,* Hill *life gets dry...if you only knew. What am I talking about? You know all about that, though, don't you?"*

"Well, I don't know about all—"

"I'm preaching to the choir, aren't I?" she laughs. Councilman laughs back.

"You could be if this conversation were off the record.

"And what if it wasn't?" Shannon smirks back. *"Of course it's off the record."*

"Yeah—whatever," Councilman replies with a sarcastic cough. "Nothing's ever quite off the record with you people."

"That's because we thirst for souls in search of fame...people like you."

Councilman gives a nervous eye twitch: *Aiiight, wench, you got me on that one.* There's an uncomfortable and momentary pause.

"...So, what's the word, bird? You down?" Shannon poses. *"We've been nice at it for nearly an hour, and you haven't*

asked for so much as a number. Tuesday nights can get sour and lonely when you're me."

"Well, I'm not you," Councilman grins stupidly. *"I'm married."*

Five years later, Shannon hitches a flight on *El Al Airlines,* ending up in *Israel,* land of *Revelations;* a classic Shannon move. The girl who always itched for action away from the echoes of marbles walls, and mumbled special order speeches on the *House* floor that even put the speakers to sleep.

A few bed board-knocking favors, a wink with a nod and a kiss later, and here Shannon is, patching that shapely, feline roundness firmly into a *Middle Eastern* bureau chair, ballin' with professionals covering the *Intifadah* beat, in search of *Pulitzer Prize* pinnacle.

Councilman thinks sadly about how pressed she must be to get back home, before musing into thirty seconds of brain-freezing rated X.

Damn: I should've hit that. Maybe when Shannon gets back. I'll send an email, shower accolades for the great story, congrats on the new gig. A friendly 'how's Jerusalem?*"*

Remember me? I'll say. Summer of impeachment and backlashing midterm elections? Let's get up when you get back.

If you get back...make it back alive....

chapter 10
PHILADELPHIA TO D.C.
DAY 7

The shoeshine stands are remarkable astrological points and stars in a constellation of events and organized thoughts. Because I moved around so much within *D.C.* limits, tangling from job-to-job, getting busier each one, several stands were selected after a never-ending search for the perfect shine. The shoeshine, I learned late in my young life, is the quintessence of professional man, or the man that simply aspires to such….

"You dropped sumthin'!" The familiar and irritating sound of a hustle heard while scrambling to work down *K Street* through *Farragut Square,* tripping over that babbling bama-idiot who called you out on the dreary state of dullness, on your finest pair of dress decks.

The first time it happened, I gave this hungry cat hanging at *Burger King* on *16th & K Street* the oddest look of gratitude, mixed with clear confusion. I'm from Philly—there were no such things as roaming shoeshine hustlers where I grew up, because blue collar folks there couldn't afford it.

I proceed to stop.

Drop my head.

Pat my pockets.

Look for fallen cash.

"Naw, brudda, you dropped a shine," he replies and sucks his teeth.

That's when I realized how out of touch I'd really turned, and how insincere his intentions, and the intentions of every other back-scuttling badger in this city were. There wasn't anymore I could do but laugh and go *"A-h-h-h",* in stupid awe of my own non-street-smart stupidity.

Shines reflect alpha-male vain for greatness. Your suit can be busted, untailored, cheap, or ruffled and aching for a press at the corner dry cleaners—but your *shine?*

Your shine can blind *all* assumptions.

It's a little more than several dollars that can buy you

corporate ladder clearance.

At the age of fourteen, I remember rolling from bed every Sunday morning upon the rumble of grandmother's voice, rattling my reluctant ass to church. She opted not to go, and instead, pursued weekly religious terrorism on one hopeless wax-eared teen. I didn't go to service unless pants were perfectly creased, with the shirt sufficiently starched and ironed to compliment dusted shoes.

Dusted, because grandmother barely understood the mechanics of a shine, the way the husband of the church teen choir understood it.

He'd stare about...

Inspect me for flaws...

Overbearing look of pity in the man's eyes.

Worried and disturbed was he.

I saw it in his eyes: *This boy ain't gonna make it.*

"When are you going to shine those buckets, son?"

"They already are, sir," proudly gathered and arrogantly audible.

"No they aren't."

"My grandmother says they are!" a little defiance creeps into it.

"You call a damp rag wrapped across a dusty, heel-torn shoe like that a proper shine, boy?"

"Well...yeah...my grand—"

"She don't know, boy!" he groans and puffs, citing a bit of *New Testament* verse to underscore the point. I was indignant though, and continued wearing those raggedy, rag-washed *Stacey Adams,* till I could wear them no more. Two summers later, it hit home during a short stay in *North Jersey,* land of lifetime Mayors and the endless *Turnpike.*

"Newark gangstas don't tolerate bad shines," Uncle Ray shoots back at me one chilly, hustled day. You didn't answer Uncle Ray, of course—you only listened.

What he really meant was that, I couldn't hang with him if I didn't do something about my jacked-up, fusion fashion statements. I desperately wanted to tag along with Uncle Ray on his excursions into *Newark's* underworld of smoky dens and strip joints.

He checked me into a local shine and barber spot, urban hole-in-the-wall rehabilitation; a frequent watering stop and city shrine of local Black union bosses, Black mobsters, perpetrators looking for hook-ups, high-brow politicians looking for a dollar, and vote and strip mall businessmen.

Indignant and stubborn I was at fourteen—consistently. Consistently ripping myself away from social standing, financial stability and normalcy.

It took me a while to figure it out.

I was notoriously loaded with self-absorption.

I thought I was better than the game that had been perfected long before me. That's where my road to enlightenment started, in the twisting bowels and circled streets of *D.C.* It became apparent, and stuck to clean-shaven skin like midnight shadow. I was aware of its existence since, well…since birth. A raging bull of milky discharge, squeezed from the acne of sociopathic grace.

The lessons stuck.

Unable to register a what, when, why and how, blame eventually fell on *Rome,* banked against the polluted swells of the *Potomac.* Such examination seemed less difficult when spinning effortlessly in the world of faulty compromises, legislative conferences, deals, panel discussions and agenda building.

It was all smoke-screened spiraling days of *Rolodex* expansion, power-spouse seeking, party hopping, thousand-dollar plate leaping, snotty middle-class networking activities typically reflecting the soul of a place, with no soul to speak of.

It was not what I expected of soul.

Instead, *Washington* chiseled, broke then re-shifted the human jaw with blazing precision. My existence in this town had become a cruel and wasted joke.

I was ready to leave it.

chapter 11

LOGAN

DAY 8

Local legend consumes local talk on the subject of the assassination attempt. His profile on the upswing, a once nationally unrecognizable city Councilman now has a national profile. Politics is all lore, perception and image. Events are construed and misconstrued to play on the minds of the many. How far one goes with it depends on how well one spins it—or not.

He's now more than local novelty. Councilman is part-time national preoccupation and political mythology. It's as though he gave the convention speech that never was or ran the campaign that never existed.

Fuse that with accounts of witnesses watching Councilman pull his handgun in pursuit of the shooter, the legislator soon receives the accolades of *King Richard* returning from war. It's now customary to live in the sprawling *Delaware Valley* metropolis and shake the hand of the beloved *Councilman At-Large* at least once.

Political groupies perform their ritual of speculation and prognostication: "How can one man shake nearly two million hands in one term?" A *Philly Bell* editorial pipes on with the above line, giddy journalists who were once unmerciful skeptics, all now suddenly basking in the fancy of Councilman's legislative footwork and presumed political fortunes.

The rumors start.

Will he run for Mayor? Or is Congress really Councilman's style? Can he win a gubernatorial bid now that the gun-toting rural part of the state appreciated Councilman's ownership and use of a firearm?

The city politicos and pundits instigate a vicious cycle of innuendo on the talk show circuit, working for a larger audience and several more advertisers to pay their bills. The consultants blow up Councilman's phones, eager to snare the legislator into a pre-mature campaign announcement, thus, starting a very early campaign season that will only serve to feed greedy coffers, and crony cash cows.

They tell him what they think he wants to hear, offering prizes, gifts and glory. Councilman's smart enough to politely brush them off without offering a definitive "no." He doesn't lie to himself, though. It's in the back of his mind, floating about the deep and treacherous caverns of the politician's ego.

Councilman now appears from smoke and obscurity, elevates to city legend and now, national prominence, with little tree, root or branch to lean on. The story is a tale of many spins—a trailer of countless movies, a portrait of many faces. No one knows quite for certain how, when and where it all started—except to say that the legislator is as full-blooded a city brethren as any other municipal power-broker and public servant, gauging the pulse of *"Illadelphia"* inhabitants.

Councilman's first run for office caught little attention in the headlines, even though it managed to upset the rather undemocratic, city political machine, used to picking and predicting voter choices. At that time, he was a resettled, small-time policy nerd and skirt-chasing whore who moved back home from *D.C.,* promising change in a city where, the unemployment rate and low standard of living sucked life dry.

There was an available *At-Large Council* seat opened up by the jail sentence of a corrupt Committee Chairman on the take from contractors and other businesses, with insatiable appetites for government cheese. Come to find out, the Chairman was somehow steering multi-million dollar procurements and sole-sourcing contracts out the *ass.*

He'd figured a way to insert slick worded and carefully mandated language in budget support acts outright referencing certain major *Philly* businesses, thereby forcing several big city agencies to award local and federal grants based on the letter of what became law. It was all perfectly legal and legitimately earmarked stuff, even though taxpayers would get *shit* in return, since the businesses were hardly qualified to offer any good or service—they were all merely overpaid consultants.

What raised the brows of city auditors were the many functions, lunches, dinners and gala events organized by the Chairman, and paid for by businesses or "friends" of his *Political Action Committee.*

Then, there was a money trail to numerous visits at an upscale and unlicensed *Center City* dominatrix loft, where these "friends" steadily fed the uncontrollably perverse bisexual addiction of a politician on the take.

Naturally, the Chairman's face, once the most low key and backroom of his Council colleagues, was plastered on every headline as one of the most embarrassing political moments in city history. A recipe for political upset soon emerged.

The Logan "kid" back from D.C. had little money, but lots of energy. At that time, pre-Councilman was young and fearless, caring little for the possible threats from city crime lords unleashed by unhappy party bosses, fearing a change in the city's political equation. But, he was also a grieving father, prompted into a grim sense of something-to-do by the senseless hit-and-run of his six-year-old son, and a wife who mysteriously disappeared soon after.

Death was of no concern at that point.

There was little to lose.

It was a story emblematic of the city's larger sense of loss, hopelessness and cynicism. After a brutal primary season, Councilman won the seat, beating out a line of succession candidates endorsed by "Illadelphia's" strongest political chieftains. With so many candidates crowding the hotly contested *Democratic Party* primary, votes got split and scattered all over the place into several different directions of loyalty.

At the same time, the legislator enjoyed a sudden surge of resentful residents, looking for a change agent who could do away with the "pay-to-play" games inside *City Hall.* With the timing just right, Councilman cleaned it up in the primary, beating out the competition by five points. When he slid through the general election, the legislator engineered the ultimate coup de grace of political theatre: Councilman registered *Independent,* effectively flipping his finger in the face of party heads, who thought they could turn him.

So Councilman could *"do no wrong,"* invokes one radio talk show host adamantly refuting the claims of several callers, who question the motivation behind the assassination attempt.

There are some who believe something isn't quite right about this guy (patently confirming the traditionally suspicious attitudes of native *Philadelphians*), that perhaps the local crime syndicates put a price on his head because, Councilman didn't deliver on a pledged guarantee.

Others view it within the context of his perceived "strong-arming tactics", of a city official used to getting his way despite the charge of opponents throwing fits in his face.

"I'm just sayin'," yells a nasal-dripping caller from Manayunk, "the man is like a schoolyard bully. It's only a matter of time before somebody starts coming after—"

"But, what are you doing about it, sir?" the host shoots back. *"Are you as concerned an advocate as the Councilman?"*

Awkward silence follows into several more seconds, before the producer gets fairly annoyed by dead air, signaling the host to repeat."

"...Well, are you?"

"Well, that's not the point...I mean...yeah, I'm concerned. But, but, I'm not sure some politician...my taxes pay these crooked baby-kissers to do what we as the people ask them to do."

"So, yes or no?"

"That's not the point—"

"It is the point when it's my point to push, sir. It's my show. Yes or no?"

"No, man, so I'm not. You made your point, chief. Still doesn't change anything. That Councilman's a thug and you know it!"

The host hangs up on the caller and launches into what sounds like a scripted endorsement: *"Well, if it's a thug who can negotiate deals between warring drug gangs, help turn my public schools from prisons into world-class centers of learning, decrease my subway fare to less than a dollar, and force these mini-mobster mass transit administrators to cut their inflated salaries, then I say 'three cheers' for thug life!*

"We need to get this guy to run for Mayor. Councilman, if you're listening right now, I'm making a personal plea on this show. Councilman: call in. There's an open line for you. Come on my show and announce your candidacy today. Tell us you're taking on The Brick. Tell us you're running today. Come on: make that leap, we know you've got the fire in your belly!"

Councilman tunes into the show today, smiling on the other end and quietly mulling the talk show offer. But the exhaustion consumes him, and the legislator finds himself tuning out the radio talk shenanigans and showy pretense, changing the channel, in favor of the thickly strapped "boom-bap" of the city's hip-hop scene.

Dropping the windows of his ride, moon roof stretches

open to draw in the *Old York Road* winds traversing the sounds of Councilman's speakers—heavy bass sound waves, thumps flowing clean like salmon in upstream wake, native beats invading unusually muggy air for that month.

Tie loosened, Councilman leans steadily backward in the driver's seat, simply letting the day and people pass—they appear to move as though he remains motionless. There are kids in full run following Councilman down side streets as if there's a Presidential motorcade cruising through *Logan.*

It's like a stranger's re-acquaintance with a memory far removed, from the deadly constant of a present preoccupation.

Councilman needs to figure out who was aiming to kill him…

And why….

chapter 12

CITY HALL, PHILADELPHIA
RECENT EVENTS

The *Pennsylvania State Legislature,* along with the unanimous blessing of a beleaguered *Philadelphia City Council,* manages to seize over two hundred million dollars from the bureaucratic *Loch Ness Monster,* known as the *Philadelphia Parking Authority.* The city's Mayor has a mouthful to say on the matter: "This *shit* is not right!"

It can be spun, chopped, sliced, priced, examined or marinated to anyone's particular liking or taste, but the fact remains that, nothing can clean Mayor's words which dropped fast like jumbo eggs on freshly-waxed, cheap kitchen linoleum.

These are the moments caught in time and infamy, moments mixed with human comedy, laced with great tragedy and consequence. It's a city executive's political death wish, or an unexpected jinx awaiting any public official, caught unaware before being madly unrepentant.

The office goes stale today. A few ants in a nearby corner of the room, stop as if caught, preparing for inevitable shoe pounding. *Mayoral* staffers, even *Black* ones, turn pale. A few young, inexperienced, teenage summer interns turn to each other before locked lips in uncontrollable amusement, finger-pointing at the spectacle before them.

Pausing, unflinching and unbelievably irritated, the ear-whipping velocity of the outburst shakes even Mayor himself. It's not shock in response to the words chosen—it's the tactless, quarreling nature of it, and the man that said it. You can't describe the Mayor as a spontaneous sort, nor as a creature of lost prudence overwhelmed by the animosity of the moment.

After a term, Mayor of *Philadelphia*, muddy *Gotham* on the *Delaware,* is losing face through loss of cool. Yet, cool made him. It's what inspired the man to aspire, and what Mayor aspires to, which ultimately inspired, just barely, the fourth largest city in *the Union* to make him its second African American in charge. There were quite a few who thought it wouldn't happen again, given the mess the last *Black* Mayor left.

But, the cunning kingmaker defied the odds and predictions, leveraging his political chips, jumpstarting a network that took years to build. His strength was in his class and composition of mad cool; Mayor personified it. Sculpted and wrote the script on how to pose it. Cool brought him to where he is, takes Mayor to where he's going, dropping him in the seat where he now sits. Cool is the splendid circumference of Mayor's power, the barrel filled with ammunition, and the tunnel dug for control.

Cool is *not* acting the fool.

Cool is what got you elected.

An echo, a ring, now another echo of reason, taps Mayor lightly on the shoulder: "Sir…u-m-m-m, Mister Mayor, sir," levels to a whisper, "there…is press…in the room," now a piss of air through crusted, dry lips, "sir."

Staring at the nervous aide's chapped upper lip, in awe of its defiance for balm or Vaseline, Mayor salts loudly: "The press? I don't give a…" and the rest is an unfortunate, turbo-charged ripple of cascading expletives, sounding deliberate enough to catch several rolling cameras, and the ear of one lone *Daily News* reporter on the *City Hall* path, desperate for a good story to chew on; pressed even further for scandal to pursue.

At this point, time stops…

Objects are now solidly frozen.

The only rotation of force is the walls, old government mahogany adorned with unread literary classics, legislative tomes and volumes of legal code. The sun's rays piercing the large, rectangular windows moves a billion particles of *Center City dust,* heat-hitting clouds of antiquity, while every living thing and person within small-talking range of the Mayor's ears, straddles this unseemly profane moment in suspended animation.

Unbeknownst to those who didn't work on his campaigns, this is actually classic form. Called by many in *"Illadelphia"* political circles as "The Brick", Mayor's reputation and legacy are both solidly framed on a marble foundation of strategically reserved disposition; hence, the meaning behind the term "Brick".

Stationary.

Unmoved.

Un-phased.

Nothing in the *City of Brotherly Love* could move without

"The Brick's" stamp of somewhat quiet, despotic approval. When Mayor was in *City Council* years ago, his district nudged along with how he decided it would nudge along. That annoying political cautiousness somehow paid off when City Councilman at the time, snagged a Committee Chair appointment. Newspaper columnists privately labeled him the *"Black Don of the Districts."*

Despite his outwardly mild demeanor, few city politicos wanted a taste of "The Brick's" nasty side. When he found out about his "Black Don" label, Mayor, who was Councilman at this time, let zoning regulators loose on the *Philadelphia City Paper* publisher's commercial real estate ventures, forcing the cornered newspaper exec to ultimately fire one of his most-celebrated political writers.

A trusted political advisor to the Chairman didn't feel that move, insinuating a slippery slope into *Third World* politics, the irony of such in a city where democracy was born.

"The Brick", angered and taller, shoved a finger in the short, pudgy man's chest: *"That's some racist bullshit, Frank, something you'll never understand. Now, just because your misunderstanding, fat,* White *ass helped get me this far, doesn't mean you can talk to me any way you want. I can throw you off the train, too. So shut the fuck up and check my polls!"*

When angry parents, stung by a series of library shutdowns, improvised a staged, unplanned, noisy drum-beating protest outside "The Brick's" lavish *Center City* office, the thick-haired, block *Afro* wearing Councilman, played a slick game of standoff, daring them to enter. Portraying the parents' demands as "somewhat reasonable," he pretended as if he would sympathize with their cause. But Councilman back then also suggested for the morning headlines, that he'd *"worked non-stop, sleepless hours with community leaders for months on this issue"*, and that the latest *"outburst"* was an *"unnecessary ambush."*

"It is, simply, a politically motivated plot, out of many, to weaken my solid base of support in this town. Those who stand by me and continue to place faith in my efforts understand how objectionable this incident is. Plans to resolve the situation have already moved forward. We can't go anywhere if the very few continue making noise when they could be coming up with solutions."

Within hours of the morning news casts, daily paper drops and radio exclusives, the parents were transformed: yesterday's valiant activists, next day's disgruntled militants sporting heavy blocks of maternal attitude on their shoulders. In one crushing blow, they'd become a rag-tag group of angry *Black* females and misled *White* liberal "lesbian activists" (as one pro-Brick columnist put it), with nothing better to do than "make noise." The chatter on row house doorsteps painted a portrait of neglectful moms who should've been at home *"watching their bad ass kids."*

It was an excruciatingly embarrassing public metamorphosis the parents never forgot nor forgave. All they wanted was to keep the neighborhood libraries open, so their latchkey kids had something to do after school, rather than roam the streets or play video games all evening.

The parents feared an opening to other, more disturbing fiscal and fractious educational issues. First it was a slew of city recreation center closings, soon after, it was the libraries. What next? *Philly's* kids were bored, restless and disengaged—rising violence, public school test scores and slipping graduation rates, reflected something gone awry in the city's social fabric.

Instead, "The Brick", playing microphone politics, fronted compassion before cameras and press conferences. All the while, he was quietly draining money from the library budget to pay for new football stadium cost overruns, greasing the palms of his construction company buddies, who promised cash for a Mayoral bid and skybox seats.

The protests made them nervous—"The Brick" obliged: *"Be cool. I'll take of it."* He privately cursed "those ghetto-bitches from *Girard*" in bouts of power-tripping rudeness, while smoking cigars with his closest confidents.

Said mentioned was growing bored with the Council anyway. Thirsting for more leverage, the coveted seat of Mayor seemed within "The Brick's" speed and grasp.

In the meantime, the parents had a plan of their own. Hungry for payback, they'd proceed to silently groom a young political upstart from a barely noticeable section of the city, known as *Logan.*

chapter 13

CITY HALL, PHILADELPHIA

DAY 9

Several floors above Councilman is the slowly sinking and unpopular Mayor, gradually losing mandate in his first term. Some re-transplanted nuisance with an anonymous column from *D.C.* is cramping the city executive's style, writing mounds of player-blasting hate, in an effort to promote term limits.

The balls on this boy, Scribbles, Mayor rakes, *for someone who doesn't want to show himself.*

What "The Brick" doesn't want to admit is that, the weekly commentary is killing his public image. Beset by unconvinced public whim, Mayor's advisors, cabinet officials, lukewarm supporters and staffers, remain gouged and scratched by media backlash. As his political-plaster cast cracks under the pressure of changing winds, the young Councilman-At-Large from *Logan* runs a citywide shadow campaign to jackhammer and unhinge "his Honor"—without even mentioning Mayor's name.

Mayor's take on this: *Leave that to the trifling, rodent journalist leaning on the back pages of the daily paper's op-ed; the cockroach egg who pisses on* City Hall *like a toilet sport.*

As he silently manages to uphold proposed public school library and city park budget cuts, shifting millions into a new *South Philly* stadium project (a typical modus operandi for the "The Brick"), the same invisible, twisted *Daily News* writer comes at him with a pound of shtick and unforgiving printed violence.

"Schuykill Boom Town Sinks into 'The Brick's' Swampy Marsh," pitches the headline on this warm sticky day.

Who was this Nick Scribbles?

Doesn't matter—voters are eating it up. Also, Mayor can't do a backroom end run on this cat, Scribbles, because of some special contract deal between *Daily News* and the *D.C.* publication, *The Chamber.* In addition, *Daily News'* publishers are owned by a multi-national media conglomerate, which can kill "The Brick's" future ambitions for Congressional retirement when he decides to make that run.

"With The Brick steering the city ship, expect no cool Atlantic *breeze from* Jersey *pushing choppy* Valley *waters into refreshing drought relief..."* scribbled Scribbles—the balding, anonymous *White* kid with his back turned in some sarcastic head shot, hiding what Mayor hoped was a busted mug.

"No rain in the forecast, just the usual stiff, tense, Philly *heat, followed by very few answers and humorless mood; unless it's coming from* Logan's *First Son in the City Council. Otherwise, expect sweat, clustered commuter streets and cluttered subway cars.*

"Ultimately, The Brick's fortitude is crushed by the absence of effective public relations: an inherent inability to simply relate. Rather than hold a town meeting or two, Mayor chooses press conferences arranged in reactionary frustration and political anger. When unleashed, Mayor's tantrums and delusions of self-appointment cause many in this town to ask: how much does Mayor really know about recent attempts on the young Councilman's life? And if he doesn't know much, then, why the slow pace in the investigation?"

The column unstitches old wounds and gnaws open new ones. The latest accusation linking Mayor to the assassination attempt is a bit over the top, and outrageous enough to get people talking in a town that's well known for entertaining entertains conspiracy theories.

It isn't funny.

Accusation isn't thoughtful analysis.

It stings hard and pricks long.

Rather than a shot across the bow, it's a torpedo smacked into the deck of Mayor's political battleship. Once *Master and Commander* of his political fate, sailing into war victorious, he's now sinking, a shredded bit of shark food.

"The Brick" sniffs for blood.

He rummages through waste and mud for ammunition, picking away at his nails in fearful contemplation.

Alright, slick, it's your check, Mayor thinks. *My move—check on you.*

So Mayor checks it the only way he knows how, exploiting the political left and struggling to upstage local media with a few whistling notes about the way steely, old-money industrial *White* towns like to character assassinate their *Black* mayors.

"Yeah, that's right," "The Brick" chirps in an exclusive phone interview with the very *Black* and pro-Brick *Philadelphia Guild. "There's an attempt on my life. It's not because I'm a dysfunctional Mayor, no, it's because they hate the fact that we have a Black mayor. I'm chocolate-Black, and they can't stand that* (tugging into a personal library of catchy public quotes). *Rather than unite the city, there are forces in this city who would rather replace me."*

"So, you're saying that racism is still very much alive and well in Philadelphia?" the reporter begs.

"No...I'm not saying that..." Mayor thinks about easing the rhetoric a bit before answering because, he'll need *White* votes, too. *"I'm just saying that this is a classic saga of good versus evil, poor versus rich. It's beyond racism. Our town is better than that,"* Mayor lies. *We've matured—always have. That's why we're the* City of Brotherly Love.*"*

As "The Brick" blazes in his soapbox glory of phrases, even he has a hard time believing, the *Philadelphia Guild* reporter on the other end of the phone line makes a fist, positions it, and pumps his arm in a soundless jerking motion that sizzles with sarcasm. Later today, he confesses boredom with the story, and with the joke of a big city Mayor.

Yet, Chief Editor says keep it: "Goodness, man, this paper's survival depends on citizen grins and priceless awards ceremonies. Are you mad?"

"It's stale, Chief."

"Then unwrap and freshen it a bit more, boy. Call The Brick" up again and get him a little riled if you have to. But, don't mess it up, son—I mean that." Chief Editor gives the reporter a look like it will be the end of an end if he crosses Mayor too much.

So, small *Black* paper reporter calls Mayor again, patronizing the press secretary into a follow-up front-page feature that could galvanize support from the deacons, preachers and civil rights throwbacks.

Black Mayor now sniffs…

Spliffs…

Puffs…

Blows smoke on the phone, and through the ass of the rookie reporter. *Philadelphia Guild's* staff writer, green out of *Cheney University* and bucking for recognition, is eager to wipe the *Black* college-stigma stain from his fading blue collar.

"Mayor, do you have any comments relating to the assassination attempt on the Councilman? A Daily News *columnist came short of outright accusing you of deliberately stonewalling the investigation..."*

Mayor's teeth now grits, gums bubble: "I prefer to let the investigation take its course. I put much faith and confidence in the work of our police investigators. You really should contact the Police Commissioner for further comment on that, son."

I'm not your son! Why am I suddenly everybody's damn 'son'? thinks the perturbed journalist. *"So, that means you have not aggressively pursued any leads in that investigation?"*

"Haven't pursued any leads? Son, we found the shooter dead in his car in South Philly. *If that doesn't wrap it up—"*

"But, you just said to let the investigation take its course. If it's as wrapped up as you say it is, then why have an investigation taking its course? Plus, there are indications of a larger conspiracy at work." Rookie reporter soon senses Mayor's increasing level of irritation on the phone.

"I really can't comment on the nature of that investigation."

"Any comment on the Daily News *column?"*

"Nothing that I find significant at this time."

"So, you believe that it's correct in—"

"No, it's not correct," Journalist hears Mayor's chair squeaking violently in the background, an indication of a nervous response, *"it's absolutely incorrect."*

Mayor didn't say off the record, yet. Keep pushing, reporter thinks. *"Then it's a fabrication?"*

"Certainly is!"

Mayor is terse.

Short.

Tense.

"The Brick" looks at his watch with fantastic repetition. The press secretary now goes for the mute button on the phone speaker: *Boss, boss, before you go on*—until Mayor glides his hand and blocks the motion, giving him a look of *I dare you to touch the phone!*

"Okay, sir. Do you think the Councilman has anything to do with it?"

"I don't know what the Councilman does outside of his time on the public payroll..."

"So, you're saying that you don't know rather than just saying no? Sir—"

"I didn't insinuate anything. I said: I don't know."

Both men now speak over each other in a way that alarms Mayor's press secretary into a frenetic east-to-west pace on the Executive Office floor.

The journalist continues, ignoring Mayor, *"to the possibility that it was politically motivated. Also, Mayor: do you think the Councilman wants your seat?"*

Mayor's voice slightly rises: *"He can't get this seat! The boy hasn't been where he's right now that long."*

"But, do you think that's his plan?"

"Look...no one in this town knows what the Councilman wants to do. Why don't you ask him yourself? What I know is there are forces in this city that seek to unseat Black mayors, if they feel certain interests are not being represented."

"The Councilman is Black, what about him?"

"Like I said: certain interests.... Why don't you check him out?"

"You want to go on the record with that, Mayor?"

"Son, I may be a bit off the chain at times, but I'm not stupid!"

As the conversation gets juicy, Mayor overhears the digital recorder now being clicked off. Rookie reporter ends recording, his voice fading into "u-m-m-ms" and "a-h-h-hs" before "The Brick" slips in one final time.

"On the record, however," Mayor chimes in carefully, "I do believe those nefarious interests I spoke of earlier are capable of backing my would-be opponent."

Now the *Philadelphia Guild's* front page gets a rare pair of bells and whistles this week.

chapter 14

5TH & LOCUST STREETS

DAY 10

Scribbles unleashes verbal fury in the *Daily News* upon reading the *Philadelphia Guild's* feature, linking Mayor's obvious dislike for *Logan's* "Kid Wonder", to longstanding racial insecurities flowing through "Cream Cheese's" city's veins.

"*To our metropolis' center*, teases Scribbles in his recent column, *"stands an embattled Mayor who is backed into political oblivion and organized neglect, but constantly cornered by justified state mandates. What a mess!"* Scribbles flips into his laptop this hazy morning in a brown-hue franchise, located at the corner of *5th and Locust. "A brittle executive, broken and falling into logistical, legal and legislative disrepair. He claws for dear political life. The fuzzy fracas over the* Parking Authority *money is the tip of the iceberg....*

"Over on the West side of the city, a Penn *scholar gets props for dropping dime on the 'authenticity assumption', as displayed by our honorable Mayor. Even African Americans in politics lust for the eventual prize in any political play: power. That's human—and contrary to sickening notions, people of color are human, too; which makes everybody on GOD's green earth imperfect. The ideological side chosen is ammunition in the special quest.*

"Rising tempers and seat posturing have as little to do with Black *politicians searching for authenticity as the* State House *had anything to do with the* Parking Authority's *decades-old chronic mismanagement, fueled by zealous ticket-writing, overspending, lax oversight and rampant hook-ups. The more money into the school system, the better, and we'd much rather see the kids benefit from it than have the bureaucrats squander it. It's really not that deep, the state simply caught on to the game."*

But even Scribbles knows it isn't that simple. Sure, the state caught on to the game, but the state is also made up of entrenched *White* rural *Republicans* who resents *Philadelphia's Black* power base. They want the city completely back, and are pulling national strings to make it happen fast; conspiring with every institutional tool at their disposal.

White legislators in farmland *West Pennsylvania* could care less about *Black* kids without textbooks and school bathrooms in disrepair.

Another column for another time, Scribbles promises.

Today, he's after "The Brick"!

Not because Mayor is Black.

Scribbles just thinks "The Brick" is full of *shit!*

Sipping on frozen mocha through a straw, Scribbles sucks on downtown air and stretches overworked arms above his head. It's late morning, the empty zone from early gridlock to misty lunch hours. The café is silent.

Waiters, waitresses, cashiers and customers are like schools of birds, fluttering about branches only four minutes ago. Now, they're not chirping anymore, much like still urban pigeons before a nuclear blast. This will be the journalist's career bomb-drop, Scribbles plaintive and professional *Hiroshima.*

"Black power aside, human error is…well…human. It wears no exclusive, limited version of brown, beige or yellow mask, nor does it really have a political alibi to hide behind—it's just there. Philadelphia's problems, like Philadelphia's permanently displaced and permeating poor, are all an unforgiving fact of Philadelphia life, more so than its potholes and lead-infested drinking water. The fact remains that, for better or for worse, city government is managed by a man who just so happens to be Black, disregarding, for the moment, the presence of those "Vanilla" hands behind the scenes that Mayor speaks of.

"However, there is a fascination with unnecessary role race plays, in allowing certain key players to determine who the key players will be—all the while, jerking the true interests of their constituents. Lost in the vicious verbal salvos lobbed across the cotton field, is intelligent discourse on bread and butter issues."

White man calls the *Black* man out! Mayor can hear it now.

Very unacceptable!

Passé', and void of historic sensitivity, it's very in your face and politically incorrect.

Yet, very classic Scribbles, though.

His hometown people will have to get use to it.

act 3:
roots

We cross our bridges when we come to them and burn them behind us, with nothing to show for our progress except a memory of the smell of smoke.

—Tom Stoppard

chapter 15

ELEMENTARY & ADOLESCENCE, PHILLY/D.C.

REWIND: FLASHBACK

Washington, D.C. had sold itself on an emotional auction block, just like the slaves of a done day, who'd been sold and whisked away only moments from the White House. *The city's lure provided an unfamiliar lust the future Councilman had searched for all his life, offering him the excuse to leave hometown behind without any regrets. It was an easy sell—more so for politician to be than his family.*

They thought it was the random college choice of a young adult still unsure about what direction to take. But, he sensed there was more to this place, the backdrop of an education that went well beyond textbooks and cloudy academic hype. Now a city politician, Councilman reflects warmly on those critical lessons years later while campaigning along the narrow stretches of North Philly *streets, shaking every hand in earnest, kissing every forgotten cheek and passing out every trashed flyer. Years later, he'd feel so vulnerable.*

But, during Councilman's youth, invincibility was stone cut and marble hard. He believed he could handle anything, or at least, control it, like the unemployed cowboy wrestling with the bull of many challenges he'd face throughout.

Years ago, long before elections, polls, bills and scandals, Councilman recalls gazing into the eyes of Lincoln Memorial *one glazy night to find utter peace—a warm rush of romanticism bubbling through teenage veins. The grandiosity of the perfectly chiseled monument is in stark contrast to the unpleasant weariness of his life before D.C., of days spent daydreaming in the back seat of no way to channel his youthful energies.*

Then came thoughts of that mulch-filled smell south of Route 301, *yonder into* King George County *some forty-five minutes away to piston of summer boredom, and cackling crickets, where* Virginia *marsh steamed and perforated. Every month had consisted of the long, steamy drives south of* Maryland, *recognizing every tree and blade of grass along* I-95.

When the family Buick *with* Pennsylvania *tags pulled into great grandmom's rocky rural driveway, pimple-cheek "Kid Wonder", in no wonder of this cursed jail of country solitude, would trip from the vehicle, in a gasp for stuffy air.*

Afterwards, cousins from distant counties in sound system-equipped jeeps would crash into country apathy with promises of distant Babylon. *They'd speak of spoiling beautiful women, over-priced automobiles and cosmopolitan debauchery—that fire of manhood, douched by frozen country lemonade, re-emerging with primal anxiousness.*

That was D.C. *then.*

He'd loved it...

Back then.

Tons of warm summer air blown into strands of thick curls, as his cousin's jeep flew up 301 North *towards* Branch Avenue *into the unknown: wild parties, intriguing rumors of wild parties, hot clubs and pretty honeys tickling with* Spanish Fly *sensation. It was an understatement to suggest "Kid Wonder" couldn't wait to get away from the drudges of* King George; *sedentary, simple-living* King George.

In fact, King George *could've been obliterated in a sudden nuclear blast and he would've cared the least, while fifty miles away, winding and grinding into the wee hour summer nights, conquering the intersection of* M & Wisconsin Streets, *or throwing dirty, crumpled dollar bills at exposed ebony thighs, once snuck into the grittiest of* D.C. *strip clubs.*

That was D.C. *then: a gallery of nostalgic firsts—first lap dance, first alcoholic urination and vomit sequence on the side of the* Dulles Toll Road; *first gambles, and the first of devastating blowouts. First breast rubs to nipple kisses, on to first favor of oral satisfaction. Then were the first jumps off jagged cliffs into glistening pools of uncertainty.*

Every summer of adolescence presented itself with a cannonball-dive into juvenile absurdity—if young "Kid Wonder" could get away with it. Older cousins with jobs, bills to pay and other cruel adult responsibilities, had justified the occasional day trips away from cranky elders and wrinkling geriatrics appearing to pass gas for regretless fun, while sitting on screened porches.

Disguised conversations about who'd "poked" who's sister, who-was-who's daddy, and what the White *folks did, done, were about to do, or scorned the Negroes for being too lazy to do themselves, droned endlessly.*

Mosquitoes could drain no more blood by drop of dusk.

Washington *had become the antidote; its spirit was fresh and alive, the aroma of power and expansion as addictive as the hardest street drug. All of these elements combined to create the foundation for a future in an uncertain world, and nothing in the city happened without the constant evolution of keen observations taking place, unnoticed by most.*

An appreciation for Washington *beyond guilty pleasures had fomented into an obvious realization that, this was (after all) the nation's* Capitol: *that molten core of democracy, that thumping central nerve of modern order, from which a kind of global stability sustained itself.* Washington—*a corridor of final law, the ultimate determination of power, the root of what was what.*

Governments had sprouted, fell then revivified into reflections of what Washington *decided they should be. Since the young man's ambitious mind outpaced the gravity of what everyone else took for granted, appreciation then transformed itself into obsession.*

College was only months away, and "Kid Wonder" made a conscious decision to land in D.C.

chapter 16

CHILDHOOD PHILADELPHIA

REWIND: FLASHBACK

When girls didn't distract, the drives through Washington, D.C. *were also suspect in analyzing its meaning and plot, in a quest for personal theme. History had been a quietly favored childhood cushion since I'd read* Civil War *volumes upside down at age three.*

While others took cheesy field trip photos of groupie treks down Market Street, *gazing the* Liberty Bell *for sake of just doing it, me, a runny nose first-grader, stretched myself to peak the diagrams, and outdoor historical brochures on* Independence Mall. *I look back and treasure the stories about eccentric, old statesman who shocked himself in a thunderstorm only to discover electricity. Second grade social studies quizzes grew into something much more.*

"Hey ma, what's this word?" a question leading into the first important lesson of my young lifetime.

"Let me see...p. o. l. ...H-m-m-m...that's called politics," grandmother answers.

"Politricks?"

"No, boy—po-li-tics."

"I keep seeing it in this book, I keep hearing it on TV, when we watch the news van."

"Oh yeah..."

"Yeah—it's everywhere!"

"So, what's the word again?"

"Politics!"

"R-r-r-r-r-i-g-g-h-t," grandmom growls delightfully, the growl of a voice that raised a household of five kids alone, and from hands that scrubbed White *people's floors for a generation. That was her growl of approval: the Virginia-ease, sharecropping version of a good film review, or a high-strung network anchor.*

I'd grin.

She'd grin.

Then grandmother would pull a sweet meatloaf or a fresh

pound cake out of the oven, and we'd grin in unison, all day.

"So: what's politics?" I finally mounted enough courage to ask, because normally, she'd either encourage or force me to inquire through the worshipped, but aging Webster's *dictionary, levitating above the living room mantle. Books and words and more books were an absolute in the* Logan *household. Hence, difficult nouns, verbs and adjectives were examined with ferocious conviction, "since they wouldn't let* Black *folks read until recently," grandmom would say. Word absorption was compulsory.*

"Go look it up," she scowls, skillfully holding back on the politics question. Grandmother knew something I obviously had no clue about.

At my fifth year, the reason for her occasional outbursts on racial history, strangely linked to my unanswered questions, was still very cloudy.

I first made color distinctions based on objective, clear and simple reasoning: one dude had peach-colored skin while the other dude, in contrast, had brown-colored skin. The "Black people/White people" thing wasn't an instantaneous jibe; sometimes, one was lighter or darker in various tones than the other.

In all reality, as far as this planet was concerned, there's no such thing as "Black" *or* "White", *just a whole lot of people of different shades. Hearing all this talk about* "Black *that" or* "White *this" as a kid, added to further childhood confusion, on top of the confusion already there. This led me to imagine persons as black as coal, and others—white as chalk.*

The Civil War *and* Reconstruction *books—authoritative chapters by the likes of* Catton, Foote *and* Twain, *started clearing this up a bit. Slow and eager studies of* Tom Sawyer *and* Huckleberry Finn, *finally confirmed my suspicion: "black and white" couldn't be a grouping of colors on the ultra-violet spectrum.*

These were ideas: fancies of the most distorted funnels of the human mind. Sometimes it was an agenda...other times—a scientific hypothesis and intellectual laziness.

The heart of this dynamic somehow engulfed the essence of who I was and continued being. It also fueled a methodical insanity, a quagmire of bruised emotions that brought me to certain points, wasting much time and many relationships. This became my hidden political spin to master the political stage, soon becoming the central theme in every campaign I instigated.

I'd figure it out later....

Following an unsuccessful expedition into Webster's *dictionary, small, post-toddler fingers were still tugging away at grandmom's skirt, still asking: "What's politics?"*

"Politics is decisions."

"Really? Decisions? What's that?"

"It's how we make up our minds about things."

"O-h-h-h-h... but, don't we do that anyway?"

"Yeah, we do," grandmother lectures patiently, prying away at some lost wisdom. "But, politics is different. Special. Politics is the real big decisions that affect everybody and makes the world go round. Sometimes it's when we make these decisions as a whole group; like a whole group, like a whole neighborhood or block of people. But, most times, the final decisions are made by very powerful people."

"Who?" I remember how confused I was then, just a small inquisitive boy getting to the bottom of it all. I wasn't getting it. And why should I?

"Powerful people. People with money and power."

"Who are they?"

Grandmom rolls her head.

Tightens lips.

Flings eyes in circles.

Patience is lost.

No more questions!

I'm tired of all these questions, boy, *grandmother thinks.*

It would be an answer that had its place for another time.

Politics would wait.

Years later...

...I sometimes wish that answer had come a lot sooner.

chapter 17

2ND & LINDLEY STREETS

REWIND: FLASHBACK

Dropping the ball that day put my eyes on the prize: politics. There was slow motion within earshot when my nine-year-old son's skull and back, cracked the entire windshield of a speeding sedan on Lindley.

What was I thinking at that moment?

A split-second sermon on physics, gravity—and like, Damn—didn't know my boy was that stocked to break a whole windshield. *But, the shame of that split second was enough to put me into instant grief, and an obscene scream of "N-O-O-O!" ...It was really some sad shit, an uncontrollable reflex of emotional vomit.*

One moment he's happily playing...

The next instant, my son's lying on the street.

Long limbs contorted and twisted.

Wide eyes brightly blinking...

One last look of youthful innocence.

And...I...

I-I could see his finger twitch...

Just enough to point at me...

Son whispering through dying eyes: "Dad."

And he was gone.

Guilt had led me by the hand that day. It was my cup of cope, a constructive deal with the despair of losing my only child.

My son!

My last name!

Inside, I'd burned with guilt, grieving, turning to no one; simply hiding behind a stoic public self. Kick in the door, and you would've seen a completely different person, of course.

I was melting away inside.

Disintegrating.

Breaking into shattered glass of broken heart.

But on the outside, I'd appeared energized, passionate about the notion that my kid didn't die in vain; that he was now poster boy for new causes.

"No-no-no—you see, it's a larger issue of unprotected city streets without speed bumps and any care for our kids," I'd told folks. When the news vans came, I'd given a stirring performance of instant angry dad with public axe to grind. I was raising the stakes. Making an issue out of a no-brain non-issue.

But, it was all a lie.

Politics was performing my inner-suicide for me.

My self-destruction...

I really didn't care.

I'd blamed myself, but needed blame elsewhere, needed the comfort of another explanation.

My wife blamed me!

I wasn't even finished telling her what had happened, and she's fast with the blame, slapping my head in a rapid, wicked and non-stop volley of open hands.

"I DON'T UNDERSTAND!" my wife cries, "I DON'T UNDERSTAND—WHERE WERE YOU?"

WHAP!

She slaps me.

"WHERE THE FUCK WERE YOU? I DON'T UNDERSTAND!"

My wife's rapping the shit out of my face and head while I'm struggling to hold her, hug her, defend myself from the sharp stings of the assault.

That was the last broken straw for the woman.

She could never forgive me for something I had no direct involvement in, but it didn't matter because, I'm his father, and I should've been where my son was.

My son was kicking a soccer ball on a wide sidewalk in front of an active public school. I was too busy trying to get into his teacher's business and pants, not noticing that the ball had drifted between two parked cars into the street and I...I told him not to cross the damn street without me! And, if he's to cross without me, to look both damn ways!

SHIT!

That boy...such a knucklehead he could be sometimes. Just like his father. Boy just knew he could get it; just knew he could outrun tons of speeding steel on a busy city street. But, I'm the father. I should've watched him. Paid more attention.

My son's teacher was grinning the "we-can-make-it-

happen" grin, and I was too focused on how to make it happen without his mother finding out. My boy probably noticed; sharp kid. Smart, couldn't run anything past him because there was not a beat skipped.

... Son probably got angry and went after the ball to spite me, probably was pissed off. "Here goes dad again, now with my teacher." He wouldn't tell his mom, though. My boy would get mad at me, but he loved the concept of us too much; loved the family, and we loved him back.

I know that's how it went down—I would've done it like that. Stubborn blood, good soul—I miss him so much!

My wife didn't think so. Hear her tell it, and I was driving the car (which sped off by the way, that spineless, coward bastard!). I already had a long rap sheet, and erected a big ass doghouse with my name inscribed on it.

Too many nameless women I'd messed with.

Too many promises I'd broken.

Too much money lost.

Even after the bullshit, she stuck through it with me—loved me; swore undying loyalty to me. That sense of loyalty is where our son got that from—it wasn't from me, because I kept on betraying my wife's trust. Before my son died, I'd cooled down, though, seeing the light. I'd become fearful that if I didn't stop, GOD would punish me. So I was good—satisfied and content.

And then this piece-of-ass (teacher) comes along and I'm seeing her every day, when I drop my boy off and—the chemistry was just there. You can't cut biology off, especially when the scent from his teacher was that strong.

I was back to my old game.

No care for consequences.

I didn't even have to tell my wife what I was doing when the car knocked our son into unforgiving asphalt.

She knew...

The woman could tell by the guilt draped about me like worn linen. That was it for her! We'd already moved to Philly *from* D.C. *against my wife's wishes and better judgment. My idea; and as usual, she always went with my big ideas, always putting her stuff on hold in the interest of mine.*

"The Good Wife" she was.

D.C. *wasn't working for me. I was getting homesick, getting tired of* D.C. *I wasn't doing exactly what I'd ended up going there to do in the first place, wasn't successful by some twisted measure of achievement we both set. I got to the point where I'd begun to hate everything about the place, and everybody in it. Nothing personal, I'd just become fatigued—some late twenties emotional crisis I should've sorted out before getting married, I guess.*

"Let's move back home, move to Philly,*" I say one day.*

"Why? What's wrong with where we are now?" my wife replies.

I'd shuffled about it, and shit, couldn't give a straight "because" to her "why." But, I talked about everything else, about how less expensive it was in Philly, how closer to my family it was, how more down-to-earth the people were. The woman huffed about the crime and homicide rate; I'd shot back with statistics a reporter friend back home had shared recently, about how the shootings were mostly ex-felons on ex-felons, lugging beefs from prison cells into the streets. Statistically, we had nothing to worry about; besides, we'd move into a nicer part of the hood.

I'd lined up fictitious job opportunities to put a good spin on it, even though I hadn't started looking yet. The odds were stacked on that since the unemployment rate in Philly *was about forty percent for brothers. But, I wasn't just any* Black *man; I had a resume of policy gold. I'd hustle and get plucked in no time, and I did, making much less than what I was making in* D.C.; *but doing something I loved.*

My wife would transfer to a new school, finish up the graduate work at Temple *or* Penn University. *She was leaving* Georgetown *and a grant behind. I didn't care, as long as we were moving back home.* Selfish prick, *my inner voice says to me.*

Eventually she pretended to reluctantly buy into my idea, having that "here we go again" look upon my wife's face—emotions stirred with a lot of love and patience. Yet, I know she didn't believe me. I'd hoped that she had, but the signs were there.

The woman was real irritated.

I'd just uprooted the whole family, and I felt that my main man didn't care, he being seven-years-old at the time. As long as my son had some friends and toy soldiers to play with, I thought he'd be cool. Plus, he'd have his grandmother, aunts, uncles and cousins to look out for him. Yet and still, my boy wasn't happy because, his mother wasn't happy—she being miserable.

The signs were there.

I knew that shit would be coming, based on the way my wife moved through the house: how she'd impatiently flicked dirt from her fingernails, slowly blew air from her nose, and bitched-to-moaned under a mother-load of whispered curses; even walked sluggishly and moody—desperate and beaten, all in one step.

The tension had thickened.

She'd be in the bathroom, and I'd be in the bedroom, wrapping the last knot on my tie, with thoughts of ignoring her, hoping the woman's consternation would wither into diseased silence. I'd then run downstairs into the kitchen which wreaked of a somber dark-brown, acting as though I'd be doing something critical to any given morning routine, but not really doing shit.

Plainly, an alternative to my wife's angered motives upstairs, as I'd preferred passive absence over passive presence. Better to run like a frightened ass to the kitchen, where I could lament the morning sorrow, rather than face the turbulent storm of her building scorn, watching the woman sink knee-deep in depression, as we'd sunken further into marital discord.

"You guys have issues," that voice nags again.

"You don't say," I snap back.

I would talk to myself, from the bedroom, to the hallway, and in the kitchen; I'd talked the cabinets, opening them in a fret of sounding busy, yet, I wasn't doing a damn thing but killing time. At times, I'd raise quiet anger to counter my wife's annoying assaults, I'd think of killing her—well, not literally, just was finding a way to shut it down, and shut the trying woman up!

Our kid would watch us and laugh sometimes. I'd escaped into that laughter and settled into a sea of calm, amid the ocean of extreme chaos. I'd looked stressed, my son looked...uncaring, and when he'd caught my eye on his eye, the boy approached me with a toothless, ridiculous grin, and a slow-nodding head.

She, on the other hand, didn't find it so amusing. It was buildup to an emotional disaster. Making it worse, I'd resorted to old, callous habits. My eyes were drifting.... Suddenly, Philly *had begun to blossom with so many beautiful women, and "untapped" joy. "Where'd they come from?" I thought in amazement, "Sure weren't here when I left for college."*

No love at home meant looking for "love" elsewhere.

Biology had kicked in. Even before the teacher, I was experimenting here and there: smooth-legged, lovely hipped girl at the coffee shop, woman in pink at the local deli, graduate schoolgirl with the bi-sexual edge, and let's not forget, single-mother stripper with thick, jiggling ass, who was as smitten with me as I was rock-hard for her.

Sure, I loved my wife, but I hated the atmosphere I unjustly blamed her for. She'd smell the scents of unforgivable on my collar, breath and lips, clogged about in my pubic hair. I'd come back home to my wife after a short evening of unrestrained trysts, gently tugging at her panties, waking her up, and she'd comply, gently giving love back to, perhaps—showing me what I'd missed.

She knew.

But, let the rope go so far.

Eventually, he'll hang himself, she probably thought. "I'll just let him hang!"

Meanwhile, my wife silently held on to our second child, tucked away in the pocket of an unhappy womb. I hadn't known until she'd clutched her stomach in frenzied pain one day, pushing me away and mumbling: "I won't let you kill this one." That's when I'd accepted how fucked up it all had become; the death of our first, interrupted a fresh start and focus on newfound joy.

Visions of our boy's body surrounded by yellow caution tape—it all moves fast. Crime scene. News vans. Microphones stuck in tearful faces. Hours of lonely crying on the living room sofa while wife throws things in unbridled anger. Picking casket. Picking plot. Paying undertaker on stretched credit. Funeral. Eulogy. Gospel songs that make you cry. An impassioned, politically-timed sermon by Mayor, looking for second term—words about an unsafe city, unsafe streets, kids in danger. Black kids becoming extinct! Press conferences. Car with busted windshield found, but no driver, no registration. "Stolen tags," the cops say.

The city mourned. I took to the street in a disguised tantrum, leading picket signs and megaphones on City Hall's *steps. It was better than staying home. "We the people" screamed for speed bumps; Mayor's pity soon evolved into hate, because money was shifted from pet projects to answer the voters' rage.*

Through it all, she kept her pride, maintained composure and grieved. We'd lived in the same home, but saw very little of each other. Then, one day, she was gone....

I haven't seen my wife since.

And though I miss her...

I have no energy to find the woman.

There's only failure, guilt and I...
Living in an empty house.

chapter 18

A CLINIC IN PHILADELPHIA

REWIND: 5 YEARS AGO

"Miss Blue's" story is, through the accidental design of her hardened life: a tale of tealeaves and sad faces. A little girl, born to a deck of cards forcefully dealt, able to run wild and climb trees till last breath, but unable to break free from the trap of whatever destiny awaits her.

"*This is…my life*," "Miss Blue" chokes on the corner of a last tear, and we must wonder what life the introspective woman speaks of. Is it the one she leaves behind, where her husband is left in an empty home, and the memory of her dead son unshaken?

"Miss Blue" is radiant cream and auburn princess, one with a broken soul starving on bare living, and the evil of anguish that engulfs her. Though her beauty—as intense as it is, known to fool many who stare and prejudge it as a portrait of stability, is really mixed curse and survival crash course, the cosmetic armor she didn't choose but learned to manage.

On this sudden, damp day when the tapping insanity of rainwater scurries into asphalt puddles and clogged street drains, "Miss Blue" crumples inside like a tightly balled paper in a fist. She is a stand-alone of no real consequence to the other people sitting in the lobby of a community health clinic, merely someone else in an ordinary waiting room, lamenting the "ordinary" life the young lady just left.

The rapid *click-clack* of computer keys rushes through a surreal blur of faces, cheap paintings and plastic chairs, as a receptionist calls her name: *"'Miss Blue'…"*

Self-absorbed husband who kills his son is not ordinary! "Miss Blue" thinks while sitting in this strange land of coughing drug addicts, the balling yells of their fixed babies, and swells of the under-employed, unemployed and altogether under-appreciated. It's somewhere in a fairly obscure *Southwest Philadelphia* neighborhood that gathers attention, only when bullets fly.

She sits still, refusing to attract unwanted attention, despite the usual looks of envious women who also wait; the waiting room "Miss Blue" always dreads—the stares she can handle and shoot back.

Waiting rooms symbolize uncertainty.

Uncertainty, being the challenge that it is, forces her to wave a flapping white flag of surrender.

The woman holds her chin up high, though.

Others, however, are too busy chewing on their nails to even notice.

Misery is so *damn* inconsiderate.

Collective misery is just a hot *mess!*

"Miss Blue," the receptionist continues calling the randomly picked name from the front of the waiting room, beckoning the displaced wife/widowing mother, who doesn't want anyone finding her; the fake identity has worked thus far, so she plays along to the point where she's convinced of her new life.

She's "Miss Blue", daughter of ball-and-chain, priestess of misfortune, lost woman who already went through three name changes, and probably nine more lives before she settled on this one. There's a deep sigh at the mention of the name, because it slowly drips with much mud.

"Miss Blue" wipes her eyes and rubs small cakes of make-up from her fingertips. She slowly rises from her chair with measured poise, a sudden burst of energy and proud concert. "Miss Blue" sways and carries her untold story, despite the gritting stares of insecure women; still, she does not care, as the woman's accustomed to it: "Miss Blue's" duplicity of pain and promise—the intersection crash of beauty and brutality.

The fetus in her womb had been kicking for days, small and angry; there's a feeling that, based on the arrival of some new dynamic, mother and father doesn't want it.

The reasons had confused fetus' small mind.

But there's a vibe it couldn't ignore.

"So why have me?" fetus pleads.

No answer.

At that point, fetus chose its own direction.

Without warning, mother is watching dark, thick clumps of blood fall into a toilet, a terrible case of miscarriage confirmed by a doctor, unable to offer more than the sorrowful hand, placed against her shoulder.

"One other thing, Miss Blue. Something really peculiar

came up in your blood work that I think we should discuss."

This is now a day later after the first clinic visit. There's a doctor who corners her, struggling to explain something new, something "Miss Blue" doesn't want to hear.

"I know you're not feeling well, Miss Blue. I understand that. But, in the meantime, we really need to admit you and perform additional tests."

"Wha...what?" "Miss Blue" is a little dazed...

Unsure of what to do...

And where she should go next.

"Miss Blue, I don't think it was stress alone that terminated this pregnancy."

She really can't deal with anymore of it.

"WHAT DOES THAT MEAN?" The young lady feels a chill, a race of ice up the spine in fear of any answer the cold, replayed reassurance of the doctor's hand will provide. *He's done this many times*, "Miss Blue" thinks. Feels doctor is detached, tolerant, uncaring—but pressed to care because it's his job; young, ambitious activist post-med student reaching for Hippocratic oath greatness on the sores and broken bones of the downtrodden.

But there's something audibly different about his tone: *"Well...I'm not sure,"* the doctor shrugs, like a kid who just dropped a full cone of ice cream on the street, now moving his hand from the woman's shoulder while moving a deliberate step back for distance.

"WHAT DO YOU MEAN YOU'RE NOT SURE?"

There's clear irritation in "Miss Blue's" voice.

She snaps at the lack of clarity while eyeing him.

"Initially, I was under the impression that...perhaps...you'd acquired some sort of infection, an STD."

"Huh?"

"Let me finish," the doctor's anxious because the woman has already slid from the examination table, fists clenched, tell-tale signs of animus creeping into the veins of "Miss Blue's" neck, as though she's bucking for either a slap or punch—violent stocks of the trade when hustling the ghetto health clinics. *"It's not that, really, it isn't. But, what I'm seeing concerns me because I haven't...none of us..."* pauses after referring to mysterious colleagues, *"have seen anything like this. It has viral characteristics, but nothing we've seen like—"*

"Viral?"

"Yes...but it's strange because it appeared very organized. I...I-I don't know. But—"

"Miss Blue" moves towards the door.

Gives an odd stare.

"Miss Blue, we really should—"

She leaves the room.

Dumbfounded doctor is left alone with a stretched hand.

"Miss Blue" pays for the diagnosis in cash.

Disappears....

councilman's north philly interlude

Logan Street Journal Entry

chapter 19

MINDSET OF MODERN "ILLADELPHIA"

GOING PHILOSOPHICAL

There's a distinct, funky sameness about North Philly *that outlasts the century that it's in. An annoying similarity that hits me like grandmother's painful plucks to the forehead, as well as the nagging yelp of the German Shepherd seven houses down; equivalent to the repeating, schoolyard bully, as he pushes your sense of calm to typhoon edge, as he bangs the tip of his index finger in your temple so hard, you end up swinging fast for his nose.*

I can't shake the feeling that the place will never change, never progress because it doesn't want to. North Philly *appears satisfied with the narcoleptic condition that plagues it, that keeps the location from moving forward. This is my town; the town of a town that I wish was something more than it wants to offer at the moment.*

But, it's where I'm from.

The offending air is also atrocious, rank and pissy, like that Logan *corner with the twenty-four-hour Laundromat, where limping, one-legged cats and one-eyed dogs congregate. Each following suit of the other, ghetto-stained clones, but different in size, shape, genetic composition and straight mix—yet all providing a puzzling glimpse into the cracked sidewalk conditioning of animal hustles.*

Ghetto-stained clones seriously searching through rusty aluminum trash bins, ravish ripping through plastic bags of human refuse, waste and unusable food, amounting to the everyday pursuit of survival and power, for those claiming themselves the most fit to survive. Through patient examination of urban cats, dogs, pigeons, squirrels, rats, roaches and flies, we can manage the eloquent quest of modern social and political commentary.

Dozens of college classes in political science, classic philosophy and literature, justice and law, comparative social sciences and economic theory are rendered useless upon long walks through treacherous examples, of urban milieu. Lectures become nostalgic blips, stuffed into the mind like mixed bread crumbs in Thanksgiving *turkey, voices of forgotten college professors proves no more effective than the buzz of mosquitoes, eagerly preparing to feed into the flesh of a human earlobe.*

Only one lesson appears to represent itself in full, practical clarity: "It takes a clinically unstable and insane individual to run for office." *The unpredictable nature of the statement catches every student in the classroom off guard. This is the reason behind lack of scattered laughter, dropping jaws exposing the roof of our mental chasm, or those whispers you hear, moments after an outrageous comment, strategically inserted into an otherwise dull college lecture.*

I quickly sigh before laughing, showing little care, but cracking the code. The professor and I see eye-to-eye on that I'm learning more about the business of politics. We're suddenly two parallel fingers, connecting in a contorted gathering of the minds. I'm becoming nimbly aware of the process unfolding, before realizing that this is what I signed on for. This is where I will end, in relative misery, dragging my feet through the mud of fiscal ruin and social dysfunction, once accepting that I could never defer thousands of dollars in government loans, used to finance a useless education.

With that, I take to the streets (which is why I'm here, strolling through the crap and extreme hatred of North Philly), shooting the proverbial shit to figure the mystery, before outlining a series of questions prepared for others, who are also dwelling the same squalid landscape in shakedown of irony, truth, focus, fullness, meaning and purpose; scraping legacy from life when there are innumerable signs in the road, confirming your irrelevance in the world's grander scheme of things.

I always come back home to Logan, *for clarity. Something in the lack of progress answers questions about the person and the politician I've become.*

Ghetto-stained clones clutch for food, struggling in mortal claw-to-claw combat for portions of sidewalk, alley space and gutters at the end of a sewage stream, are key lessons looming larger than life. We politicians, we public servants are no different. In fact, we're even nastier, perfecting the art of ghetto-combat over scraps of ego and earmark.

There's nothing more sickening than grandstanding men in well-tailored suits, battling on rhetorical soapboxes and podiums, or lacquered sound bite-bully pulpits, since every case epitomizes individual interests actively itching for position and status. It's not really human nature, I figured, it's actually nature itself...period.

Riding mass transit today, inhaling intoxicating fumes far into concrete havens and urban living, I delve into the antithesis of sustainable human civility, happening upon some very nasty incongruities. You find out a lot about human nature and social evolution just by riding a bus. These are moments where I discover the ability to set myself apart from those who simply choose to ignore and detach themselves: my colleagues in the City Council, the journalists who watch and gossip over us, the prognosticators of political spin who think they know it all when they really don't; the ignorant rich who claim to care, but know no better because there's no profit in them knowing. From the most plain-as-day-is-plain-as-the-sky-is-blue...sometimes—save for the shades of muffling gray

The powers that be, the people who run this city or gain from those who do persist as part of it, or they may choose the road to acceptance, acknowledging some bizarre, grossly familiar comfort, in what deserves little positive reinforcement or applause. In being unaware, or opting the path of total ignorance, one slowly separates one's self from the truth, and develops a strange immunity to pain. But, regardless of where the powerful ones reside, how much has been acquired, who they know, where these people work, or what car they drive, these people should know that they have little chance of escaping the hard truths of "Illadelphia".

The dying bus routing its way through North Philly, runs a slow hustle through the unresolved agony of broken homes and charred memories, depreciated values, gentrified blocks, and timeworn-lives, abducted by the worst and most unlivable of human condition.

When I reach my destination, I find my colleague, sipping on an afternoon meal's ice tea, pondering the availability of the waiter. He festively pulls a cerebral rewind into twenty years, discussing how so much has changed over time: the restaurant we sit in was never here before; the downtown block, where a collaboration of city planners and contractors decided to revitalize it, once politicians made good on promises.

"How fascinating," my colleague wonders. "This was the last place in this GOD-forsaken city you wanted to find yourself. Now look at it: clean and beautiful. I remember when brothers were shooting dice on the corner. Now, it's a coffee shop full of yuppies—that's some funny *shit.*"

This may be top among the numerous reasons he moved so far away, three thousand miles to the other side of the country. The memories here are so fresh and so bad. Anything and any place is more comfortable and soothing to the senses than where my associate grew up: where his oats were sown, grounds were stomped; where it was once the funky, crumpled, urban fantasy he'd parted with.

He breathes, slowly inhaling as if high, smelling air, waiting for a quick, passing wince of recollection. Accosting disturbed, yet eerily fond memories of home, my colleague describes a time of dark, abandoned buildings, torn barbed wire fences, laced like tattered shoestrings across cheap, red-light district property.

Instead of wondering why and how such contradictions between the sustainable and the nauseating co-exist, we silently grope in amazement at the stretched figure of fifty-story towers smothering smoothened streets, newly pressed like heavily starched dress shirts.

Is it really that bad?

Or did we, now beings of social comfort, pleasantly appreciate the danger passed, cursing the former whom these modern marvels left behind? Who is most responsible for this "it's broke and I can't fix it" mentality, despite the availability of means to the positive end? To no end, we blatantly bribe our memories with our optimism, since the possibilities seems endless in the informal stares accumulated, during this casual meeting between two old friends.

A spontaneous combustion of riots, social revolution, criminal upheaval and political neglect contributed to the past, regrettably contributing to the final outcome of the future. Eventually, this promises to reach the pinnacle of its own ugly and pitch-black precedent. This urban nightmare will transform itself into an unresolved pain that contrasts with the marbled columns of the structures, blazing into an eye-pleasing skyline.

There would be a terrible contradiction and mishap of broken priorities if everything we witnessed and examined that day were to collapse, and instead, twist into a malignant *Babylon,* a crippled institution we fools of apathy and ignorance created. We assume everything we do is for the purveyance of good deeds, now awkwardly slapped into the middle of old anguish—while making insincere steps to reshape, change and correct it.

Charles Dickens' pen, we dreaded, will soon emerge, and blaze across the skies of this *New Rome.* We will perform a pilgrimage to this same table, this same restaurant, discovering a displeasing, urban campus, bulging over the cloudy horizon—aligned just past buildings and row houses, burned and untouched for twenty years.

Then we'll applaud the effort.

The potential it once held proves unusable. There's irresponsible reliance on misappropriated government funds, malfeasant urban planning, and its damaging, but resilient culture of color complexes, class conflicts and generation gaps. The street institution, once glorious in its own right, will gradually wane into neglect, accented by collapsed surroundings and human thievery.

Its once competent reputation will be an unsettling reminder, circumvented by the reality of its many ruins. But, in all fairness, it will persist. Persist like *Roman* customs and *Celtic* debris, like *African* rituals and *Eastern* religions.

It will serve its purpose.

(My critical lapses can sometimes be a little too critical.)

act 4:
enter the stage

Twenty years of votes can tell you much more about a man than twenty weeks of campaign rhetoric.

—Senator Zell Miller (D-GA)

chapter 20

OFFICE OF THE MAYOR, PHILADELPHIA

DAY 11

Scribbles and Councilman suddenly become a dynamic duo, through no association, other than the journalist's pack of weekly columns. Though they've never met, Scribbles endorses Councilman's policies, and the politician, as expected, meets the erratic writer's expectations. However, this unofficial arrangement is beginning to impact Councilman's situation in a rather negative way.

The Pennsylvania Black Legislative Caucus doesn't care for the At-Large Councilmember's bold interference on *Philadelphia Parking Authority* funds. Those funds were supposed to go elsewhere within the city's state-run school budget. Bypassing them, and running directly to the State House Speaker for action, isn't the protocol expected, lacking the humility of an aspiring legislator, struggling to curry favor with the city's political elite.

Essentially, he didn't kiss the collective ring.

Unbeknownst to them, however, the very rural, gun-owning, *Western Pennsylvanian* Speaker contacted Councilman, deeply disturbed by the news of the assassination attempt, yet impressed with the *Philly* legislator's ownership of a concealed weapon.

The burn of being overlooked soon singes, and festers into the mortality of wounded pride. It's disrespect to no end when such maneuvering doesn't occur with the blessing of the city's highest elected and executive official, a man the *Caucus* waited years to install into the state's most powerful urban borough. So, there's Mayor, calling from the comfort of *City Hall,* lobbying for Councilman's final political fall. "The Brick" joins his *Caucus* colleagues on conference call, fiercely picking away at his nails in the frantic fury of a political conspiracy unfolding.

"I propose a boycott," Mayor spits.

"Of what?" questions a skeptical legislator on the other end of the phone.

"You mean who."

There's now a pause. Though on separate points of the state, Mayor could tell they're perplexed.

"We take this reporter, Scribbles out of the equation—that's Councilman's man; his promoter, it seems. Let's make his boy look bad, ruin Scribbles' credibility. Turn he and his newspaper into civil rights pariahs. Put a white sheet over Councilman and Scribbles' heads, and they become enemies of the people, arch nemeses of the community, traitors to our city, and villains to our race. Besides, the *Daily News* doesn't have enough *Black* reporters, anyway, so we'd be doing everyone a favor."

So, on they march, as the Caucus decides to organize a fairly substantial and amply publicized boycott of the *Daily News,* and its infamous shadow columnist. The accusations are highly charged, vaguely defined. Every press conference place Scribbles at the scene of the crime; Councilman, they claim, is his trusty sidekick.

With the city's African American clergy on board, every speech or sermon puts Scribbles and Councilman within the same sentence. Every *Black* city talk show rarely hesitates to name the two as *Black Philadelphia's* greatest threat. These slick political maneuvers worsen the fears of a traditionally dispossessed constituency who will, by their own slick calculation, ultimately blame Councilman for the root of lasting problems, and the birth of Scribbles.

The flashy assertions of racial impropriety and injury are engaged, as though they actually matter. But, the boycott itself is a dangling piece in the political jigsaw puzzle.

There's a larger racial tug-of-war being waged in the city.

Yet, *The Pennsylvania Black Legislative Caucus'* strategy will speak to a widely felt frustration, aimed towards the city's thin, but solid *White* ethnic majority, still very intent on preserving its interests at the expense of politically disemboweled segments of the population. The dispossessed and *Black* will describe it, within the most vivid terms, as a situation where they were given less chance to control their own direction in the system, trapped within the constraints of majority rule.

Scribbles and his columns find the notion and rumor of a boycott, somewhat confusing, belittling the effort as sermonic noisemaking.

"Something to stir the natives," gripes Scribbles, assuming

that if these problems do exist, and that it's his position that the racism they accuse him of is from a resolved *American* past, that there are other ways to address it, other than public tongue lashings.

Sales of the paper actually soar.

The Scribbles boycott garners national attention, raising the column's profile and increasing subscriptions from as far as *California.* Gains in revenue from a newfound *New York* readership, replaces any losses in the *Tasty Kake* capitol.

The editors nervously permit the gathering storm to continue: *Let's see how far we can ride it before tanking Scribbles*.

Whites in the city, for the most part (with the exception of the daring few), feel they're rid of the racist legacy, outlived by their parents. Whites are indisposed to accept, but accepting what they perceives as cultural sanctification: diversity.

Such views only serve to enrage the Caucus even more.

At this point, Ankh quickly enters the fray.

chapter 21

CENTER CITY TO NORTH PHILADELPHIA

DAY 12

"Racism and its institutionalization," speaks *Black Mafia* boss in a televised "opposition speech", *"is the pipedream of delusive individuals in search of answers to their own weakness. Imminent pleasure and short-lived stability feed the ego, and help dismiss the aptness to differentiate between basic right and wrong. It resolves any guilt felt from the ignorance of social misdeeds. Because of this, Scribbles must go."*

One way or the other, Minister Ankh has been persuaded to join the boycott, which takes this citywide protest to a whole new level. Yet, unbeknownst to the circle of powerful *Philly Black* politicos who orchestrate the series of open protests, Ankh itches to insert himself in the affair, hungry for more coverage, eager to announce his larger public intentions.

Mayor eggs Minister on, despite warnings from advisors. There are worries regarding criminal appearances, should more information about Ankh's suspected underworld activities surface in the media.

"Doesn't look good, boss, considering Ankh is staging a resurrection of the Black Mafia,*"* says one *Temple University* professor with his ear to the street, in a private luncheon with Mayor, at a posh *Chestnut Street* establishment.

"Black Mafia? *That's* nonsense, *professor. I haven't heard that term used since I was a teenager. The* Middle Easterners, Russians, Orientals, *some of them* Nigerians—*they cut all that shit up and took it over, right?* Negroes *are doing low-level, street-corner stuff these days. Where did you hear this from?"* Mayor takes a careful, calculated sip from a hot cup of honey latte, while the professor shakes his head.

"Brick, you've been in City Hall *so long that your head is now stuck up your* ass,*"* the professor laughs, bringing back a bit of the old school frankness they'd enjoyed as childhood friends. The professor then becomes serious, starts pointing his finger at Mayor, moves in closer so no one could hear him.

"I'm telling you, Ankh is making moves. He's consolidating fragments of the old street guard, into a new movement. Except this *time, he's playing it smart, making it all appear very political and race conscious—it's all* bullshit, *though. Ask your police commissioner—I know he knows, but doesn't want to tell you, since he'd have to investigate just how much you and Ankh talk."*

"What are you talking *about? I don't—"*

"Brick, don't bullshit *the* bullshitter, *my friend."* The professor gets real tense and frigid. The exchange between the two prompts a Mayoral bodyguard to suddenly step a few yards away from the professor, slowly unbuttoning his suit jacket, in preparation for a likely showdown. Mayor quickly offers a heated glance, motioning the trigger-happy plainclothes officer to stand down.

"I teach college for a living, so you can't *sell wolf tickets to me, brother—I* know *you and Ankh meet up quite a bit.... I also know you're much interested in more campaign money for a possible re-election run against the Councilman, that you're being real selective about what you see and don't* want *to see."*

Mayor falls silent.

"Now, I'm telling you: watch it. Ankh don't smell good, in fact, he might *try to run for your seat, too. And I'm being told it goes a lot deeper. The minister's getting bankrolled from some powerful donors—no one knows where his money comes from, but it's not from selling dope or pushing some shit that 'fell off a truck'. Somebody real powerful is backing that boy up—*you *need to figure out who before you do business with Ankh."*

"The Brick" didn't listen, driven by vengeance and payback on Scribbles. He connects with Ankh shortly afterwards today, setting up a meeting to discuss what kind of noise Minister could make.

The boycott gets more interesting.

When something as a boycott, protest, or an "uprising" becomes a reality, the question becomes: "Why do you complain so much?" This reaction is evident in the exasperating sighs of *White* city residents, growing impatient and tired of infuriated "street" leaders like Ankh, lucidly baffled that *"The Blacks"* seem unlikely to give up—anytime soon, on the rallying cries for racial justice.

But Ankh doesn't care.

He'll be speaking at a church later this week, a few days following his private meeting with Mayor, discussing plans for an even larger rally. Minister, on a totally different front, presses forward (occasionally touching base with Mayor, however, through multiple cloak-and-dagger channels).

What was and is still not realized is a reflection of the insidious attitudes perpetuated within our society, so we beg to differ and add clarity," says Ankh. *"It was the ignorance of several hundred-year-old concerns, cheapened and placed on aging backburners. Yet, some are audacious enough to contest this boycott as an expedient form of advertisement for race-baiting activists. How* dare *they."*

A group of journalists cram to the back of the church's sanctuary, becoming unusually attentive.

Ankh's tone isn't sharp as before.

Mood isn't as combative.

Demeanor and emotional aroma is…

Pleasant?

Minister is suddenly poised.

Crawls his way into the center…

What are Ankh's motives?

What's the new plan?

Elected office?

The next man's guess is the best guess—next-to-the-man, next-to-the-man, who can't figure out the moves of the next man next to him. But, his rhetoric tonight seems bizarre, and unseemly tepid for Minister. *"The importance of ultimate freedom for the dispossessed is not what specific acts of benevolence can the dominant society accomplish. It is an issue of survival, of our self-preservation as a people in this democratic community. Many people fail to recognize this, and will perceive freedom in its casual, non-liberating motif.*

"Freedom, to the dominant in our society, is arranged as only one minor level of democratic principles, therefore, establishing that freedom is not complete. It is mechanically restricted and attained in stages, the difference being that, freedom in the majority rule system is an equalizer, only disseminated when there is majority consensus. The catch, however is that, one group's freedom is not legitimate unless there is a consenting majority decision. This has the effect of politically and socially displacing most groups, particularly those relegated

to 'minority' status.

"James Madison *warned that the minority should be protected against the sometimes, dangerous whims of majority rule, while he surely remained unmindful of the slave population, spreading like blazing fire, and* Native Americans, *violently pushed past the frontier into extinction. Yet, while getting real academic for a moment, I wonder if the majority should even care. Why expect something that will—as expected, never transpire in the first place?*

"Democracy seems plainly deceptive and trivial, once the traditionally disadvantaged group must experience a system of unjust proportions. How can an individual's freedom be the same as another's? It's common sense to conclude that we all differ in many ways—therefore our individual versions of freedom come in different shades, shapes and sizes. Hence, the dispossessed groups' want and need for complete freedom is a belief in liberation, the latitude of which is a challenge for the majority of Americans *to accept.*

"I think that the insanity of race is not the popularly conceived notion of Black *reaction to it, it's a problem consistent with the dominant society's inability to accept the full context of a dispossessed group's freedom—as that group, not the dominant institution defines it. And, the dispossessed group, unwilling to conceive freedom beyond the limits set, since freedom is obtained, not given, compounds it. That cynicism may also include the dispossessed group's unwillingness to realize the dominant society's inability to comply with the full context, of their shaky definition, of what freedom is. Therefore, to me, freedom is relative.*

"The formula suggests that whereas Group B has judged that Group A prevents them from spreading into suburban neighborhoods, Group A contends that at least Group B exercises the full right to buy a home or start a business, when the poor and colored folks who lived there couldn't do so more than fifty years ago.

"The 'diversity' of culture does not hurt. In fact, even I will admit that it's a healing component for a racial hemorrhage. But it's the 'diversity' as it's now being defined, that must be questioned. What are the real motives? The accomplishment of a truly diverse environment is definitely not one of those motives. Diversity in many ways is multiplicity assumed, respected and

accepted only for the purpose of preserving certain interests, and also, to relieve a sense of guilt. It's supposed to become a diversity of differing interests, able to reconcile under 'one nation, one GOD', not because it's the patriotic or national thing to do, but because it's the only real goal to assure that nation's survival, as well as the survival of its citizens.

"To get along is not that simple a task, but it's a task we must endure."

The church crowd of a thousand roars below Ankh's dais.

Structure walls and columns shake.

Cameras flash and flicker.

Pens smear notepads with runny shorthand.

Television producers buzz with hype this evening.

Ankh looks as though he's preparing to upstage every public moderate in the city. Did the man bump his head on the way to church?

Some register it as a personal/political epiphany in the making, and there are others who simply stop, point a finger, and look back to see if they're the only one who saw it.

The birdcage of Mayoral cronies didn't factor this in as "The Brick" bristles at the surprise competition. Doesn't dig the new front to his left flank, when Mayor already has Councilman on his right to deal with.

So did Ankh just give a stump speech?

Let's guess, the people are saying: "This fool in red, black and green really thinks folks will vote for him?"

But what exactly is he running for?

chapter 22

16TH STREET, PHILADELPHIA

DAY 13

Flying high and drawing cloud circles in the sky is *Philadelphia Guild's* staff writer, Tat Nurner: rookie, front-page green-paper kid, straight out of *Cheney University's* urban journalism program; a pressure cooker of courses, barely surviving on recognizable accreditation. The entire school is on the life support of generous alumni. When interviewing for jobs at some of the larger mainstream newspapers, Tat figures that editors call him in, so they can split a gut and gawk a laugh or two about the school he went to.

With that, Tat works hard to counter the ridicule with a last laugh of his own. He will continue believing, however, believing greater things awaits him at the end of the long, dark tunnel the beleaguered journalist often travels.

Minus the laughingstock receptions he receives on the big paper interviews, Tat's destined to reach the heights, which was once believed as unreachable, according to the Nurner family motto: *"What's* killing *you is really keeping you alive."* This served them well through slavery and sharecropping, through *Southern* exodus and *Jim Crow.*

The Nurners are all accomplished doctors, lawyers and military officers, who inspire testament of strength through a kick in the mental jewels. Uncertain at age five as to what that truly meant, Little Tat Nurner got the pep talk from his pops on the lessons, from knee-scratching bicycle crashes, lunging into life, like a war-seasoned soldier on recon missions.

"Risks are acceptable," his father tells him, *"quitting is an unknown concept that I* don't *want to ever hear you talk about!"* So when Pops, tenured history professor at *Cheney,* gave a resounding and fatherly *"ABSOLUTELY NOT"* to acceptance letters from *Temple, NYU, Columbia, Maryland* and *Syracuse,* Tat maintained his cool, calmly.

Nurner fathers (on back to two fathers before him) at Cheney *tradition, isn't about to kill Tat. Ivy League and first-tier schools be damned! And if this doesn't work out, pops could do the hook up and install a teaching gig at the university's history department.*

But Tat, as city legend announces him on the local media circuit, will do it much differently. He now breaks stories like wars—each analysis, exclusive and investigation as cliff dropping as the last, heated as the next; every word and syllable reshaping policy in the *Delaware Valley* mass of brick and stone. For Tat, this is the culmination of dreams, wishes and plans, working the *Black* press beat, suddenly gets as glorious as hustling the "Big Paper" circuit.

Tat can stand out.

He *is* standing out.

While everybody else in the *Black* paper league covers award ceremonies and community dinners, Tat goes for the scandals and big quotes. Create a league of his own and eventually, some day, take over *The Philadelphia Guild,* transforming it into something greater.

Suddenly, editors at the mainstream papers want Tat.

He rarely returns the calls.

Tat's aggressive, and that's good enough to call his own shots, now posting his own stories, yet young enough to get routinely chewed by his cautious, politically pandering Editor-in-Chief.

"Slow down, Tat."

"Alright, Chief."

"*Slow* down, Tat!"

"I said *'aiiight',* Chief. *Damn!* All on a brother's back."

"I *mean* that! Don't *start* on me, little man. I know this game, and have played it, *way* longer than you. Slow down!"

"I got you, Chief. I hear you. Slow down."

"Don't get like that *White* boy, Scribbles."

And this pisses Tat into a dreamy, heavy-handed *pimp-slap* of the brown hue from the Chief's face—the mere comparison without opportunity to allow rookie from *Cheney*, the benefit of his own standard; instead, Chief stoops to the *"White boy"*.

Compare me to the White *boy, you brainwashed fool*, thinks Tat. *Why not compare the* White *boy to me? What's the harm in that? ...Why do we* always *have to follow a trend, rather than start one?*

So it's Tat that silently pats his back as the metro area's

brightest, most talented, raw jack reporter; the savior of *Philly's* largest, oldest, struggling, *African American* newspaper, rearing, and ready to take things to new levels.

"I can do *better* than Scribbles, Chief."

"How so?"

"We got Brick's grin already splattered on the front page. Naturally, why not an exclusive with the Councilman himself?"

"What makes you *think* the Councilman will go for something like that with a paper like this?" Chief challenges.

To the Editor's surprise, the young trenchant city legislator aiming to craft the populist tone takes the invitation. Councilman appears more than game to the idea, as though he's been waiting all along for the financially fledgling, but respects weekly newspaper calling him up.

The interview is finally scheduled, and the fifth floor office in City *Hall* buzzes with a burst of skittish gaiety and fevered commotion.

Everyone knows Councilman is hurting from Mayor's boycott assault, and the emergence of Minister Ankh as a potential political rival does not bode well for the political aspirations few are privy to. But, Tat calculates that the legislator also understands that this particular paper could, rest assured, bust him out in the most terrible way for not agreeing to the interview.

Eventually, the talk show circuit gets word that Councilman is perhaps too set and proper atop his *City Hall* tower to bother with the average folks below, particularly those that read *Black* newspapers. It isn't a political risk worth taking in a city as polarized and jaded as *Philadelphia.*

Whatever the reasons, Councilman now seems eager to tell all.

* * * * *

Tat arrives to *City Hall* shortly after, sling pack stuffed only with digital recorder and pad for each hand. There's little fanfare or big entrance, only handshakes, an abrupt, boisterous exchange of niceties, mixed in with comments on the weather and city sports. Moments later, Councilman and Tat are plunging into deep conversation, and the shadow of a front-page feature begins to evolve through candid exchange, a painfully meticulous verbal water boarding of prickly Q and A.

It's the hallmark of the journalist's personal style, getting to the point while begging the questions—questions of answers Tat's already predetermined for his benefit, and his alone. He makes up his mind long before the interview, pegging any politician as phony as method of low expectation, a formula that isn't gone unnoticed, and irks the most experienced city politicos who reluctantly agree to being skewered.

"Why are you an Independent, Councilman?"

"Well, actually, Tat…I was once a Democrat, and then a Republican."

"Interesting."

Tat gets a look from Councilman like the revelation is something significant, or unparalleled in either of their times.

A Black Republican, the young reporter thinks. *Go figure on this mental-train wreck! So, here's where I'm supposed to get wide-eyed, and my mouth is suppose to foam in rage—where the interview stops, right, Councilman? There are few rejects like you, obviously. …Or, is that the way you want to make it seem? You want me to feel pity or admiration?*

"Let's talk a little bit about that. This is a different kind of interview, Councilman. I want people to know you, get a *real* sense of who you are behind the political mask and all that. Are you okay with that?" Tat asks.

Councilman simply nods his head for affirmation.

"The Republican thing—that's interesting; I didn't know that. Does that make you different, or considered to have 'sold-out', as they say?" After all, this is an overwhelmingly Democratic city."

"No," the politician answers flatly, acting as if he's ignoring the last statement. "It serves as the foundation for a point I'll get to later on. But, I felt I could trust you to be objective here. I was a Democrat, too, now. Don't forget that part of it," he laughs. "But, I grew tired of party politics. There really is no difference between the two."

"Tired of what?" Tat bemuses. *Tired of the same plan? Tired of the same conversations that cause you to do something dramatic, creating your own plan and conversation, just to replace theirs?* The rookie newspaper man has seen this type before: *they've either been this way all their lives, or they get caught in the urge to try something new—like experimenting with drugs. In this case, it's not heroin, PCP or crack—it's politics.*

Tat notices the pause.

The thinking.

My question puts Councilman into pause—he expected more from me. I honestly don't care. Chief will, I'm certain. His Caucus friends and the Mayor will love this. I just want the story, the real story.

"Tired, Tat, because, in the final equation, it doesn't matter. Republican, Democrat, Muslim, Christian, Left, Right—it doesn't matter until they *all,* make it seem like it does. Like it does make a major difference, as if there is suppose to be a difference, because the powers that be, want so much for a difference to exist. This is what caused me to switch around a bit. To evolve."

Councilman leans in.

Uncrosses legs.

Folds worked hands on slippery oak desk.

Sunlight eases into the office, yet, loud horns from *Broad* and *Market Street* hits an office window in bouts of short, angry beeps. An alarming police car's siren now goes off to who knows and don't care where. The shrilling whistle of faulty, transit bus brakes could crack wood from the windows if they were open.

"Since this is a *Guild* interview, I'll speak to your target audience for context. Our people, especially, are real funny that way," Councilman states. "We find a difference or two, split into our respective camps, and then we find eight million different ways we can die at each other's hands. We know compromise when it comes to dealing with the *Romans,* but only provocation once dealing with ourselves. You can't tell everybody this—it's the way it is, I suppose.

"A *Black* Democrat, for example, may have an easier time dealing with a *White* Republican than with a *Black* Republican, and vice-versa. The only difference between the *Black* Democrat and the *Black* Republican is their chosen side. Yet, they both move to a trembling sweat once Master's whip cracks. We don't seem to comprehend Master's intentions as he conquers through division of mind, body and soul. Instead, we play into *Rome's* hands, and swaddle ourselves on Master's whip. Those involved in this game, rarely seem to really understand it. They don't seem to comprehend Master's intentions: continue to annex the mind, divide the body, conquer the soul."

"Who is 'Master', Councilman?"

"You don't know what I mean?"

"Let's assume for a moment that I don't."

"The way things are."

"The way things *are?* That's not a who, that's a situation."

"But, situations can control us as well."

"Do you mean *White* people?"

"No. I don't really, I mean Master. It's a metaphor for the type of system we submit to. A metaphor for what we've become, and how we allow what we've become to subjugate us."

"Okay, moving on." Tat is clearly annoyed. There's a thought that Councilman is patronizing him, offering something of an Ankh-like template to fend off the critics.

"Anyway, being *Black* and being Republican was like being night and day at once. It's...taboo, anyway. And it wasn't all that election-worthy for a," Councilman put his hands up in a quoting motion, "*'Black'* politician seeking office. I couldn't expect arm-opening receptions. I could've gotten *mugged,* man, taking campaign walks through *North Philly,* talking about I'm some *Abe Lincoln* or *Teddy Roosevelt* progressive. Teddy who?"

Councilman falls into his own hidden sense of humor. The journalist cracks a smirk, but remains steady in his usually unruffled, hyper-professional manner. Tat's not impressed, but pleased that the politician is comfortable enough to offer the point.

"It was like a deliberate 'double-consciousness'? Is that a correct characterization?" Tat wonders.

"Yes. Somewhat—you could say that," Councilman responds. His "double-consciousness" is pre-meditated, a voluntary reflex to Councilman's life's experiences—a willful kick in his own ass. Some people like punishment, and there are others who are molded for it. Unlike most of the politician's persuasion, he's aware that there's such a thing as a "double-consciousness", and with this knowledge, proceeds to live it.

It's Councilman's dream to be as such.

"The real purpose of my strategy at that time was two-fold. It had nothing to do with history or tradition so much. I felt we'd pretty much played all our political eggs in one basket for too long, giving too much loyalty to those who could be equally wicked.

"By that point alone, what is the difference between the two parties? They're both owned and operated by the most corrupt of men—why do we even try to distinguish the two? As a whole, we're as loyal to a political label as we're interested in it for ulterior and selfish motives.

"Our counterparts practice partisan games out of selfish motive. Most of us, on the other hand, are more interested in showing just how partisan we can be, rather than using the party system as a vehicle for the best means possible. We're the only people I know of that refuses to strategically align ourselves with both parties, because we are *hopelessly* obsessed with one. But, we regretfully forgo any chance at the exercise of real power. We restrict our ability to maintain and strike issues with strategic flexibility.

"The reason for the elected official I am now is centered in this philosophy to some degree. There's nothing moral in excessive allegiance to one political party, simply because that party's platform looks good. And there's nothing moral in being completely sold on the other party because you think you're special. We're so easily sweet-talked into these escapades."

Councilman: purportedly anti-Black or heaving pro-Black? Tat fails to see which side he stands on. *It's all just Black to me,* Tat wanders into thoughtful similitude. All he wants is his story, his interview: a serious glimpse into Councilman's mind.

Councilman sighs heavily.

Catches a short wind of breath.

Spins his chair for a brief moment.

Now glimpses out the window into *Broad Street.*

Rotating towards the opposite direction and, without real purpose, Councilman aimlessly looks about a bookshelf of required reading. By his mood and telling frowns, Tat figures he's comfortable enough to disclose more.

"Let's be human for a moment," the politician begins, "and I mean that seriously. I don't mean to say this for media consumption and, like some of us do, revert back to truly believing that all we are is black or white, without considering shades of gray. I'm not into flashy rhetorical ploys; leave that to the preachers and the activists. I'm being for real.

"What happened in our system of democratic beliefs was not simply an innocent change of political guards. Dangerous patterns do exist, and these are patterns we must follow for our survival. Most politicians who decide our fate fail to mention the underlying political motives, the shadow money passed from terrorizing, pale-faced bigots into campaign coffers. Fail to mention their *true* voting records, since most of us citizens, fail to even do the research.

"The citizen's word, to which the elected official is supposedly bonded, becomes irrelevant, muffled, his mouth filled with the political sock in it. This lack of awareness on our part is all very timely, in the context of what could always change into the bleakest of futures."

"*Why* are you telling me this, Councilman?"

Councilman pauses…

Leans forward again.

Man with expensive gold cuff links, camera-ready smile, and city government desk, break into nervous coughs and a hurried laugh.

"Because, man, it's evolution. Spiritual evolution, that is. You think we get up here through superhuman powers in a cape and spandex? We politicians are people first. We grow, hurt and evolve, just like everybody else. Our problem is that we do it expecting to one day, have taxpayers flip the bill. I'm willing to admit what no one else wants to talk about—having growing pains. My growing pains were philosophical and ideological; I didn't drink, snort, needle and *whore* it all away to finally wake up and realize I was now complete. Didn't you go through similar struggles to get to where you are, Tat?"

Reporter gets bitterly annoyed and defensive at deflection.

"I'm asking the questions, Councilman."

"That recorder still on?"

"Why?"

"You want this interview, right?"

"Yeah."

"Then scratch everything starting from 'it's evolution'."

"You never said that was off-the-record."

Sixty-second silence…

Tat's interview is imploding.

"Councilman?"

"I've got a good afternoon to wait for you to rewind."

"Well, sir, we'll just have to end it there, I suppose," Tat says, puffing arrogantly, assuming he's dodged the politician's hardball.

"Fair enough," Councilman states and rises from his chair, in mid-drift to the phone. "You can talk to Chief about it."

Tat huffs a moment.

Shoots a glance at the politician.

How'd he know his name is Chief? "Chief wouldn't care."

"*The Philadelphia Guild's* publisher, who's Chief's boss, who might get a call from a few of your larger advertisers, would be interested."

Tat pushes "rewind" button.

Several minutes of candor, blown across digital dead air.

Recorder shuts down.

Clicks.

Forwards, in one breath of journalistic anxiousness.

Councilman is pleased.

Thanks young reporter for erasing sound bites.

"There's a principle to this thing. I'm not trying to be different for the sake of being different, I'm just telling you like it is, friend. We need to drastically change and look at the way we do things, we need to look at our collective condition from a different angle."

"When did you finally become such the 'Independent'?" Tat curiously asks. "Do you believe that this is why your life was targeted?"

Councilman avoids second question.

"During my last days as a Republican, I kept running into spooks: cynics and self-doubters who argued persistently for 'bootstraps' and 'self-determination', when we were the originators of all that. All this time, they skipped and grinned while reciting rented talking points. A lease on the soul is what I would call it. They were on the political take: consultants, lobbyists, staffers, and talking heads—party brass monkeys, looking for a cheap high. The same gut-yawning, ear-throbbing talk that blamed 'liberals', 'poverty pimps', and 'race-baiters', as if they were doing so *damn* much to change the world when they weren't."

So, Tat writes in a footnote for the future article, "*In disillusionment, exasperation and the need to survive with a fresh conscience so he could sleep with at night, Councilman became an Independent.*" The journalist then performs a mental note: *Councilman grows weary of defending the "party", when there are greater cobs of corn to shuck, larger balls to throw, realizing a better path to pursue upon the next century. Blah-blah-blah!*

"But politics is what makes this small world spin, the politician continues. Minus wars, police brutality, tax and budget cuts, and racial profiling: forget *a-l-l* about it. Let's pile into the franchise coffee houses over steamy cups of rich, sugar-thick cappuccino, and pontificate about how we get systematically pimped!

"To mention the term to the dispossessed," Councilman rambles as if interviewer is no longer in the room, appearing as though the effects of the shooting has somehow traumatized him, "is introducing a foreign language. Confusion rears its vexed head when thrown to the wolves of misinformation and virtual unknown. Ignorance reigns. Silent screams of incredulity: 'What's that? Who?' The explanation is lost in universal astonishment, spun on yarns of hype, bugged-out by Biblical bile, and bigwig bantering. That's politics.

"Every decade partisan baritones reach chalkboard-scratching crescendo ending time, reason, fairness, justice, and maturity as we all know it. But, if only we did know, since certain segments of the general population have little to no control over their political fate.

"Time, motion, thought, touch—all essential interactive elements of human existence, are folded into suspended snapshots of animation when you finally *realize.* The mug dodges micro-sized, atom-splicing minutiae, in quest for a correct analysis of this dreadfully *Orwellian* situation: everybody in this game either looks or thinks the same." Thirsting for a third-eye burst, Councilman talks of his brain getting twisted, turned, tagged and tackled.

"Few souls, Tat," the politician rises from his chair slowly, hands folded behind his back, "dare to brave a squared, in-the-face peek at the terrifyingly dismal state of politics, a coming catastrophe of dangerous, global proportions. Claims of representation are simply veils hiding the appetites of political ego and glory; preserving party dominance and platform become the foremost priority, as public needs are placed between backburners.

The problem with this ongoing, tired, whiny debate between left and right, is that it becomes obsessed with itself like a busted hip-hop re-mix, obsessed with one outdoing the other, and less moved by that enchanting, *"Fantasy Island"* dialogue towards compromise and productivity. Democracy, instead, becomes the chained beast of Sunday talk shows, polls, sound bites and Teleprompters. What's overlooked and conveniently neglected is lack of representation, thereby creating an atmosphere of resentment, distrust and, ultimately fear."

The reporter posts occasional planned coughs throughout the course of the speech, signs of boredom that doesn't appear to faze Councilman any. As long as Tat continues taking notes, the legislator will press on with the platitudes, remotely hoping that someone out there—even the journalist sitting across from him, will grab it.

Still, Tat, eager for a fresh expose, doesn't buy it.

A politician, unplugged and unchained by something deeper, *always* prints a good headline, but each time there's something missing, since the politician is the martial artist of decoys and deflection. Tat now wants to talk about the dead son, and the mystery of the missing wife.

There's this weird cut-off, emotional wall shielding Councilman from any inquiries into his past. Voters simply accept that about him in a way they did no other politician in recent memory. While in office, Tat hasn't seen any photos of the family, no happy snapshots of the son, no prettier snaps of the wife.

What's that all about? Tat thinks to himself.

"Councilman, I'd like to ask about your family, I—"

"This interview is now over," is the last thing Councilman says before making an exit from the office. "I have a hearing to prepare for. One of my aides will answer any policy questions you may have."

No problem, though. *The Philadelphia Guild* will get it: an exclusive with a future mayoral candidate?

"There must always be the potential for some sort of national self-examination, Tat," the reporter replays the part of the interview he believes is safe to record. *"An urgent and laborious meditation concerning public pride, public safety, and public unity. It presents the opportunity for all to rally behind a common theme of patriotism, and a rigid thread of civic solidarity, themes presently missing from the general social fabric.*

"With the future now here, there's a desperate need to grasp the fresh and unprecedented; the need to challenge the tedium of a stalled world dominated by the repeated, devastating emergence of stale thought, lacking true democratic passion and direction. Ideas must formulate beyond the infant perception of what sounds good. Ideas must now work. In order for ideas to produce the tangible results required, they must to some extent, contribute to the common good. It's a mission I believe I've been destined to carry out."

"The Brick", Tat feels, shouldn't worry. Mayor's spot is too small a move for Councilman. Guys like him either need to aim higher, or have privately planned to scale it.

The reporter has a feeling that this interview is now getting far beyond the bottled up pain of Councilman's deceased son.

chapter 23

CITY COUNCIL

DAY 14

While penning another *Pulitzer Prize* hopeful, Tat failed to ask some of the more important, or city-related questions: *"What about that recent tax hike, Councilman? Doesn't the city already have a surplus? So why inflate city coffers with the loot of hard-earned work?"*

Instead, *The Philadelphia Bell* beats *The Philadelphia Guild* to the questions. It soon becomes a beastly turn in Councilman's career and reputation. People now start paying attention to what he's really doing on the fifth floor of *City Hall.*

When the words "tax hike" blazes the pages of *The Philadelphia Bell*, many in the *City of Brotherly Love* shift uncomfortably over morning coffee, grits and eggs. The hike becomes momentarily ominous.

A double whammy of tax increases wrecks *Philly's* solitude: the City Council rips a hefty twenty cent telephone tax, and Mayor follows suit with pre-Memorial Day weekend property tax increase: a thirty cent hike. This is all backed by the legislative arm-wrestling of the kid from *Logan.*

Little notice is given to how greasy Councilman manages it. It's all pressed on a backdrop of rising food and fuel prices, unabated by long car lines at the gas station and frustrated citizens, scurrying about the grocery store aisles in search of relief.

Tax hike? It feels so…tyrannical; so unholy, and disproportionately cruel; disturbingly and disgustingly metropolitan. But, these changes are forced by the winds of expansion. The city's budget figures are coarse with the smell of it. The increases in spending are steadily rising, as the tri-state market expands, unfazed by citizen chagrin, environmental atrophy or irate voters. But, few residents, if any, in this modern urban latrine are voting anyway.

Apathy sets in like an odorless virus.

"Who cares?" privately quips Members of the Council, Mayor, and his Cabinet. There's little accountability come

Election Day in this Gotham of nearly two million. They're all guilty, every citizen, man, woman and child old enough to understand what's going on. They were halfway crunched in dawn's rush hour on *Roosevelt Boulevard* before they even realized they forgot to vote and, thus, left their fate to the bruising egos of self-interested statesmen last election.

In the real political world, tax hikes are as volatile as a lit cigarette near a leaking gas pump. Many *Philly* couch potatoes miss something, merely musing at the ease of the City Council votes overwhelmingly favoring Councilman's proposal to increase taxes, as a way to steady the shrinking city surplus. One Councilmember goes nostalgic, before activist on the rest. Another swipes a calculator, crunches some numbers, and surges forward with his vision of fiscal logic.

This is becoming an era of crunched budgets amid rising expectations, and an affordable desire to live as well; as the modern century could provide.

So what about a tax hike?

As unfair and as burdensome as taxes are, one has to kindly remind themselves of what those paycheck devouring critters are suppose to provide: sustainable public services, continuous trash pickups, regularly shoveled snow when white flakes fall (if they ever fall again), and relatively well-educated, over-achievers in public school.

Since *Philadelphians* discover paradise is better without municipal sick-ins, seasonal trash worker walk-outs and annual public school teacher strikes, raising taxes seem a surefire way to keep the budget balanced, and the neighborhoods served. In *Philly,* thirty cents more seems hardly a worry since all of the above are, for the first time in the city's long life, being received on a tasty platter.

Yet, the issue at hand will show itself in whether or not the hike will serve the greater *Philly* good. After many curving rhetorical maneuvers, *"I believe that will happen,"* is what Councilman offers on morning talk. Certainly, this is a City Council and government hardly beset by public whim, come election time (although that will change with time, economic uncertainty, the scene of multi-office rises plaguing tree-heavy skylines and abandoned parking lots that could've been recreation centers).

But, it's also apparent that *Philly* can still be an affable industrial town where the working person can have his/her voice heard, as loud as picket signs and bullhorns can carry them. Hence, that's where accountability will lay solid.

The Council, so far, is giving every indication that it knows its course. These members, many new and fresh for the most part, do not appear all that desperate for political tokens.

The times are very good to this lot.

Few could dream of anything going wrong....

act 5: conspiracy

The government is psychotically racist and robotic.
The matrix of entrapment is socio-economic.
—Immortal Technique

chapter 24

NORTHWEST PHILADELPHIA

DAY 15

Lieutenant Halkos and the *Philadelphia Police Department's* Central Violent Crimes/Fugitive Task Force jumps to the first belief that Councilman was the target of a failed mob hit. All angles lean in the direction of the notoriously violent d'Stanfa crime family, an organization with origins secretly shoved in the hidden alleys of 9th Street's food market, where dried pigeon dung is inches deep, and the strong smell of finely cut meats, mill about like a murdering musk.

Big d'Stanfa, sources say, fumed in hot rage, because the politician's latest zoning legislation indefinitely stalled what would've amounted to a half billion dollars worth of luxury town home projects, and outdoor shopping centers, restoring the entire middle to south end of *Delaware Avenue's* pier. Say "Big 'Deez'" stands to make mad cake on whatever deal is in the works.

Some case it as "retirement loot".

One informant replays a conversation with the crime boss some time back: "*In comes Councilman 'whatever-his-face' breakin' all the contractor's balls on zoning violations, illegal labor practices and, get a load of this* shit *here—environmental impact studies.*" Big "Deez" fumes: "*Who da fuck made dis guy me?*"

"d'Stanfa ring a bell, Councilman?"

"Yeah. I've read about him in the papers," Councilman throws back during a casual chew on a stick of gum.

"Ever meet him?"

"No. Don't reckon I've had the immense pleasure. He thinks I boned his billion-dollar empire."

"Have you ever met anyone that's associated with him?"

"No. I don't believe I have."

"Has d'Stanfa ever contacted you?"

"No."

Second-tier police detective shoots peripheral laser beams into Councilman's living room, while managing a shot of retina into the whites of the politician's eyes.

Searching…

…Searching…

…Searching for data…

On a mission to discover if there are lies amuck.

He can't see or sense any at the moment.

Pauses…

Halkos continues scanning the room.

Councilman watches carefully.

"Why do you ask, detective?"

"No particular reason, Councilman."

"Gotta be."

"Gotta be what?"

"A reason," Councilman quickly quips. "You don't ask questions like that without reason."

"Well, I *just* did, sir. You let me continue asking, and you can simply answer."

"Certainly. You can then sit down, wait, and sip on some fresh *Kool-Aid* while I call my attorney. We'll wait for a few hours before he gets here, about enough time to pass where you'll be trapped—trapped within self-defeating thoughts about how you've got better things to do with your time and people's money."

"I see your point, Councilman. I was just wondering, was all."

"About what, if you don't mind?"

"Were you ever on the take from our local neighborhood mob?"

"N-o-o-o."

"That's an emphatic 'no' or an officially prepared 'no'?" Halkos says, smile looking like dripping cheese.

"So, you're *saying* that we need to wait for my lawyer?"

"I didn't say that, sir. Did I say that?"

"It's implied, you've established that I'm a *suspect* in an assassination attempt on my own life."

"Yes or no, Councilman?"

"What do you think?"

Bastard!

City Hall heavyweight watches city payroll pawn give the heaviest sigh, as the detective throws a leaning, casual glance, at what amounts to yet another crossroads in his career. But, the decorated officer has heard that the politician is far from being like…

Like what?

Petty.

There hasn't been a story, to date, of Councilman exacting revenge on lowly public servants for a pittance of nickels and dimes. Halkos finds some degree of relief in that knowledge.

But, still: how far do I go? How far can I take Councilman? Every man has his breaking point. Do I size the public official up, or keep it cooled down? Do I anger and piss Councilman off? Is he a suspect?

Halkos took a few more seconds to think, deducing and reaching dubious conclusions that a stack of investigative papers won't bring.

"You don't need a lawyer, Councilman, you're fine…I just need to be thorough. You can understand, sir." Halkos' eyes steadily lower in humility.

The focus of the Lieutenant's query simply shrugged and let go: "I'm intimately familiar with how thorough our city's finest can get. I appreciate your diligence, Lieutenant, because it's my safety and life. But don't throw stones where there's no water."

Halkos figures that someone is still tailing Councilman.

The print of the shooting attempt suggests that.

Whoever it is…

Has been following the politician for some time.

"Big 'Deez'" men?

Halkos doesn't know.

Yet d'Stanfa wouldn't make it so obvious.

Whoever it is…

Follows Councilman strangely.

chapter 25

A DARK ALLEY, PHILADELPHIA

DAY 16

Councilman fails to mention anything to Halkos since the politician figures it's best to keep things on the low; he doesn't want police getting wrong ideas, or their presence scaring away those who follow him. Councilman thinks this approach could go a long way closer to discovering the truth behind the shooting and the series of strange events that led to it. But, the politician realizes it's a dangerous proposition to fool law enforcement. Still, the risk posed by those following him is far greater than the clueless suppositions of the city's violent crime investigators.

It's why the city official was carrying a gun in the first place, that early evening, a week before the shooting. He knew he was being followed—strange men in customary mystic black suits were sizing the politician up for some unknown business.

Crisp, sixty-five degree air frosting *Northeast* winds into moonlit vapor, Councilman goes for a vigorous run towards *Belfield Avenue,* adventuring past daily stresses of work and that funky, rat-infested corner at the subway stop and elevated rail station nearby.

Running swiftly…

Across *Broad...*

Through *Lindley...*

Down *Lindley...*

Across *Belfield* the politician races, thinking the shortcut across the outer south edges of *La Salle University* will keep him relatively clear of a random mugging. As Councilman reaches *Tabor Road,* past the local auto "chop shop", and ancient shrine of stolen hubcaps, he isn't prepared for the impromptu stop by two *White* muscled thugs, who throw him against the hood of a dark sedan; a blazing flashlight beams in on their target.

"Where you off to?" asks Thug #1.

"Running." Politician comes to a sudden stop, regulating his breathing, in case there's sudden need for quick escape.

"From what?"

"Nothing."

"Then why you running?"

"I'm training."

"Training? Running that fast? Through this neighborhood at this time of night?" Thug #2 interjects feeling the need to get in edgewise, his perspective itching to interject and take lead.

"I need the exercise, fellas, and I'm almost done, though. So, maybe you guys need to *piss* off."

Both goons snicker.

Thug #1—a tall, mutt-looking bastard on the left with large-sized craters on his face, spits shreds of a chewed, unlit cigar: "Yeah, I bet."

Thug #2, the shorter, jittery partner in crime, slips in: "That's all they know how to do—run; run fast."

They? Who are they? Politician ponders, finding himself more offended than frightened. "What's this all about?" Councilman curiously asks, figuring that the two men know who he is.

Suddenly, the larger cat with the questions bucks the city official behind the knee, disrupting his center of gravity, crashing the politician's skin and bone into fender.

"I ask the questions, *Councilman!*" Thug #1 growls as his partner chuckles on, amused by the politician's expressive mix of fear and chunked pain.

Councilman grimaces…

Sucks in the pain.

Man-up, man-up, Councilman quickly thinks. *They'll be done soon.*

"Relax," whispers Thug #2 directly into the politician's ear, as he searches the city official, frisking for a weapon in the crevices of Councilman's running gear. Politician, tense and guarded, manages to insert sarcasm into the conversation, suddenly two-siding the exchange.

"How much you think I can stuff in a pair of shorts and a T-shirt?" Councilman soon regrets the burst of confidence, as the buzz-cut thug with *Napoleon* complex and cackling laugh steps in, nestling the blunt end of the flashlight into the city official's lower rib-cage, just enough to force out a large blast of air from the pit of the victim's chest, followed by a saucy taste of blood bubbling to the politician's throat.

"Keep that trap *shut!* Don't get cute," Thug #2 orders.

Councilman quiets.

Humility sets in.

City official recoils in obedient horror.

Incident lasts for a fast, fifteen-minutes.

The side street where it happens is conveniently hidden.

Alley thickly glazed with darkness.

Finished with intimidation, giving no reason for the visit, the two men leave the politician gripping his abdomen in pain from multiple punches.

The car leaves.

The street falls dark.

Councilman stands silently as traffic flies by.

Five minutes into re-composure, licking his bruises and returning to peace, the city official runs the fastest mile he's ever run. Wishing home and grandmother's fried fish were both only inches away.

chapter 26

NORTHWEST PHILADELPHIA

DAY 17

Halkos takes to being straight about the situation faced by the anxious legislator, whether the detective likes it, doesn't appear cool in the face of desperate circumstances.

"The dread-locked, homeless 'John Doe' with the hole in his head was at the wrong place at the wrong time, Councilman. That bullet was meant for you. My suggestion: either get lost for a while until we find out exactly who put the hit out on you, or stick around and let us detail a few plain clothes for your protection. Transportation will be provided, compliments of the city."

"That's mighty fine of you, Lieutenant, but I've got enough protection." Councilman fears the possibilities, but plays it cool. During such moments, he thinks back to the day his son's untimely death.

"Please, Councilman, I'd really like for you to reconsider."

"That's alright—besides, that's a waste of taxpayer's money, having the department ferry me around like the Mayor."

"This courtesy comes directly from the Mayor."

"Regardless of who it is, Lieutenant, I *respectfully* decline the offer. Extend my gratitude for the gesture, though. In fact, I'll send him an email."

"Well…all we're saying is that you can't rely on that unlicensed firearm."

"Check your sources, Lieutenant, my hardware is legal. I can carry it, too."

Pause…

Councilman's factoid sinks in a little.

"So, how long do you suppose the investigation will take? Any kind of time frame, Lieutenant?

"I couldn't tell you."

"What had you settle on the mob?"

"Lots of activity and chatter in *South Philly.* Our informants get a little jumpy when we mention your name and the shooting. Plus, the shooter did previous work for a d'Stanfa capo by the name of Timothy Bigletani, otherwise known as 'Biglet'. Does that name ring a bell?"

"No. No it doesn't."

"Sure, well, *Delaware State Police* found his remains burning in a melted *BMW* somewhere outside of *Middletown.* We suspect d'Stanfa got pissed that the shooter missed, and took it out on Biglet for screwing it up. Biglet's moment of judgment was soon to come, anyway, he was strung out on too many different substances."

"Who killed the shooter?"

"We think Biglet did it to eliminate any leads."

"Lots of theories…lots of thinking, Lieutenant. But, nothing really concrete."

Halkos swallows before gulping on lingering spit.

"No. Nothing concrete. But, we're doing our best. We'll eventually find the link to d'Stanfa himself. Right now, we only have hearsay."

Hearsay won't bring my dead friend back.

chapter 27

NORTHWEST PHILADELPHIA

DAY 18

Councilman doubts it's the city's entrenched *La Cosa Nostra.* If push came to shove, d'Stanfa would approached him with a cut in the pier project, which the city official would "respectfully declined", and the beat would go on until the old man could unearth some mind-changing skeleton in Councilman's closet.

Physical threats?

That would be too crude, potentially too public for a modern crime boss in search of 21st century legitimacy. It's better to funnel money into union accounts, using the cash as laundered retainers for aggressive *City Hall* lobbyists able to construct a compromise.

"Big 'Deez'" is a creative businessman with only *business* in mind; violence is often a last resort. Shrugging the thought away, the politician figures d'Stanfa could find a few other thankless, squirming, bankrupted politicians on the Council to bankroll, two or three more souls sold to the devil for two or three more votes against the bill while it was in committee, waiting for it in case it skipped out.

To Councilman, the mob-hit theory is too easy—too convenient and accommodating. He's not buying it. Not d'Stanfa. The signs are leading to something much grander and nefarious. Something beyond the conventional scope of Lieutenant Halkos' investigation is looming in a shadow of dead branches that smacks into virtual detours, leaving for more questions.

The longer the questions are left unanswered, the longer the haunting uncertainty. Instinct simply tells the city official that the d'Stanfa crime family may want him dead, perhaps…or, they may have carried out a hit, but didn't necessarily authorize it.

Why was Bigletani killed in such a grisly way over something so trivial?

Autopsy reports (from a department insider who owes Councilman a favor) suggests multiple, small knife wounds killed the young mob capo. Quick, dirty puncturing, and closely aligned knife or dagger wounds; lacerations found, after painstaking picks and pulls of charred skin—suggests the flesh was cut and the wounds mortal. But, it wasn't the same knife matching every opening. If city official is seeing this right, then one of two scenarios occurred.

One: A psychopathic, blood-lusting mercenary sadist tortures "Biglet" for fun. It isn't on d'Stanfa's dime or order, either. Tortures high ass Timothy Bigletani for hours into the Delaware *night, as he frightfully screams in relentless pain and fear....*

But wait...why kill a man while he's in the damn car? Why do it while he's driving? How do you murder a man while he's driving, or not driving, but clearly preparing to drive off? Why slay while he's parked in an area where the screams can echo, since his mouth isn't gagged to dull the sound? His windows are open, too?

...What's up with that?

Or...

Two: Someone throws dozens of various sized, angled knives into "Biglet", with such precision and speed, at such fair distance and such force, that he dies silently and horribly, rather than quickly. Another section of the report discusses a broken windshield. Somebody real talented does this...or a bunch of bodies in rapid motion throwing knives?

Red letters stare back at Councilman: *"Inconclusive." The New Castle County Medical Examiner* doesn't understand, or has never seen anything like it. What she does note are *"vital arteries struck. Lacerations significantly deep and fatal."*

For some odd reason inexplicable to him, Councilman can't help but think: *Ninjas?*

A childhood interest in *Eastern* fighting, *Kung Fu* movies and anime unveil tangible suspicions: *throwing stars could've meant "Biglet" was assassinated by black clad, face-covered soldiers of the Nonuse, or "the art of stealth,"* he ponders, but, thought is still cloudy.

"Assassination" is the key word because, ninjas do not murder—they're trained and retained, instructed to kill without prejudice. An often-used weapon of choice is *Shuriken* ("throwing star"), a multi-edged, sharpened, star-shaped weapon of pain that the trained hand can throw in simultaneous, almost semi-automatic motion.

It's a very ancient, clean way of killing, since it leaves no trace of modern ballistics. No fingerprints, no markings, meaning, no clues for baffled detectives and caustic profilers.

The examiner found twenty-seven cuts, with eighteen identified as the "vital arteries." That makes sense. Each ninja traditionally carries nine *Shuriken*—"nine" being the lucky number. Twenty-seven cuts means there were three assassins out of sight and sound that put poor "Biglet" into eternal sleep. He didn't know what or who housed him, how fast or how they did it.

What in the *hell* are ninjas doing in the *Tri-State* area?

Why were they killing mobsters?

"Big 'Deez'" wouldn't have hired ninjas because he once publicly stated his distaste, distrust and bigoted disrespect for the "gooks", as he crudely calls anyone who remotely favors *Asian* ancestry. So much for that, we suppose. And what would d'Stanfa know about Japanese assassins? He mostly used "family" for projects of that sort; with the exception of outsiders he'd planned on snuffing out when their usefulness was used up.

Councilman doesn't figure Lieutenant Halkos into the equation, because Halkos wouldn't see this one for a while. This was out of the Lieutenant's league and personal realm, as far as Councilman's concerned. Ninjas?

"*Please!*" he could hear the police Commissioner chuckling. "*Give me something solid, Councilman,*" the commish would say. "*A killer is on the loose and we got a city to protect. Something I can see, eat and really sleep on. Don't waste my troops' time with this* Kung Fu *shit!*"

A few flashbacks and recent events will connect the dots.

There are larger powers at work.

This is bigger than "Big 'Deez'".

Bigger than the city…

Bigger than the hard river breezes hitting *Penn's Landing*.

chapter 28
SOUTHERN CALIFORNIA
DAY 19

Nearly three weeks past the shooting, Councilman receives an early morning call from his emotionally shaken grandmother, her *Southern California* paradise shattered by the rudeness of a home invasion gone awfully extreme. Alone upon grandpa's death, and adjusting to the challenges of single elderly life after fifty odd years of marriage, the woman calls her politician grandson in defeated tears, crying of injustice; barely pulling herself together over the aching tightness of ulcer—from a broken heart and weak stomach.

"Someone broke in!"

"Grandmom—what? *Who?*"

"They broke into the house," elderly woman begins, speaking in broken bits of language, "house in shambles and pieces! Everything ripped and destroyed!"

A burglarizing tornado of fishing hands went spinning through her *Long Beach* crib with such brunt impact, that every corner, inch of floor space and tile, is covered with personal effects, furniture, appliances and paper.

Many items disarrayed.

Mad glass shattered.

Memories strewn about like road kill.

Nothing is missing.

Everything is there.

Just out of place.

Interesting how someone can do that much damage and not take a damn thing, the politician thinks. Jewelry, antique keepsakes and collectibles, left behind by the rummaging "burglar"? *Doesn't sound like a burglary.*

The connection isn't fully made until his grandmother notes the eye of the vandalizing storm in her late husband's study, a house garage converted into a *Frankenstein* fantasy.

Sloppy, yet mysteriously organized chaos of wires, monitors, tools, screws, nails and other assorted items, gathering dust of last touch. This is where the most damage is done, according to the elderly woman.

Her deceased mate made sense and logic of what's in the garage, only *he* was able to convincingly extrapolate method from brain processing madness, creating fused balls of protons and electrons.

Councilman's grandmother used to joke about how her love would spend hours—days even, building "the next atomic bomb", as though the old man was actually doing that. She joked about it to ease the rattling nerves that worried something disastrous was about to happen, when saws started buzzing, and hammers banged endlessly into the night.

But the old man was a harmless engineer with forward-thinking prowess and great intentions, as far as he was concerned. A bit too stubborn for his own good, even at the expense of raising his kids as fully as he could have. But, in the mind of Councilman's grandfather, all he wanted was to save the world from its own humanity.

Humanity ravaged the elderly guy's precious earth with war, famine, pollution; it was humanity that plucked trees from the earth like wine bottle corks, spit gaseous fumes into the air from car mufflers and industrial pipes, carelessly dumping poisonous runoff and toxic waste into oceans and river ways.

Seasoned engineer, commendably imposing his aged common sense, wanted to bring an end to it all, feeling as though he could at least save the two most precious resources on the planet: air and water. Thus, born from frustration and fear of ecological devastation was the *Macro Ionization Device*–affectionately dubbed, *MID*.

Councilman now vividly remembers his grandfather's summer lectures before the condescending college circuit, struggling to crack the hard heads of balding, bifocal-wearing professors, ensconced in their own marble column routines and egos. They perceived the degree-less nuts and bolt "mechanic" as some cheap, impulsive, rebel inventor without credentials or a patent; their rude scoffs, coughs and snickers, testament to baseless disrespect and disregard.

"There are many myths in the field of macro-ionization," the old man tried to dazzle, *"ranging from ignorance to downright stupidity."* Councilman's grandfather lectured until he'd crash and burn his lesson with tactless and unfortunate upstarts of that

classic family pig-headedness. His wife on down to his grandson would try to tell him: "*You have got to level the rhetoric a bit if you want to sell the idea.*"

"Nonsense," the seasoned engineer blasted back. "I can do just fine showing those *Ivy League* hotshots just who the authority is." He'd lecture on, driven by a need to prove things: *"As a pioneer in the domestic treatment of energy by a process of what I call macro-ionization, I feel it is high time for the slaughter to commence."*

And so it did.

"First, a brief history," Councilman's grandfather gently shifted the audience after castrating it, moments before. *"As an informal student in this fascinating field, I performed many experiments in the macro-ionized treatment of the local water supply. What I found is a way to clean it without releasing pollutants or eliminating nutrients."*

His grandson, now the young politician fifteen years later, reminisces closely, seeing the auditorium, scanning the dwindling crowd of students, instructors and socially half-baked professors. Those present were mired in their own coughs and hushed laughter. All Councilman did back then was focus on the guys in the back: *Who are the guys in all black?*

"We complimented this technique by using an automatic, salt type of water softener at the time, but we were aware of the negative health effects of the sodium in the water supply, as well as the weekly task of feeding several heavy bags of salt into its bulky brine belly," the old man indicated before wheezing a bounty of a laugh.

A few female undergrads found the engineer somewhat charming and delectable, spitting a groupie snort loud enough to force a blush. The cats in the back were not phased. They kept lips tight, foreheads wrinkle-free and pens moving. At most, there was a swift hand straightening of black suits, white shirts, and *Secret Service* detail ties. Writing of copious notes continued into note pads without interruption.

Given the dispersed layout and disinterest of the crowd, the rate of absorption was astounding to young politician to be. These memories fuddled his brain into rupturing migraines because "they" always showed up, assiduously absorbed into the lecture, rather than the man.

Everybody else was, like, *"To hell with the lecture—who's*

the crazy old geezer? Why are we here?" The black-suited introverts in the back, however, kept it quiet when it ended, bouncing out swiftly before anyone curious enough would ask: "*Tell me, why do you guys sit in the dark writing for two or three hours? Don't your eyes burn? Are you really human?"*

One day, Councilman's grandfather disappeared for forty-eight hours—forty-eight skin-peeling hours. Forty-eight hours when his wife smoked two packs in frenzied, rare nicotine fit. The local police were called and soon after, he'd returned in a daze, soul broken and psyched.

It was spooky, spine-chilling for his wife to see him like that—downright dire and uncanny of the seasoned engineer. It was the first time he'd appeared stunned in disbelief.

"Who was it, grandpa?" his grandson grills exhausted old man. *"The men in the black suits?"*

"I'm tired, son."

The old geezer was clearly tired and out of mood for questioning. His face simply wrinkled, aged and drained itself of color.

"*You go to bed and get some rest. Your mind is in overdrive."*

chapter 29

PHILLY VIA CALIFORNIA

REWIND: FLASHBACK

Before "Kid Wonder" skipped off to Washington *for college, post-teen's grandfather drove more than a week across the great expanse of national frontier, to reach* Philly *for the shortest continental visit known to regular men. The car wasn't even in the driveway when the old man started rambling about secrets, more secrets he wasn't supposed to tell because—the seasoned engineer didn't know what the secrets were.*

His grandson was stunned: "What made you drive all the way here? Why didn't you just take a plane?"

"Secrets...gotta keep the secrets. They won't find me if I drive. I threw the scent off."

"Who?" his grandson asked. At this point, the old man looked out the window for something he had little idea about. "Who's keeping the secrets?"

"Powerful men," his grandfather trailed off.

"How powerful?"

"Powerful."

"I heard you, but what do you mean by powerful?"

The old man, now shaking with a mild hint of Parkinson's, *catches his grandson by both wrists, drilling the most fright-filled stare into the young man's eyes.*

He suddenly pulled back, dipped into his stripped leather case and presented a book; gold-trimmed and tightly bound by an intricate stitch of string and cow skin. This was no ordinary book, for it was thick and voluminous, carefully shut by a hard external flap of reticule, buttoning into a looped metal slot.

"This now belongs to you," the engineer states, talking with such chilling authority, that the gullible teen became hesitant to question him.

"...What is it, grandpa?"

"Plans for an alternative source of energy. It's a lifetime of curiosity, questioning, hypothesis and work," the old man preached in distant tones. "The blueprint for something

magnificent and historic. I'm giving it to you. You must protect it."

"Damn. Grandpa, I can't take this, I—"

"YES YOU CAN!" he angrily barked. "YOU HAVE TO!"

* * * * *

"Kid Wonder" leads his grandfather to his own bedroom, where there's a collage of posters, stickers, pop-culture mullion thrashed about into an indoor wall mural.

"You have to," the seasoned engineer insists; his previous boom now down to almost a whisper. The old man's voice rang firmly, last remnants of youth barely registering, but managing enough to impose momentary reign. "Yes you can, son," he kept whispering, "yes you can." His grandfather needed him to take it, protect it. "Perhaps, even, the world might need you, boy. Right now, neither of us can talk about it, can't tell anybody about it. There are important folks after this. They fear it—want to destroy it.... I don't know, they probably even want to use it, get it before somebody else does."

"What—what is this?" Suddenly, the boy understood the presence of the black suits in the back of the lecture halls. "This all about...what, the MID?" Old man gave a slow nod in affirmation.

"Son, I only named it that to throw them off. It's much more than that. I tapped into something I didn't really mean to."

"They're not out to hurt you, are they, grandpa? 'Cause if that's the case then we need to call the cops and—"

"No one is calling any damn *cops! No one! You don't understand...we can't call anyone. Keep this real quiet, boy, I mean it—understood?" Roughness soon transformed into a tender, soft touch of senior love.*

"One day, when the dust settles, I'll tell you all about it. Right now, they won't think to come after you. You're not into this. The time will come however, when they'll realize you have it. When that time arrives, you've got to be prepared for it."

Two weeks later, the teen's grandfather was slumped in rigor mortis on his Long Beach *office floor. The dust he spoke of never really settled since the cause of death is still unknown.... No signs of struggle saved the fatal concussion from a nasty bump to the head, the ugly wound investigators attributed to an "accidental" fall on gritty linoleum tile.*

chapter 30

WEST PHILADELPHIA

DAY 21

"Raw, I need a favor."

"Shoot. What you need?"

"Big favor—a hushed favor. Like, if you say anything about this to anybody, I'll *kill* you and throw your miserable *ass* into the *Schuykill.*"

Councilman isn't laughing at his joke. He appears a bit more serious this particular evening.

"Aiiight, bruh! Dude, the *Schuykill?* Throw me at the *Jersey Shore,* at least. I could use the vacation. I—"

"Seriously, this is high-end, Grade A, government cheese, my friend. The only reason I'm letting you peep this is because you're the only cat I trust who can decipher it."

"What is it?"

The legislator shrugs like a befuddled kid.

"Don't know too much about it—just a little. I'm not telling you what I know right now though. You read it and we'll huddle later to discuss the findings."

"C'mon, man—what is it?"

Raw Mikey is a thin, pasty, marshmallow-colored, PhD student a good five years into never grasping his dream of a Doctorate, and digs it the way he has it; the lifestyle affords the freedom to do what he prefers to do, on his time, at his convenience. A-h-h-h, the luxury of photographic memory and knowing almost every damn thing, Knowing it all allows Mikey less worry; he can never fall behind because he's always ahead.

Raw keeps a low profile, very grungy, and has little stress. If he needs loot, Raw knows where to get lots of it, and what numbers on the street to play, or which databases to hack.

"Break the cycle," is his outmoded motto. Commuting to work each morning reminds Raw of a gruesome sci-fi flick once seen where some cursed planet grazer, in search of human flesh to appease its galactic appetite, methodically ingests billions of people.

Needless to say, the channel was turned—not due to stomach-grumbling nausea while eating a plate of saucy spaghetti, but his mind was triggered by trifle annoyance at how the filmmaker could be that *damn* clever to make such a connection. So rather than hate the game, Raw hates the players (that same, slap-to-the-forehead reaction when your idea beats you to the punch, that lip-dropping "Now, why didn't I think of that?").

Raw attempted "normalcy" for a minute, working for "the Man," slaving in the workspace cubicles. While maneuvering and swimming through fifteen miles of *Interstate* urine, he managed to make that same connection like everybody else. Thoughts became as effortless as stiffened cows munching on grass before the butcher's slaughter; or like pigs who'd prefer snorting into cornmeal tonnage and clumps of assorted garbage, in squealing anticipation of the ax that determines their fate as either sausage stick or gelatin-laced *Jell-O.*

"Each morning, we're the figurative sheep herded onto macro-economic pastures. We completed the social construct that sits atop our backs, like race jockeys whipping waddling asses for speed. For this, we met the ultimate torture tool of our Maker: stress. Costing us three hundred billion annually in lost productivity, and counting. Why do we, then, get all crisscrossed when hearing of all the latest corporate scandals? Isn't the modern American workplace, in and of itself, a mass, stress-boxed scandal?" Raw recently wrote in his wildly popular anonymous blog.

"Shag the stress," he used to tell his politician friend. *"I don't need that kind of stress in my life."*

And, yes: don't forget the chicks. Enough about stress—let's talk about the girls. Raw is in endless quest of the perfect campus women untapped, but dripping with horny-toad anticipation, for a pass at what their parents had warned them against.

Sex is what occupies Raw's mind at the coffee shop intersection of *36th* and *Spruce,* amid the sweet smell of *University of Pennsylvania* punany, mixed with the grind of his mocha and Councilman's chai.

"Nice threads, Councilman. I could get use to seeing you thugged-out."

All clothes on the man, some tags as *Philly's* next Mayor, tell a story of total electoral ignorance. The incognito is heavy, the commercial hip-hop and subtle bling: thick as the latest video sensation. A red *Phillies* cap is pulled down low, dark *Hugo Boss* sunglasses covers any trace of sight. One hefty-breasted girl in luscious grace, of the type of action Raw Mikey salivates after, swings towards Councilman for an autograph without knowing it's him, thinking it was somebody else well-known, somebody who rocked several city nightspots, several nights before.

"You got the wrong man, young lady," and before the politician could manage a recanting apology or gentler word more, she pushes her hand in perpetual disgust, truly convinced it's "him"; you know, the guy at the club the other night who *"rocked the mike, right?"* Buxom beauty just knew it was the emcee that now poses a front, as if he can't be bothered with the virtues of his own work.

"Can you check it out, Raw?"

"Sure. Where is it?"

* * * * *

Raw Mikey is now on the trolley, racing to *Center City* before heading to the orange-colored subway line underneath *Broad Street* to *Fern Rock Station.* He follows his lifetime friend's instructions for the walk down to *Godfrey Avenue,* then into the woods, just a few hundred paces west of the recreation center on *5th Street;* the spot where they both got rushed at age twelve by a menacing gang of gluttonous, *White* teenage skinheads-in-training.

Raw, back then of half-wit age, broke the cardinal rule of *Northeast Philly* racial engagement by hanging out with "The Brothers." There were unwritten codes in unofficially segregated *Philly* about that. The skinhead-wannabes couldn't tell what his friend, young "Kid Wonder" was—Black, Hispanic, or mutt.

It didn't matter.

He was "Colored".

Stained.

Dirty.

Contagious.

As the two boys scraped, punched and somehow wiggled their way out of certain death, it was enough drama for Raw and "Kid Wonder" to forge a friendship for life.

There it is, at the base of the thirteenth tree from the edge of the brush line, is the reason for the insane subway ride and nostalgic marathon walk from *Fern Rock Station:* a non-descript metal box with a combination lock. Before grabbing it, Raw looks around nervously to see if anyone followed him. Feeling certain all is safe, he tasks himself with the most thorough review of its contents.

* * * * *

Hours later, Raw's sitting in his politician friend's black *Audi "Q7"* in total darkness at *Fairmont Park,* on this mild *Philly* evening.

"I'm not following." Councilman is confused by what Raw is describing through a combination of complicated scientific terms.

"Your grandfather, if I covered this right, developed a means of cleaning water by use of some very complicated ionization process. What he did is totally purify water, but also maintained and strengthened some of the original nutrients in it, meaning already, you piss off the bottled water industry that's trying to replace tap water.

"The language I just read to you is from the patent your grandfather submitted, where he only tells half of it. Your grandfather doesn't tell you about the type of process, nor does he go into how he managed to produce a grand unified theory."

"…A what? Raw, what's that?"

"A grand unified theory—a GUT. It's when you combine or unify strong electromagnetic particles with weak nuclear energy—"

"I didn't know there was such a thing as *weak* nuclear energy."

"I hear you, but let me finish. You combine those two elements then merge them with stronger nuclear energy particles."

Councilman's face goes blank.

"What I'm saying is that GUT is *mad* power to the *nth* degree. It's said that such power is impossible to build. If you build it, you tap solar system energy."

"…Keep going."

"Well, your grandfather created his own…species of GUT. I don't know what he means by this, but your grandfather keeps talking about how something 'told' him about it. He doesn't tell you about the completed positioning of the process, either…nor does your grandfather mention, in the patent, the development of a special technology to enhance the force of the process. That information is contained within another set of notes separate from what's been formally submitted. These notes he gave you fill in all the blanks."

Raw nervously peaks into the pitch-black street where they sit, a deep and extremely dark line of trees leading towards *Belmont Plateau.* Nothing but shadow can be seen for yards—the most unsettling scene.

"Hey, u-h-h-h…what's the deal? Why you park here?" Raw isn't digging the cloak and dagger ambience.

"Seclusion," is all Councilman says, as he looks out into the trees with a cold, frozen stare. It's clear Councilman is bottling up quite a bit in his head.

"What, from civilization? Yeah right—what about cops coming through here?"

"Relax, I know the schedule."

"Alright, 'Mister Mayor-to-be—Man with Keys to the City. What about the cats after this?"

Councilman burns a quick look of hostility, mixed with bewilderment.

"What? Who are you *talking* about?"

"C'mon bruh, *who* are you talking to? All this man-of-mystery talk—the cats that tried to *kill* you. Thugged-out at the coffee shop so nobody recognizes you, turning away that hot piece of ass like you did while sippin' on Joe. I've known you too long, slipknot."

"I don't know, Raw. I don't know," the politician says and shakes his head, before rubbing his temples onward to the eyes. "But…yeah, I think the people that shot at me were actually looking for this, or they supposed I knew too much about it already based on my pro-environment record. So, rather than ask me for it, they decided to get rid of me, steal the info and ask questions later."

Raw shakes his head: "Man," he responds as his brow lowers; the most serious look even Raw has ever seen his friend make. "This is real heavy. I see now."

Slender, pale, chopstick fingers withdraws papers from a briefcase-sized pocket folder. So intrigued by Councilman's grandfather's ideas on MID is Raw, that he spit out a short, digestible thesis for layman's consumption.

"You're grandfather put together a conduit for recyclable energy. I mean, this is real, and he wanted to obviously go public with it someday. But if you're an oil executive, or owner of a multi-billion dollar bottled water company, you don't want this out. In fact, if *MID* drops, you lose money—serious money: *I'm-back-in-the-poorhouse-selling-used-cars money.* Inventions like this you, one: pay the creator off. Two: kill him or, three: just put it in storage so it doesn't go public."

Yeah, Councilman thinks, *they couldn't pay grandpa off. He was too stubborn for that. That's what the missing forty-eight hours was all about.*

"But, there's more to this," Raw goes on. "If you're the government, you don't want other governments getting their hands on it—you *feel* me?"

Zipping his head into four directions, Raw monitors the moonlit street, cautiously watching a lone set of headlights pass by. He lowers his voice to a barely registered half-whisper.

"Yeah, *MID* is a tree-hugger's wet dream—a Democrat's pep rally. See, this bad boy runs some kind of organic power process to completely cleanse water. I mean: cleaner than bottled water, and it continuously recycles water. Your grandfather called it 'infinite recycling'.

"And…this nasty little ball of ionization found a way to recycle gas for several weeks, he started working on recycling for months at a time. Your grandfather's got enough material in here to start work on his version of *GUT* as the sole source—he already cracked that equation. This is, like, almost bigger than relativity. He just never got a chance to implement it. You would almost never have to go to the gas station…again? Well, not necessarily, maybe once a month, two tops.

"*MID* keeps recycling the gas, re-using it and then cleaning it—*Ethanol* it, for lack of a better term. There are few, if any, emissions; all this while the gas is still in the tank. Imagine that! It would throw the oil industry into the unknown. *Saudi Arabia, Iran,* all those annoying *Middle Eastern* countries surviving on oil bank would *crash* into immediate purge mode."

Raw's laughter spit a squeamish snort that slices the nervous silence between the two friends. He continues on: "And that still doesn't cover the *GUT* your grandfather somehow managed to prove."

"What makes you say that?"

"Because when he found the *GUT,* your grandfather tripped out. All he wanted to do was save the world—not destroy it in a flash. *GUT* is like the *Big Bang* repeated; it can get unstable enough to turn itself into a destructive force. Your grandfather didn't want to mess with that any more than he'd already had. It's like playing GOD, and your grandfather had enough sense to leave it be."

Raw sniffs hard.

Thumbed his nose for running mucus.

Grows silent…

Now shifts in his seat.

"But, these cats after you—they don't have the same sense he had. The power is too ridiculous to ignore. Yeah, they know—they know all about it."

chapter 31

QUANTICO, VA

DAY 22

"Counselor" grows increasingly impatient with Councilman. The politician is a non-schemed interruption of planned space and universe, a ripple in time, the knot of minutes throwing the daybook into disarray. Councilman's unpredictable nature has become intolerable—impairing old plans that were designed decades bygone before he was even a thought, or blast of sperm.

Councilman's status as an irritant has, unbeknownst to him, propelled the city politician's reputation onto the master list of most wanted targets, by the people Germani worked for. There exists consensus to eliminate the legislator while in pursuit of his grandfather's invention, however, there's a problem in terms of how to proceed with the plan.

"Councilman must *go*," so orders the quiet, dark council of men known as "The Members" who run things, many of them past tired and torn of the rhetoric and destabilizing social revolutions from forty years before. "And it's incumbent that you find a way to dispatch him *fast.*" Traditionally, they're in *no* mood for uprisings, surprises or sudden attacks.

Germani's employer took few chances on matters like this. The *MID* invention represented the culmination of many dreams spun endlessly in the underground offices of "The Members'" front agency, located in the bowels of the *Quantico, Virginia Marine Base,* a forty-five-minute drive outside *Washington, D.C.*

Officially referenced as the *Office of Research and Development Acquisitions (ORDA)*, much of the surface work entailed weapons of mass destruction analysis conducted by a full regiment of professional scientists under the operational command of the *2nd Marine Logistics* and *Intelligence Battalion.* It's a little-known, barely noticeable operation with a federally funded billion-dollar budget, emerging as a tightly coordinated quasi-government outfit, existing on a mix of Congressional earmarks and private foundation funding.

The 2nd *Marines* don't know much about it either.

But, unbeknownst to many on *Capitol Hill* who'll go along with funding the hidden line item in yearly budgets, *ORDA* was also called "The Sentry"—by those in the know.

The Sentry was formed back in 1790 as a security arm for Congress, as they fled *Philadelphia* from a brewing revolt of unpaid *Revolutionary War* soldiers. Running for their lives on the road from *Philly,* the old Congress took little notice of "The Sentry" guards' savvy organization skills. As time passed, they solidified a secret charter, long before reaching that legendary piece of land that's snug tight in the corner of the *Potomac* and *Anacostia River* intersection.

Over time, The Sentry's responsibilities would expand. In its modern version, *ORDA* has collect data or "confiscated" intellectual property, deemed a "threat" to national security. What's really happening is that *ORDA* has found ways to transform that "property" or "technology", into something useful for larger national "interest."

The *MID* defies every bit of science *The Members* knew of, yet validates every wish they'd made. It's of the highest priority to secure it before another competitor does. There are many competitors with many interests and threats adverse to national security, but ORDA-cloaked operatives have to acquire it through much more concealed efforts considering Councilman's high public profile.

It isn't that easy…

Both retrieval of the *MID* and the death of its owner must "appear" accidental. They can't cause any more trouble than already caused.

Fate however, can at times, rise as unpredictable as weather patterns—there are times when GOD is viewed by the dark council as unfairly malicious, cruel and impractical. No sphere, *Tarot* card reading mystic, or future-telling oracle can manage the merciless caprices of the Heavens—if one were to believe in the power of angels, as ardently as "The Members" of the covert dominion don't. Since termination of previous deviants inches close to changing history, further success is affirmed by the absence of unusual but periodic blips, stirring social discontent on the horizon.

"The Members" are by no means absolute agnostics or demon-worshipping servants bound by fire rituals and pentagrams.

A prerequisite of their status depends primarily on a chronic belief in the power of Man—his sole purpose to achieve through conquest, in spite of humanity in the interest of greater stability.

"The Members" are agents of any Godly blueprint set forth if there is, in fact, a GOD. GOD, to them, is a common good, and good is what the men define, according to what their intentions are.

Stability and prosperity at any cost, *is* the common good. The group's common good won't/can't be attained through blanket notions of justice, peace and trifle whims of idealism. Justice isn't permitted, even as theory or concept, because its existence (contrary to democratic thought) is really the result of what "The Members" determine, in their combined efforts prior to the conception of one miserable, antagonistic *Philadelphian* Councilman, hardheaded enough to posture for national mark without *their* consent.

There's no room for predictable lapses in security, no breaks or exceptions made for anyone failing to place operational tenets above personal distractions.

This includes Germani.

He knew so when choosing acceptance of this calling upon the terrifyingly painful insertion of code into his nasal passages.

Strapped to a metal recliner, without drugs to calm or caress the senses, Germani was converted from civilian normalcy to corporate obligation, a status marked by excruciating throbs of piercing alloy into the darkest crevices of his brain. Blood and mucus were prodded into one of the more agonizing moments in "Counselor's" strangely buckled life.

"The Standard", as it's unofficially known, defies convention and ridicules compassion. Pain is the primary tool for use against opposing force, and the last resort only found when the brain losses function—therefore, there's no such thing as pain.

Pain, "The Standard" imbues, is the ultimate representation of the fool, an extension of weakness, and a dishonorable finality to those seen as meek and timid in the face of adversity.

There's no strength in pain, as overwhelming strength is the pre-cursor to victory.

Pain is absorbed.

It's the baneful existence of his foe.

chapter 32

CAPITOL HILL

DAY 23

Germani's ride is characteristically late, thus marking the unexpected, amid constant and increasingly lifelong expectations. Such routine occurrences are, therefore, slightly annoying, casually treated as a necessity, rather than a compulsive sense of insecurity and paranoia.

Inconveniences are treated as minor (yet predetermined) mishaps; a nothing of any matter compared to more important matters "Counselor" routinely attends to. A late driver is treated as a microscopic portion of his life's conditioning, there's nothing worth noting as a terribly head-cracking disturbance, nothing of any sort deserving for even mild thought—it has been there, Germani has done that.

Of cursory importance, dictated by protocol from a mysterious Sentry source early today, sent by e-mail, are the following steps: "*Walk for a mile towards the direction of the smallest of the three main* House *office buildings, then turn left on* First Street, SW. *Use of a quarter and dime is necessary. Use the coins to obtain the day's copy of 'The Trumpet'. Proceed to walk back and turn an immediate left to walk down the hill towards Rayburn. Stop at* South Capitol *where you'll wave a silver-colored* Grand Marquis *with* District *tags and markings, identifying it as a taxi.*"

Scratched, dented and in desperate need of paint is Germani's ride, spinning as a carousel in a split-second saturation of vehicular violence, commonly expected of reckless or unknowing drivers commanding power-steering of *District* taxis. The driver, a male of *Arab* descent in his twenties, seems well trained enough to ask his passenger for destination, but the street madness a moment before, briefly riles "Counselor."

"Where are you going, sir?"

"Follow your instructions," Germani orders, offering the responding signal, stating the need to reach *National Airport.*

Hands sweating, the driver dampens his forehead, replying

in nervous tandem through what seems an impressive handling of gear and wheel, from brake pedal to gas. The maneuvers are quick, fierce, fearless, but pre-planned to the point where rubber meets asphalt in a horrifyingly high-pitch scream, lightly tapping through the solid serenity of the car.

Blazing friction instantaneously produces smoke like flint on dry wood. With that happening, the two drive yards upon a *Capitol Police* officer on foot, who motions the violating automobile and its owner with a disapproving glare, a loud obnoxious yell of law mixes with intercepting flashes of a raised hand: "PULL OVER!"

A distressed and red-coated face relays to the anxious *Middle Easterner* who reads the officer's lips while profusely irritated by the delay. Cursing the cop in *Arabic,* the driver obeys upon approval from his passenger's narrowed eyes in the rearview mirror, from a tense back seat.

Despite his silence and calm look, Germani's mood does nothing to placate the situation. Any casual observer examining the rigid-jaw *Southeast Asian* in his mid thirties, would see "Counselor" sporting a contemporary dark silver-colored tie/shirt combination, buried in a charcoal, three-piece pinstripe; the mysterious man, nothing more than an unusually patient taxi passenger bearing deep eyes, well-exercised shoulders and large weathered hands, chiseled by constant exercise, the occasional murder prompted by sense of duty, and always manicured to perfection.

None would feel any sense of immediate danger from this man, only cursory awe: a refined, superbly dressed professional gentleman with presence and comforting impression—women of all grades and socio-economic standing go instantly nocturnal once in "Counselor's" path. His few-inches-above-the-sixth foot stature is made noticeable not by height (for there are millionaire athletes and imposing night club bouncers much taller), but by solid masculinity in manner and physique.

The *Capitol Hill* officer is fast into the usual motions—drilling both driver and passenger for license, hand firmly on semi-automatic while launching into interrogation. Soon, the driver reaches into the glove department for registration and insurance, and tension settles hotly into the faces and frowns of all three men, as the cop awaits backup.

Wickedly bored by the monotony of same beat for several

hours, the officer initiates light conversation with the impeccably tailored, bronze-colored chap in the back seat. The driver meanwhile, stares forward in the direction of the *Rayburn House Office Building* which dramatically yawns its sculpted power onto *Independence Avenue,* as if the descending slope of street angling into *South Capitol* is a series of marble steps, falling into hell.

Idling and grabbing for cool air, the *Ford "Grand Marquis'"* engine gently sputters a courteous clacking sound, as if reminding all parties that a tune-up is needed. Admonishing the nerve-stricken young *Arab* with the trigger-happy reflexes, the car has no sense of its impending fate, nor cares to bestow any sympathy on the driver who scorched its tires moments before.

Holding the driver's license and waiting on verification of the man's identity, the officer keeps a careful mental tag on the white collar in the back.

"How are you today, sir?" cautious cop asks.

"I'm just splendid, officer. And you?" Germani responds, managing a forced smile into the corner of his lip.

"Where are you off to so fast?"

"Counselor" doesn't dig the inquisitive "five-0", attempting to avoid the query, irritated by the criss-crossing examination of the back seat, not digging the edge in officer's question.

Why is he grilling me, rather than the driver? Germani thinks. *I'm not the one driving.* "Across the *14th Street Bridge,* officer."

"All right—Virginia. Shopping? Going home? Lunch?"

"Business."

"Okay."

This reminds Germani of the random police traffic stops and searches in downtown *Boston* years ago, while at *Harvard Law.* The fresh scent of deliberately mistaken profile, the type he frequently experiences in large airports at the metal detectors, not to mention boyhood bike rides in *Southern California* interrupted by xenophobic county deputies.

Germani grew fairly use to it.

They were *beneath* him.

"And, how are you, officer?"

"U-m-m-m—oh...yeah, *'splendid'*...like you."

There's something the uniformed man doesn't exactly fancy about the two brown suspects speeding past *Capitol Hill,* when every other cab leisurely strolls past in usual pattern.

Suspects? Suspects for what? the officer's id thinks in wonder. *...No—suspicious. And the guy in the back is way too damn cool about the delay...unflinching and uninterested.*

Contemplating odd behavior, but not yet pushed to red flag, the cop pitches an insincere apology to the passenger in the back, noting the *Hill* is presently in a perpetual state of increased alert, due to sporadic and intensified American military raids into distant lands. Not mentioned is that anyone looking remotely the part of terrorist will be subject to questioning and search, that includes freshly-pressed, starched suit in the rear: better safe than *stupidly* sorry enough to find face plastered on networks as the careless, *asshole* cop who got Congress blown up because he didn't do his due diligence!

"Excuse me for a moment," cop says and steps back, hand casually leaning on semi-automatic, as if merely looking for something on his utility belt that fingers can't fidget with. With index pointer pressing the wireless device attached to his neck, the officer leans his head to the left shoulder, in a coded call for backup.

Thirty seconds later, two police cruisers speed from the direction of *C Street,* lights flashing and attention stirred.

"Counselor" remains calm...

Placid.

Disposition perhaps a tenth-of-an-inch crinkled.

"Sir, please *step* from the car—slowly," motions the man in blue to the driver, young *Arab* fighting final submission to underarm perspiration and forehead moisture. Once leaving his seat, two additional officers in black military fatigues and baseball caps, instructs the driver to spread his hands on the warm hood of his decade-old sedan.

No one takes notice of smooth drizzle, crowding the air in a moist blanket. Rain clouds are smelled hovering above.

Already studying the nametag and mug of the first, overly cautious cop for future reference, Germani catches the sudden, then passing look of pause from another officer, wondering why the door seems so heavy, thick, and slow to open.

Cop shrugs it off as unimportant.

"Hooptie," officer is soon overheard mumbling.

As men in black fish into pockets and crevices of *Arab* driver sprawled in bent "X" fashion before them, Congressional staffers, curious *Hill* journalists and lobbyists, stroll slowly past the scene, waiting for action, tragedy, shootout, or blood to fulfill front-page fascination tomorrow.

"Officer #1", as Germani labels him, shoots a smile of fake reassurance to his new, *Park Avenue* sewn friend in the back seat. *Maybe he doesn't have a claymore sword strapped to his torso, I'm not going to piss him off just yet,* first fuzz in blue thinks. *Guy looks important—don't want to burn any bridges before we've built a foundation."*

And as fast as fears could turn for the worse, self-engineered prophecy beckons in the sound of spit-shined crocodile heels tapping stone, drowned by calls from a gregarious House Speaker.

"Gentlemen, excuse me! Excuse me, officers! You can pass on this one—Counselor, always good to see you. How you been?" Speaker Riplat is Texas-born, desert-conditioned and in full staff regalia to absorb the imposing radiance of his office.

Told by quizzical reporters that anonymous staffers recently complained of burning toes, worn legs and bruised ego from the constant physical demands of "running around with the Speaker", Riplat responded flatly in the tradition of his classic, down country, *Lone Star State* aloofness: "So what! Nobody seems man or woman enough to say anything to me!"

Such questioning, or the expected internal turnover of whip-lashed staffers, never deters a man steamrolling into Presidential destiny.

S-h-i-i-t, I can because I'm third in line! Riplat thought.

So destination walks to-and-fro never takes place through *Rayburn House Office Building,* or *Longworth,* or *Canon*—they take place around them; in the streets, regardless of rain, snow or sweltering *D.C.* humidity since Riplat needs *"the exercise and stamina to live long and virile for the gentle* Texas *women in my district."*

Stepping from the back seat, grabbing the Speaker's hand in a strong, bear-hugging shake, Germani towers over Officer #1 in a skillful, subtle brush of pulled political rank.

"I'm great, Mr. Speaker. The feeling is always mutual. What brings you around *Rayburn* this top of the hour?"

"Spring chicken never stops to play, he just keeps movin' Counselor, you know how it is.... We've got a problem here?"

Germani is a bit annoyed that Riplat is freely using his operational name as if it's acceptable. But, he knows the Congressman is useful for the moment, since he needs to get to the airport fast.

Riplat immediately badgers the first guard with unwelcoming, high-handed indignation and stare: *IT'S YOUR PLAY, ARMED GUARD ON FIFTY GRAND A YEAR!* thinks House Speaker with steely, grilling eyes that convey much more than what's said.

Frozen by a discharge of inward fear for job, Officer #1 gives no indication of disturbance, though his instant look into Germani's pupils, betray any measure of tightness he desired, during those last few moments of extreme duty.

With his spot blown, Officer #1 manages limp response: "No, Mr. Speaker, sir. We're fine."

act 6: brainwash

You can only form the minds of reasoning animals upon Facts: nothing else will ever be of any service to them.

—Charles Dickens, *Hard Times*

chapter 33

PHILADELPHIA

DAY 24

In *Philadelphia,* now is the season of protests; protests bubbling, heaving, reaching ideological fervor before exploding. The city is overflowing with rebellious, middle-class, backpacking suburbanites on college break excursion, and confused head-wraps, eagerly digging for the same hot potatoes their parents handled forty/fifty years before. A contingent of innocent bystanders is crushed into a stuffy, creamy and uncomfortable center, thinking: *What about us?*

Ankh loves and hates it.

There are fresh recruits bumping about in those crowds.

Like cattle-to-herd, into the pastures of his cause.

Every screaming coterie of college-age kids on the brink of voluntary detention is Minister's kind…of fools. They can be molded, manipulated, and easily screwed for money, if he needed it to happen. The group is his perpetual fundraising machine, preyed upon for Ankh's faith and passion, which bellows past the grayness of their confusion.

There's hope that perhaps he can persuade most, if not all in the crowd, to get his point. Only Ankh's point matters, ridiculing and smashing the cardboard slogans students frantically pump into the air, as they scream for a justice deferred.

But Ankh's on a much higher level.

There are greater stakes at play, and despite his infamous rants in the opinion section of city newspapers, many still seem slightly lost and unable to find his point, even if it pokes them in the eye. That's fine—only the strong are needed, and Minister resolves that most are *weak* anyway.

"*Look* at them," the amused street activist belches to his lieutenants. "Like kicked ants scattered on the institution's front lawn, by the *Man's* marble step, hands reaching out to the windless air, tripping over each other's walking canes, while on a blind hunt for my *point.* Fools…"

Ankh's reputation as the best in his line of work, pushes

every protest performance as his most memorable performance, and organizers, in turn, always save his grand best for last. Hushed, the crowds mass around each stage, buzzing into thousands of anxious conversations, panting impatiently for the truth as Minister "sees" and "tells" it.

With head blown to the size of a suspended *Goodyear* blimp, Ankh breaks the quaking anticipation with the straightening of French cuffs, the clearing of throat hoarsened by speeches, and the inability to remember what the *hell* he said years ago. It's not until brief collapse into "spiritual preparedness" that Minister controls the stage.

While kids sprawl about *City Hall Square* fraying his riddles, they clamor for the inventive style of hip-hop and Sunday church, Ankh cleverly raps together in very plain, cool, melodic *English.*

"Calm yourselves…be seated." Known for those pretentious, smacking lips the headlines and talking heads will banter about each week, yet here, Minister stands unafraid, and to his pricking point—chooses to numb a nerve or pulsate a vein—giving the students his skin-blistering version, of what Ankh knows the "truth" to be.

It doesn't matter if his truth has been repeated or many times unheard, what matters is the manner in which Minister delivers it. His truth *never* enters a room or covered a stage without bravado and bullhorn announcement, the failing tact of revolutionary talk.

The performance counts.

Not the message.

The performance will always be in the peoples' midst, or permanently transfixed on their minds, blazing a new road, gallivanting onward through the blind wall of bold-faced government lies, folks have all become accustomed to. Ankh's truth is, however, many times unknown because, it has been suffocated and strangled by the ill-boding tongues of pundits, busting him on television spots and radio shows.

Students dismiss their possessions.

Leave truth behind.

Continue rallying at *City Hall's* steps.

Block traffic.

Anger cops.

Create afternoon rush-hour havoc.

They're armed with grunge clothing, trashcan drums and confrontational looks.

"How far would they go against government decree and order without the ammunition of my word? These fools *n-e-e-d* me, yes?" Ankh smiles, eyeing his soldiers as an endless river of questions enters his mind, watching *Philly's* finest commence regnant investigations, into the scanned assemblage of protesters below.

...Today's the day she catches Ankh's eye.

The day he finally locates her.

The woman: slender, athletic, and graceful through the front of the crowd, occasionally stopping a group conversation with her own philosophical take on it. Men stare about, as saliva drenches the ground below her.

Presence is astounding.

She's beauty unchallenged.

The protest now stifles itself, temporarily fluttering into nothing more than a collection of murmurs. Instead, there are men (and women, too) waiting nervously in earnest of her full, bra-bursting bloom; her inevitable rise—the flow of melting whipped cream when it evades evaporation, plunging to overtake the edges of the unbreakable *Tupperware* bowl of banana split.

The response is fairly natural. Fetish-filled, freshly and sexually foul propositions made in sun-lit dreams that dare, glowing gray-lined tremble where the minds of men can peacefully rest the backs of heads upon white cotton; to watch night dip into streams of orgasmic fireworks upon "stroke" of *New Year's* midnight.

She becomes confiscated looks.

Passionate verbs.

Escaping nocturnal safeguards.

What men *won't* do!

Or what they would...

Shame on the puritan man who is *fool* enough to rely on religious disciplines, ancient biblical creeds, or those testicular-clogging, born-again compromises; only the fool who can't, won't, wouldn't, doesn't coddle the carnal brainwash she instigates each time the woman strolls the block on her way home.

The virtuousness.

Voluptuousness.

Indisputable innocence.

Ankh knows her as “Miss Blue”, the inebriating naivety of a firm, ripened peach, barely torn from the stem, but bursting with thick, sweet, pre-dawn dew, as she awaits the final pluck.

Few venture beyond these daydreams into her chaos.

chapter 34
WEST PHILADELPHIA
DAY 25

Ankh recognizes the sister seated before him. Watches her hanging about the local university newspaper office, discovering the young lady's columns being laid on the opinion pages of *The Weekly Eagle;* her writings charged with agitation and grief.

When asked, no one at the paper knows where she came from. They just know her as "Miss Blue", assuming she's a student. The young lady writes so well, and keeps the tone of her articles so controversial, that the young undergraduate editors simply figure it will help to keep people reading the paper. Maybe they'll snatch a few awards before job searching in the real world.

"Miss Blue's columns are eloquent, yet, they're also full of dejection and accusations, unreceptive campus goons, callous technocrats, and the castigation of community exile, due to the exceptional disposition; and sexy smile that lines the sister's face.

This worries Minister: she appears on the brink of losing it, despite her raving allure and attractive demeanor as a recruit.

"Perhaps I need to indulge in the Whiter alternative," "Miss Blue" jokes in a recent op-ed. *"Maybe I need that in a frisk for sanity, as opposed to the unavailing search for happiness through colored skin."*

"That was a serious line to write, sister." Ankh leans towards "Miss Blue" while sipping a gulp of green tea. She sits across from him with arms leaned back on a red pleather perch set, scanning the walls and windows of a small holistic food joint, nested in *West Philly.* "But I'm certain you really don't feel that way."

"How do *you* know—you read minds, too?"

"I know because that letter didn't fairly represent the strength of this strong *Black* woman seated here before me."

"So you read minds and ladies' underwear, do you?"

"Miss Blue's" style is disturbing and offensive, but that kind of abrasiveness intrigues Minister. She possesses fire, courage, and audacity that's attractive.

Tapping his glass of tea before stirring it incessantly, Ankh laughs: "Yes, I won't front: men would kill to get close to you. But that's not the reason for my approach. We'd like to offer you an opportunity."

"Who's *we?*"

"My organization."

"Miss Blue" is familiar with Minister more so than the organization, but she's aware of what he talks about. Most within *Philly* city limits suspect Ankh is "organized," but no one holds any specific or detailed knowledge. He isn't public about it, Ankh referring only to his "soldiers" or "centurions"—a small legion of clean-cut and steroid-bulky *Black* men surrounding him with determined vigilance.

They wear matching black suits, black shirts, solid black ties, and ironically, black "European" shoes. Ankh's men never really speak unless spoken to and they never seem confused or out of sync. Their movements are planned patterns. One night, more than several years ago, "Miss Blue" once watched them perfected combat specimen, clearing a ballroom of several hundred as a platoon of twelve.

A large post-conference party turned from an unusual cross section of elites and activists, into a near murderous scene of chaos involving rival rappers. When disaster broke out, and fists flew into jaws, Ankh was suddenly lifted from his chair, and speedily ejected from the building. As that happened, twelve men effortlessly knocked heads into a mosh pit of four dozen mob-swinging thugs, flipping elbows into a precision heavy force of martial artistry that came so fast, it was barely noticeable.

The sister watched it carefully that night while pressed aside her husband in marvel, observed with fascination, as one of the guards snapped bones in the hand of a missed assailant, anxious to use a hidden semi-automatic. No one else but "Miss Blue" saw the gun snatched from the man's fingers—the crack, a whimpering gurgle of pain, and one towering centurion whisking him away in a headlock.

The man and the gun vanished…

Fight was over in five.

Dancing resumed in less than ten.

"Does this mean you'll let me in on what *exactly* the organization is, Minister?"

"That comes with it," Ankh responds and frowns, his tone

growing more serious.

"What do you propose?"

"We'll teach and refine you into what you're not, but could be. Everything you ever wanted to know about paramilitary training, from martial studies to gun marksmanship."

"That's heavy."

"As heavy as heavy allows it. It's a heavy world we live in—crackers killing unarmed brothers. Then you've got brothers killing brothers; unjust wars against our *Muslim* brethren in the *Middle East*—innocent women and children being blown to pieces by *New World Order* missiles. You catch me?"

She's feeling Ankh's vibe.

"I-catch-that, I-catch-that. H-m-m-m," the young lady hums to Minister's tune, one heard many times before.

"Be a part of this, sister. Join me."

The campus thing, Ankh can see, clearly bores "Miss Blue": the trifle parades for peace and anti-globalization, these *damn* middle-class escapades with *White* radical wannabes she doesn't like anyway. Sister's better than that. What "Miss Blue sees is people playing fun and games with fate.

It's not difficult to understand the reasoning behind her distress. What she challenges is the justification for these revolutions of peace. Good: Minister and the young lady are on the same wavelength, Ankh digs that—there's no such thing as peaceful revolution anyway.

Revolution is what it implies: bloody and awesomely violent. Gruesome. Brutal.

People want to wear fashionable khakis, download chain e-mail petitions, whine all day and text on cell phones about "peace" and "one love", and all that other pop culture varnish. It's a disgusting, name brand kindled lack of taste and respect, Ankh thinks.

Minister recalls an era of platforms and true social progress, when movements were shelters for the disenfranchised.

Since when did they become clubs for entertainment?

Instead, he watched the movements evolve into superficial fashion runway statements.

"Yeah, yeah," "Miss Blue" calls to Ankh's tune.

That's right, Ankh pounds, deep in thought, *extensions of the larger Institution. Selling souls in such a shameless shedding of their history—is the mere existence, and name of an organization as important as the revolutionary changes it's "obligated" to make?*

"Perhaps such an obligation was too heavy for them to handle," Ankh poses cryptically to the young lady.

"I agree with that," "Miss Blue" throws back.

"Yes, sister," he leads on in a passionate patty-cake of choir preaching. "It's not wrong for us soldiers of *righteousness* to question the relevancy of these groups claiming unity of cause, yet increasingly distancing themselves from their stated objectives, and from the people they *claim* to serve.

"It's time that we become the soldiers we *say* we are!" Minister now has her full audience. "Leave the chaos behind, this lifetime of senseless student causes, and cowards who won't go all the way. Come with us and fight the *real* fight! Draw blood, sister, not pictures on the wall!"

"Miss Blue" nods—a slow nod, but full with certainty and confidence.

"It's time for you to put that fire to use. We'll take care of you. You're a great writer and thinker—but don't you grow tired of the games? Playing with these *fools* while they play you?

Everything she's doing is suddenly in doubt or question.

What Ankh said is what "Miss Blue" has already admitted.

She just needed to hear from another horse's mouth.

chapter 35

SCHUYLKILL EXPRESSWAY

DAY 26

"So, you found her. That was fast. Where is she now?"

"She's training."

"*Training?*"

"Training—it takes a while. We like to get it done right."

"You like to get it done right?

"That's right. We're perfectionists."

"Don't patronize me, let's get real about this. If you were perfectionists, you wouldn't be on the take from the same people you accuse of crimes against humanity."

A meeting going on between two men in a midnight-colored *Mercedes* sedan, plastered from front engine to body bag trunk, in dark tint. You can see out, but no one can see inside.

Not even a shadow or silhouette.

They're stealth in passing traffic, the driver steady, and the tires tread through rush hour like a space shuttle in open universe. What worries one passenger the most is the other.

"You waste too much time, Minister. You dance around this woman as if you're are…" Germani pauses for word choice, "…As if you've planned some new *use* for her."

Despising "Counselor" to the core, Ankh places more focus on the dark tinted windows in silent desperation, mentally clawing at the *Schuylkill Expressway* while trailing dots of automobiles, racing along *Route 76.*

The two just passed *City Line*—beautiful, rebuilt *Manayunk* on the *Eastside* of the river, is in view before becoming a distant minute from memory. Minister no longer sees runners and bicyclists along the *East Drive.* There are only hills of old trees sliced by sidewalk, street and houses.

Traffic passes unconcerned.

Where the hell is he taking me? Ankh thinks, swallowing on saliva, having a really bad stiffening sensation of dry throat.

This why he loathes Germani—the suspense, that *damn* arrogance and air of mystery, as though he can work *Zeus'* wonders or *Pluto's* schemes. A stream of gutter now flows through Minister's thoughts, a rage consuming him to douse the fear, an endless tributary of profanity, blasting negative vibes into the air between them.

"You *missed* that ramp at *City Line.* I'm *not* going to *King of Prussia,*" Ankh growls while shifting about the back seat leather.

"You keep missing the sense of urgency we've placed on this matter. You think I *care* about your meetings, Ankh? You think I care about getting you to another meaningless forum on how *'massa done done me so'*?" Germani smirks.

Minister continues staring into space.

"*A-w-w-w,* wait a second," "Counselor" starts teasing, "I see. That's right: after that recent performance the other night, you're probably into more important matters. ...Bigger fish to fry? On your way to some campaign war room session? What do I call you now? Councilman Ankh? Mayor Ankh? Congressman Ankh? Eyes getting too big for *yo'* fat *ass,* Ankh!"

A slight hint of hood leaks into that statement. Ankh wants—needs some cultural affirmation on Germani anyway.

Now is as good a time as any.

Get the bastard up-close so he can reveal what lies beneath the outer layer. The slanted eyes speak Asian, but the jaw shifted like something *Native American* or indigenous *American.* But the curled hair, fullness of lips, bass voice and rich, mahogany shade of skin eclipsing yellow, speaks of something distantly *African.*

The brother could indeed, be a brother. So why do what he does, Ankh massages his head for answers. Minister's fingers dig into the side of the dome facing the tint, digging for more insight into his unlikely employer.

"I'm bleeding for my people, Counselor. At least I have that luxury. I—"

"*Bleeding?* What? As some *vainglorious* pseudo-martyr?" Germani mocks Ankh. The activist stops cold. "A difficult pursuit, yes, I guess I can give you that—staging protests and, now, campaign announcements are always much easier. It's becoming a mighty honorable profession these days: getting paid to run. Don't know how *noble* it is, but it gets the *loot* you think you need.

"Dressing radically or in '*revolutionary*' poise; stage poetic, grandiloquent rebellion with only microphones and network cameras rolling—threaten uprising while resplendent in pretentious clothing or *Kente* cloth…not knowing exactly what the colors stand for, mind you. Wear your culture on a make-believe sleeve until you feel *"The Man's"* eyes have watered! …It isn't necessarily *Nat Turner* or *Huey Newton* posing on a bamboo throne. It's not like jumping off the *slave* ship, or better yet, *burning* it—but it has its planned effect.

"It continues to reinforce the notion, the image…the symbolism of upstanding servants and *'Great Black Hopes',* working in the best interest of 'the people', working as *authentically Black* as *Black* can be. The detail, the motives, the compelling plots, twists and themes, are *always* hidden between the lines. Lights…camera…action!" Germani flickers his hands for effect.

Minister throws an intense internalized fit to kill Germani.

A cold-blooded, no-second-thought kind of killing.

But he has to hold the urge.

Ankh, in disarray, dismisses Germani's last statement" "I'm just saying, Counselor, you missed my exit. Thought you were giving me a ride to where I was going. I ride, we talk a little business and it's done."

Struggling to loosen the conversation, Ankh now eases his tightened jaw: "Listen, we're working on her. We didn't realize there was a substantial amount of de-programming involved. We thought she was ready to go. This young lady has got a lot of issues. Many emotional screws loosened from years of neglect, misfortune, shame and pain. I'm not saying I feel sorry for her, but I want the girl intact for future assignments. My organization may have use for that kind of talent."

"*My organization,* Ankh," Germani seethes, "will make the *final* determination as to what your *organization* can and cannot do with her. That does not include any *sexual* brainwashing you might be planning. Don't think we don't *know* about that."

The order is made!

Keep your hands off the merchandise! Germani glares. *Do your job—make "Miss Blue" available! Train her and wrap this up*!

"The Members" want Councilman dead before the next election cycle.

chapter 36
BROOKLYN
REWIND: FLASHBACK

For many years, and before her marriage to Councilman, young "Miss Blue" had lived under the shadow of her "infamous" father's insanity. Meeting the legislator, falling in love with him, raising a family should've served as a springboard for normalcy in her life. That never managed to happen, given her husband's addiction for women, and the rate at which his selfishness drained her.

Yet, "Miss Blue" lunged forward with life, strangely reflecting on her old man each time she'd be faced with the shock of another affair, or another badly plotted financial decision, leaning on memories of how she'd survived her father's mental trips and plucks; caught wandering off into the dreamy stars.

At nine, "Miss Blue" couldn't understand her father's flaws and lapses, couldn't understand his trips and episodes with insanity, since it all seemed so unreal at the time. Family members had simply attributed the man's problems to a conventional case of manic depression, a lifetime battle with bipolar edges that kept everyone distant from her immediate clan.

That was years ago when they'd become lost on a desolate Vermont *road somewhere, roaming through the pines on a forgotten mountain. By all outward appearances the family seemed normal—typical father and daughter on vacation with fishing poles stacked in the back, hiking packs cramped on the floor, a full box of* Zip-locked *sandwiches, and bottled juices melting ice in the* Styrofoam *cooler.*

But, wrapped in the details was the pure realization that "Miss Blue's" dad wasn't "wrapped too tight", definitely not tight enough to simply move from point A to point B.

Her pops pushed the odometer on the aging Volkswagen *van like an alcoholic farmer, putting the whip to his oxen, carelessly unmindful of the narrow, two-lane mountain paths that curved and split when you least expected it. He'd seemed unmindful of the anxiousness and shot nerves one might draw from such risk. Never mind that a deer could come suddenly galloping from the forest edge, crash into an animal pile-up, whizzing out of nowhere into the windshield; or that a black bear could've rammed a new trunk into the family car.*

"WHO CARES, RIGHT, DAD? yells "Miss Blue's thoughts into the van, as if all alone. YOU DON'T SEEM TO CARE, DO YOU? YOU PSYCHOTIC SON-OF-A-BITCH! SO, MAYBE, I WON'T!

She'd remembered this silent act of defiance did absolutely nothing to calm her freckled nerves that day. Instead, "infamous" father continued his insane drive, throwing the vehicle all through asphalt and dirt, not thinking at all about his daughter's safety or the risks involved.

The van did its own thing, hitting curves here-and-there, careening off pavement, passenger-side tires violently scraping into roadside dirt and grass. "Miss Blue" recalls screaming loudly, staring out her window seeing endless columns of trees, falling into a riverbed somewhere, hundreds of feet below.

She'd remembered how odd it was because her old man seemed distant and undisturbed; completely numb to her sniffled, subdued cries for help on that Vermont road, twenty years ago.

Twenty years later, "Miss Blue" can't help but to think deeply about it. While hiding away in Philly in the wake of her son's death, and sudden unfortunate miscarriage, sister grows more skeptical of why she finds herself in the present predicament, linking it to a wild past that's peppered with a bizarre range of twists and turns.

During recent training sessions with Minister Ankh's men, "Miss Blue" catches snapshot-second glimpses of strange *White* men in black suits. When asking about them a moment later, recovering from a sweaty round of kickboxing, other men in the gym go blank…stupid. The suited men look so familiar…for so many familiar reasons.

"Miss Blue" goes back to a pivotal conversation several years rewind, on this pleasantly typical *New York City* day today, during a quick visit home, a time to confront her father about it.

"*You seemed determined, yet dragged into it by some unseen force."*

"Dad—tell me about *Vermont.* Why were you in such a rush? Why did you drive so crazy, as if something was waiting for you around the bend? As if you were following something, looking for it, or better, like it was supposed to show itself at any moment?" "Miss Blue" studies her aging pop's grill for answers.

Today is *not* particularly the best day to confront the issue.

Her father is in a bad-ass mood!

He looks tired and beat-up!

Literally beat up—as if some thug-sucker puffed the man's eyes without leaving a scratch on his face.

"Miss Blue" and her dad are in the antique-flavored, rust-colored collage of renovated junk furniture her mom calls "The Family Room", looking through a tinted, wall-size window into a *Brooklyn* street. It's an old, old, old, old school interior design panorama, completely out-of-place with 21st century "mega-op" plasticity of their urban surroundings.

The smell of potpourri in their quaint brownstone is distracted by the roaring sound of kids on skateboards. Occasionally, a passing sedan blasting an unwelcome torrent of *Reggae Gold* dancehall rips the fenced peace.

Today is replete with dusty skies, dry atmosphere and little rain in the forecast for many days to follow. *Hudson River* winds are a brisk reminder that the *Atlantic Ocean* yawns not too long from where the family sits. There's a scent of smog in the air, blowing into nostrils like pasty incense. "Miss Blue's" mother is in the backyard potting plants, and breaking "Bones", the family's dog's balls—his barking is a bit incessant, a bit too much to tolerate.

"It'll take me a while to register that one," says "infamous" father, deciding to ignore his daughter's inquiries about *Vermont*, while yelling at his wife to leave the family dog alone. *Can't blame the mutt*, he thinks, *if the smell of burnt twigs is agitating him!*

His wife continues bashing the dog, yet muffles her irritation so no one can hear it.

"So, you *don't* recall that?" continues "Miss Blue", "You were driving like a *demon* on that thin mountain road while I was crying for GOD's mercy."

"U-m-m-m...can't say that I do," he replies and closes his eyes for a moment, in what looks like a sincere attempt to pull it all up. "No," her father fails.

Frustrated, "Miss Blue" shakes her head.

"But, sweetheart, maybe one day it'll come to me. You want an ice tea? *Damn,* I'm parched...feel like a *damn* ice tea..."

he trails off, changing the subject, smiling. That wicked grin of shallow optimism is shown, one whenever "infamous" father wants to avoid things that make him sick!

"Daddy—no! No…no…NO! *Don't* do that!" she snaps! "I don't *want* an ice tea! I *need* you to break this *shit* down for me! I *need* to understand everything about that day…about every moment you *tripped-out* and went to *lunch* on me, daddy! My life is a mysterious trail of episodes, disappearances, blackouts and hospital visits. And you *never* tell me the whole story, do you? Like, who were those people we met at that river?"

"What people? What river?"

"SEE?" yells "Miss Blue", "That's what I'm *talking* about! They were teaching me how to fish with my bare hands, dad…. Remember? They kept me occupied while you were talking—no…it looked as though they were talking to you. We'd just met them, but they seemed to know everything about us. It was a whole town of them—men in turtlenecks and blazers.

"We didn't know them, but you walked up to them as though you knew them all your life. And then, after a day, you roll off with these men to go hunt or some *shit,* and I'm left in a strange *ass* town—four whole days, dad, with strange people that barely spoke to me."

"Infamous" father frowns.

Looks into space…

Brushes his hand in the air.

Gets erratic.

"I don't know what you're *talking* about, sweetie. You sound like the *crazy* one."

"CRAZY MY *ASS!*" she ignores her old man, "That's some bipolar *bullshit* you've crutched to cover up something else! *You* were involved with those people for some reason."

"Tell her about the runway chase, Benny," "Miss Blue's" mother suddenly chides in. Apparently, she's been standing here all along, and now decides that today her daughter won't stop until she gets answers about her father's secret life.

"Miss Blue" and her father didn't even hear the woman walk in, her quick shuffling from the backyard as stealth as the neighbor's cat that teased and tormented "Bones". "Miss Blue" planned this meeting as a single-defining moment of truth between father and daughter, yet she should've known better when the dog stopped barking.

"Runway chase?" the young lady snickers before listening intently. Her pops quickly beams thick wads of new energy. The dark puffs under his eyes fades into something discernible, almost youthful.

"O-h-h-h—ho, o-h-h-h," he responds like *Santa Claus* bugged on the fond memory of a frat party smoke bong—the man spills a wide smile on the floor. "I remember *that*; quite a fight. The point…" reflective pause suddenly gains on "Miss Blue's" pops, "… of no return, that's where it all started. I think…was that when it started?"

"Yes," the older woman cranks in hypnotically, staring into space in a way that, ruins the burst of the man's bizarre flicker of joy. "You were being activated." She then shuffles elsewhere in her unique motherly way, that special womanly demure that sifts through the house without announcing her freaky departure.

"I don't understand," queries "Miss Blue". "What are you *talking* about? Runway chase? Good fight?"

"The war, sweetheart."

The young lady now watches carefully, as the sudden burst of youth in her pops disappear.

Eye puffiness returns.

Sunny day replaced with *East Coast* overcast.

I didn't know dad was in the military. What war?

But, if the man was in a war and didn't say anything, it explains as much as it hurt.

Dad in a war?

There's a beguiling sense of pride mixed in with sudden anger, the pain of not knowing something a daughter could, at least, embellish and admire. On a level, "Miss Blue" struggles to resist, it also provides justification for her father's state-of-mind all these years. The young lady immediately begins fishing for details: *What war? When was this? Where? Did he go overseas?*

"You don't know about this war, sweetie." *Nobody does.* They won't be teaching it in Social Studies."

"They covered it on the front page, though," the mother interjects as she shuffles back into the room, returning before "Miss Blue" could engage further. The older woman holds what seems like a very molded yellow newspaper, one that's been stored away for a long time.

The man gives his wife a guarded look.

The beat-up face is back.

"She doesn't need to see that," he replies.

"Yeah-she-does. Not like the girl can't research and find it sooner or later. She's been remarkably patient…it's time you open up a little. You *have* to."

Something in the way her mother said "you *have* to", doesn't sit well in "Miss Blue's" stomach, and for some odd reason, the young lady now feels sick on flashbacks of the people they met along that *Vermont* river; the native faces twisting into weird, mashed squiggles of flesh pushed together like *Rocky Road* ice cream. "Miss Blue" tries shaking it—her dad now explodes!

"THEN WHY DON'T *YOU* TELL HER?" "Infamous" father cracks back like a cranky-ass senior purchasing overpriced pharmaceuticals.

"Because it's *not* my function, Ben. You fought the war, we didn't interface when the chase happened."

Interface?

What's the woman trying to say?

Meet?

Another word for "date" or "sex"?

"Miss Blue" whips her head in a fiercely contested back-and-forth of lost wills. Interface? That's an *odd* way to describe a lifetime of solid matrimony.

How much crack is she on today? the young lady thinks.

Her father retreats back into his cracked cotton recliner: "So *be* it," as he looks out the window—the many times the man's done so to avoid concerned family eyes. "Miss Blue's" pops plays as though more absorbed by the screaming kids and passing cars outside.

At this, the mother slides to the other side of the living room and drops a newspaper on the coffee table, several inches below her daughter's knee. Whether she notices "Miss Blue's" slipping into temporary mental illness over images of the *Vermont* trip remains unclear.

Still, the daughter of this mid-afternoon misery holds her own, fending off their twenty-year-old-chatter, twenty-year-old laughs, and mystic swirl of their twenty-year-old whispers. They suddenly become more foreign than he's ever noticed.

More alien…

Still, "Miss Blue" manages shaking it off while grabbing the old issue of *The Philadelphia Bell,* slightly torn at several edges, and stained by random food spots of many years. It's well preserved despite its dinged look, a clear front-page feature photo as crisp as the sunlight, dangling about in the living room.

The headline tells tales of a *"High Speed Chase At Airport Ends in 10 Hurt, 1 Arrest"*. The photo was taken presumably, from a news helicopter with permitted airspace over busy *Philadelphia International.*

This doesn't seem strange to the young lady, because she assumes there were cancelled flights that day, judging from the dramatic image of five police cruisers, racing fifty yards behind a convertible on a runway. Obviously, the photo is too gritty to make out whom or what was driving the car being chased.

"Miss Blue" continues reading further…

Details are drawing her in…

Drawing her in like the tangy smell of *crack...*

Fuming in an abandoned row house.

"Miss Blue's" eyes now widen!

She notices "infamous" father's name.

Written only a few letters away.

From the words "suspect" and "in custody."

GLOSSARY

Aiiight – Alright
Ballin' – Living extravagantly
Bama – Poor southern man
Bling – Jewelry
Boned – Ruined
Bones/Cake/Cheddar/Cheese/Loot – Money
Bounced/Bouncing – To leave
Brudda/Bruh – Brother
Buckets – Shoes
Cali/Cannabis/Weed – Marijuana
Capo – Mafia leader
Cat – Man
Chai – Tea
Chop shop – Illegal auto shop
Coup de grace – A death blow intended for the wounded
Cracked his sinus – To clear nasal passage/Sniffing cocaine
Crib – Apartment
Da – The
Dis – This
Dome – Head
Dropping dime – To reveal
Dubs – Tire rims
Dunno – Don't know
'Em – Them
Fell of a truck – To steal
Filthadelphia – Derogatory term for Philadelphia
Five-0/Fuzz – Police
Fly – To get smart with
Got got – Killed
Grill/Mug – Face
Hit it – To have sex
Homegirl – Local female
Hood – Urban
Housed – To beat up
Intifadah – To shake off
Joe – Coffee
Jones – Attraction
Kumbaya – Spiritual song from 1930's

La Cosa Nostra – Mafia
Mad – A lot
MSG – Monosodium Glutamate/Food seasoning
Naw – No
Neo-ghetto – New urban
Nuff – Enough
OJ – Orange juice
On the low – quieted
Oxycontin – Drug used for severe pain
Peeped – Observed
Pimp-slappin' – To forcefully hit
Propers/Props – Credit/Recognition
Punany – Vagina
Skank – Slut
Son – Man
Snitches – Informant
Spit – To recite with passion
Spliff – Marijuana filled cigar
Straight – To be okay
SUV – Sport-utility vehicle
The Man – White man
Thugged-out – Dressed in urban gear
Thug-sucker – Criminal
Wench – A wanton woman
Wifebeaters – Tank tops
Wolf tickets – Threatening or intimidating verbal aggression
XL – Extra large
Yuppies – Young educated professional

READING IS SEXY…

An excerpt from ***TANTRUM 2*** by
CHARLES D. ELLISON
A GHETTOHEAT® PRODUCTION

Benny Kindel, one time *North Jersey* hustler with a loser head stuck far up *New York City's* moral cesspool, was never the lucky guy. He played twenty bones of lottery tickets a day, which was a waste of time, and Benny knew it, never once hitting the numbers. Routine visits to *Atlantic City* casinos fizzled into roulette wheel disasters, blackjack catastrophes and finally—resorting to pickpockets of cash for that week's groceries.

But, he had his wise guy gopher jobs, constantly rubbing arms with *Irish, Russians, Asians,* fledgling *Sicilians* and upstart *West Indian* smugglers. This provided enough income to maintain a raggedy flat and perpetrating high-roller lifestyle. Benny even managed the luxury sedan with alloy wheels to spice it, the ghetto-*fabulous* trade-in for a lifetime of criminal induced procrastination.

GOD only knew that Benny was *never* the lucky guy.

"He was smart though, and that's how he got me hooked on this *Bonnie and Clyde* thing we got goin'," laughs his wife, rubbing her eyes on humored tears.

But Benny wasn't off to the smartest start that day. He jacked Mr. Hurobi for his expensive two-seater, ripped a speed record on the trooper fortified *Jersey Turnpike,* and managed to somehow slip into *Philadelphia International Airport* without a warning.

"Flight 763 has a bomb on it," is all Benny said to the clerks at the ticket counter, walking through a crowded lane of perturbed passengers who thought he was cutting his way up front. As quickly as Benny laid the chilling new fact before a phalanx of dumbfounded airline employees, he fled the scene, pop-wheeling his illegally parked, stolen car.

The ticket line was in full panic, as word of Benny's whisper at the counter found its way to a few unnerved passengers, watching a petrified counter of personnel, scrambling on the phones for security.

Here's the thing, "Flight 763" was about to take off, bound for a transatlantic hitch to *Heathrow Airport* in England. It was already moving away from its gate, Benny—in what police reports that day described as a "driven, hypnotic stupor", had no choice but to crash a gate, moving at horrendous speeds across the runway in a freshly laid coat of ugly scratches and dents, atop the hood of Hurobi's ride. It was an insane attempt to single-handedly chase "Flight 763" and wave it down.

When air traffic control finally flagged the plane to a stop, Benny was already nearby with a menacing caravan of airport police, *S.W.A.T.* and *National Guard Humvees,* closing in and ready to put a stinging beat down on the disturbed hustler from *North Jersey.* That's when the big fight started, a legendary scene of martial artistry and ass kicking that few onlookers and participants would forget.

No one could connect on how did this low-scale loser street-thug, who grew up in the elemental ghetto of *Jersey City* streets get so *skilled* in whipping ass? Benny jumped from the overheated sports car, in full awareness of his predicament and the variety of semi-automatic to automatic weapons, pointed in his direction.

The first line of attack was a thick trench of underpaid, airport police who completely underestimated the man in a black leather jacket and cotton pants, jumping from the stolen car. They moved into a fast, bloodcurdling fury of Benny's flawless roundhouse kick combinations into faces, arms, knees and stomachs which, within a matter of minutes, left behind a spine-chilling trail of nearly twenty armed officers unconscious, or gripping injuries in loud howls of pain on the runway tarmac.

As quick as he was done with the first line, Benny managed to break the arms and legs of an equal number of *Philadelphia* fuzz in blue—many of them easily disarmed by the shock of watching the man, defusing an entire throng of armed men with swift collaborations of his foot and bone-cracking shin.

Before Benny pushed on for a showdown with the *National Guardsmen* (their jaws dropped in fascination at the lightening speed with which he dispatched near lethal knee and elbow blows), a few injured cops barely summed up enough collective strength and planning, to blast Benny with a serious surge of stun gun voltage.

An excerpt from ***GHETTOHEAT®*** by
HICKSON
A GHETTOHEAT® PRODUCTION

GHETTOHEAT®

S-S-S-S-S-S-S!
Can you feel it?
Scaldin' breath of frisky spirits
Surroundin' you in the streets
The intensity
S-S-S-S-S-S-S!
That's GHETTOHEAT®!
The energy – Electric sparks
Better watch ya back after dark!
Dogs bark – Cats hiss
Rank smells of trash and piss
Internalize – Realize
No surprise – Naughty spirits frolic in disguise
S-S-S-S-S-S-S!
INTENSITY: CLIMBIN'! CLIMBIN'! CLIMBIN'! CLIMBIN'!
GHETTOHEAT®: RISIN'! RISIN'! RISIN'! RISIN'!

Streets is watchin'
Hoes talkin' – Thugs stalkin'
POW-POW-POW!
Start speed-walkin'!
Heggies down – Rob that clown
Snatch his stash – Jet downtown
El Barrio – *Spanish Harlem:*
"MIRA, NO! WE DON'T WANNO PROBLEM!"

Bullets graze – I'm not amazed
GHETTOHEAT®!
Niggas start blazin'
Air's scathin' – Gangs blood-bathin'
Five-O's misbehavin' – Wifey's rantin'-n-ravin'!
My left: The Bloods – My right: The Crips
Niggas start prayin' – Murk-out in ya whip!

Internalize – Realize
No surprise – Naughty spirits frolic in disguise
S-S-S-S-S-S-S!
INTENSITY: CLIMBIN'! CLIMBIN'! CLIMBIN'! CLIMBIN'!
GHETTOHEAT®: RISIN'! RISIN'! RISIN'! RISIN'!

Mean hoodlums – Plottin' schemes
A swoop-down – 'Bout to rob me – Seems like a bad dream
Thugs around – It's goin' down
'BOUT TO BE SOME *SHIT!*
But I'm ghetto – Know how to spit
Gully mentality – Thinkin' of reality of planned-out casualty
I fake wit' the trickery: "ASS-ALAMUALAIKUM"
"STICK 'EM UP!"
"YO, DON'T FUCK WIT' HIM: HE'S MUSLIM!"

Flipped script wit' quickness
Changed demeanor – The swiftness
Not dimwitted – Felt the flames of evil spirits!
Hid chain in shirt – I don't catch pain – Don't get hurt
No desire gettin' burnt by the fire
Thermometer soars, yo, higher-and-higher!
In the PRO-JECTS – Fightin' to protect ya neck
Gotta earn respect – Defend ya rep
Or BEAT-DOWNS you'll collect!
The furor – The fever – My gun – My cleaver
Bitches brewin' – Slits a-stewin'
Sheets roastin' – Champagne toastin' – Gangstas boastin':
"The ghetto – Nuthin's mellow
The ghetto – Cries in falsetto
The ghetto – A dream bordello
The ghetto – Hotter than Soweto"

Internalize – Realize
No surprise – Naughty spirits frolic in disguise
S-S-S-S-S-S-S!
INTENSITY: CLIMBIN'! CLIMBIN'! CLIMBIN'! CLIMBIN'!
GHETTOHEAT®: RISIN'! RISIN'! RISIN'! RISIN'!

Red-hot hustlers – Broilin' at the spot
Boilin' alcohol – The lucky crackpot

Streets a-scorchin' – Crackheads torchin'
Stems ignited – Junkies delighted
Money's flowin' – Pusherman's excited
The first and fifteenth: BLOCK-HUGGERS' JUNETEENTH!
Comin' ya way – Take ya benefits today
Intoxication – Self-medication – The air's dense
Ghetto-suffocation – Volcanic maniacs attackin'
Cash stackin' – Niggas packin' – Daddy Rock's mackin':
"The ghetto – Nuthin's mellow
The ghetto – Cries in falsetto
The ghetto – A dream bordello
The ghetto – Hotter than Soweto"

BedStuy – Do or die: *BUCK-BUCK-BUCK-BUCK!*
They don't give a *FUCK!*
In *The Bronx* – You'll fry – Tossin' lye – WATCH YA EYES!

Walk straight – Tunnel vision
False move – Bad decision
So hot – Starts to drizzle – Steamy sidewalks begin to sizzle
HOT-TO-DEF! Intense GHETTOHEAT®

"DO YOU FEEL IT? DO YOU FEEL IT?"
"THE HOTNESS IN THE STREETS!!!™"

So hot – Got ya mase?
Too hot: PEPPER-SPRAYIN'-IN-A-*NIGGA'S*-FACE!
The Madness – Sadness
Don't you know the flare of street-glow?
OH!
Meltingly – Swelteringly: *S-S-S-S-S-S-S!*
HOOD IN-FER-NO!
Internalize – Realize
No surprise – Naughty spirits frolic in disguise
S-S-S-S-S-S-S!
INTENSITY: CLIMBIN'! CLIMBIN'! CLIMBIN'! CLIMBIN'!
GHETTOHEAT®: RISIN'! RISIN'! RISIN'! RISIN'!
INTENSITY: CLIMBIN'! CLIMBIN'! CLIMBIN'! CLIMBIN'!
GHETTOHEAT®: RISIN'! RISIN'! RISIN'! RISIN'!
S-S-S-S-S-S-S!

An excerpt from ***CONVICT'S CANDY*** by
DAMON "AMIN" MEADOWS & JASON POOLE
A GHETTOHEAT® PRODUCTION

"Sweets, you're in cell 1325; upper bunk," the Correctional Officer had indicated, as he instructed Candy on which cell to report to. When she heard 'upper bunk', Candy had wondered who would be occupying the cell with her. As Candy had grabbed her bedroll and headed towards the cell, located near the far end of the tier and away from the officer's desk and sight, butterflies had grown deep inside of Candy's stomach, as she'd become overwhelmed with nervousness; Candy tried hard to camouflage her fear.

This was Candy's first time in prison and she'd been frightened, forcefully trapped in terror against her will. Candy had become extremely horrified, especially when her eyes met directly with Trigger's, the young, hostile thug she'd accidentally bumped into as she'd been placed inside the holding cell. Trigger had rudely shoved Candy when she first arrived to the facility.

"THE *FUCK* YOU LOOKIN' AT, HOMO?" Trigger had spat; embarrassed that Candy had looked at him. Trigger immediately wondered if she was able to detect that something was different about him and his masculinity; Trigger had hoped that Candy hadn't gotten any ideas that he might've been attracted to her, since Candy had caught him staring hard at her.

She'd quickly turned her face in the opposite direction, Candy wanted desperately not to provoke Trigger, as the thought of getting beat down by him instantly had come to Candy's mind.

She couldn't exactly figure out the young thug, although Candy thought she might've had a clue as to why he'd displayed so much anger and hatred towards her. Yet, this hadn't been the time to come to any conclusions, as Candy was more concerned with whom she'd be sharing the cell with.

When Candy had reached cell 1325, she glanced twice at the number printed above on the door, and had made sure that she was at the right cell before she'd entered. Candy then peeped inside the window to see if anyone had been there. Seeing that it was empty, she'd stepped inside of the cell that would serve as her new home for the next five-and-a-half years.

Candy was overwhelmed with joy when she found the

cell had been perfectly neat and clean; and for a moment, Candy had sensed that it had a woman's touch. The room smelled like sweet perfume, instead of the strong musk oil that was sold on commissary.

Right away, Candy had dropped her bedroll and raced towards the picture board that had hung on the wall and analyzed every photo; she'd become curious to know who occupied the cell and how they'd lived. Candy believed that a photo was like a thousand words; she'd felt that people told a lot about themselves by the way they'd posed in photographs, including how they displayed their own pictures.

Candy then smiled as her eyes perused over photos of gorgeous models, both male and female, and had become happy when she'd found the huge portrait of her new cellmate. Judging by his long, jet-black wavy hair, facial features and large green eyes, Candy had assumed that he was Hispanic.

Now that she'd known the identity of her cellmate, Candy then decided that it would be best to go find him and introduce herself; she'd hoped that he would fully accept her into the room.

As Candy had turned around and headed out the door, she'd abruptly been stopped by a hard, powerful right-handed fist to her chiseled jaw, followed by the tight grip of a person's left hand hooking around her throat; her vocal cords were being crushed so she couldn't scream.

Candy had haphazardly fallen back into a corner and hit the back of her head against the wall, before she'd become unconscious momentarily. Within the first five seconds of gaining back her conscious, Candy had pondered who'd bashed her so hard in her face.

The first person that had come to mind was Trigger. Secondly, Candy also had thought it might've been her new cellmate who obviously hadn't wanted Candy in his cell, she'd assumed by the blow that Candy had taken to her flawless face.

Struggling her way back from darkness, Candy's eyes had widened wide, at that point, being terribly frightened, as she was face-to-face with two unknown convicts who'd worn white pillow cases over their heads; mean eyes had peeked from the two holes that was cut out from the cloth. The two attackers had resembled members of the *Ku Klux Klan* bandits as they'd hid their faces; both had been armed with sharp, ten-inch knives.

Overcome with panic, there was no doubt in Candy's

mind that she was about to be brutally raped, as there was no way out. Candy then quickly prayed to herself and had hoped that they wouldn't take her life as well. Yet, being raped no longer was an important factor to Candy, as they could've had their way with her. All Candy had been concerned with at that moment was continuing to live.

An excerpt from ***HARDER*** by
SHA
A GHETTOHEAT® PRODUCTION

When I finally arrived back home, Tony was heated. I didn't even realize I was out that long.

"WHERE THE *FUCK* YOU BEEN, KAI?" he yelled as I walked through the door.

"I went to the range and then shopping. I had a lot on my mind to clear and I just needed to get away. *Damn,* is there a law against that?"

"Nah, ain't no law, shorty! Just watch yaself, cuz if I finds out different, we gonna have major problems."

Tony was taking on a "Rico" tone with me that I did not like whatsoever.

"Who the *fuck* is you talking to, Tony? I *know* it ain't me. Ya better keep that *shit* in ya back pocket before you come at me with it."

I had never seen Tony like this before, and it made me very upset. I knew I had to calm down, before I said something that I would live to regret.

"Oh word? It's like that, Kai? *Fuck* you forget or something? This here is *my* house! *I'm* the star, baby girl! You *used* to be the co-star, but now you just another *fucking* spectator! Show over, get the *fuck* out!"

Just when I thought things couldn't get any worse!

"Get the fuck out? You get mad over some *bullshit* and now it's 'get the fuck out'? Tony, think about that shit for a minute." I started talking slowly and softly. "I'm ya 'co-star' alright, but do you *know* what that means? …It means, everything you own, *I* own. All the work you put in, I put in, too.

"You forget who sees over the cooks and make sure ya deliveries are made on time? That's me, *motherfucker.* You *sure* you wanna have me running the street with all ya info, baby boy?"

That weird laugh echoed out of me again. This time, it set Tony off. He grabbed me by my throat, and *threw* me into the hard brick wall! When I hit the floor, Tony started to strangle me as he screamed, "BABY BOY? BABY BOY, HUH? YOU FUCK THAT *NIGGA?* HUH? DON'T YOU *EVA* IN YA LIFE CALL

ME 'BABY BOY' AGAIN, YOU *FUCKING* SLUT!"

Tony let go, and I hit the floor again. It took all the air I had in me, but I managed.

"Tony-I-ain't-*fuckin'*-nobody!"

"Oh word? You come in here acting brand-new, and you ain't *fucking* nobody? We'll see!"

Tony then picked me up by my waist and ripped my jeans off. He proceeded to remove my panties. I didn't know what Tony was up to, until he threw me onto the couch. Tony then spread my legs wide-open, as he stuck three fingers in me at the same time.

I screamed in pain…

Tony bowed his head in regret.

"I'm sorry, Kai," was all that he said, before Tony left the house for the night. I laid there until he came back early the next day. When Tony walked in the house, I'd pretended to be asleep, as he started to play with my hair.

"Kai, I hope you're listening to me. You know shit's been kinda hard since *Five Points.* You know it's hard knowing that I can't make love to you. I be seeing how dudes look at you and *shit.* I know your type, ma, you got the sex drive of a eighteen-year-old man."

I stifled a giggle.

"I just be thinking when you're gone, you out there getting the only thing I *can't* give you. I know you've been on my side since I came back home, but I still be bugging. You're a trooper, baby and that's why I love you. Please don't leave me—I need you. All this *shit,* is 'cause of you. I know that, ma-ma; I love you."

That became my driving force. The man that ran *Queens* needed me. It's true that behind every great man was a great woman. I wanted to go down in history as being the greatest.

Tony would be my link to the city. I already had him in my back pocket, so that meant I had *Queens* in my back pocket!

All I needed was the other four boroughs to fall in line.

Sure, I would step on some toes, but I would stand to be retired at twenty-five—with enough money to finance my life, for the rest of my life. AJ was right, but I had a point to prove, and money to make! After that was done, I would be game to anything else.

I started stashing away as much money as I could. I told Tony that I would no longer sleep at his house, since he put his hands on me.

Tony begged for me not to.

Instead, we came to the "agreement" that, I would *only* sleep over two or three nights out of the week, and I *had* to be on his payroll.

Tony agreed.

Every Friday morning, I got five thousand in cash.

I *never* put it in the bank.

I used some of it as pocket money, and had my checks from work directly deposited in my bank account every Thursday. I used my work money to pay my bills and other expenses. I didn't want to give "Uncle Sam" a reason to start sniffing up my ass! Instead, I hid the money that Tony gave me in my bedroom closet at my father's house.

My game plan was clear: I would be the Queen-of-the-*NYC* drug empire.

I had Tony do all of the dirty work, and I stopped managing the cooks. I became his silent partner, so to speak. With a little coaching from me, and a lot of strong-arming, Tony could definitely have a heavy hand in the other boroughs. In case the Feds were watching, I had a sound-proof alibi:

I was a student…

I worked full-time, and I lived at home with my pops.

Technically.

The only way I would be fucked was if they ever wanted to search my father's crib. Tony *never* came to my house, so I doubt that would ever happen.

An excerpt from ***SONZ OF DARKNESS*** by
DRU NOBLE
A GHETTOHEAT® PRODUCTION

"They won't wake up! What did you let that *woman* do to our children, Wilfred?"

"GET IN THE CAR!" Wilfred had shouted. The expression on his face had told Marylyn that he was somewhat scared. She'd hurriedly got in the front passenger's seat, halting her frustration momentarily. Wilfred hadn't even glanced at Marylyn, as he'd started the ignition, and drove off at rapid speed.

Marylyn then stared silently at the right side of Wilfred's face for two minutes. She'd wanted to strike him so badly, for putting not only her but, their two children through eerie circumstances.

"I know your upset, Marylyn, but to my people, this is sacred—it's normal," Wilfred then explained, eyes being locked on the little bit of road the headlights revealed. Marylyn frowned at his remark.

"Andrew and Gary were *screaming* inside that hut, and now they're sound asleep! This is not normal! I don't care *what* you say, this was wrong, Wilfred! That *bitch* did something to our kids—it's like they're drugged. Why the *hell* did you bring us out here? WHAT DID SHE DO TO THEM?" Marylyn had screamed; budding tears had begun to run down the young, ebony mother's face. Wilfred then took a deep breath, as he tried his best to maintain his composure. "Take us to the hospital!" Marylyn had insisted.

"They don't need a hospital, they're perfectly healthy."

"How can you say that? Just look at them!"

"Marylyn, listen to me."

"I don't *want* to. I—"

"LISTEN TO ME!" Wilfred then said over Marylyn's voice. She'd immediately paused, glaring fiercely toward Wilfred as he spoke.

"The Vowdun *has* done something to our children—she's given them gifts we don't yet know. Marylyn, the Vowdun has helped *many* people with her magic—she once healed my broken leg in a matter of seconds! The Vowdun has brought men and women fame, wealth, even cured those stricken with deadly diseases. It once was even told that she made a man immortal, one who now lives in the shadows."

"I'm a *Christian,* and what you're talking about is satanic. You *tricked* me into coming out here to get Andrew and Gary blessed—you're a *liar!*" Marylyn had interjected.

"That is why we came to Haiti, and it has been done! The worst is over now."

As his parents argued, Gary Romulus' eyes had opened. He remained silent and unknown to his parents. The infant had been in a trance-like state, detached from his surroundings. Wilfred wasn't even looking at the road ahead; his vision had been glued to his wife as they feuded. Gary had been however.

The newborn had seen what his mother and father hadn't seen, way ahead in the black night. Two glowing crimson eyes had stared back at the baby. They were serpentine, eyes Gary would never forget. They were the same eyes he and Andrew had seen in the hut. The Vowdun's eyes.

Gary then reached down and gently touched Andrew's shoulder. Strangely, the toddler had awakened in the same catatonic state as his sibling.

"Everything is going to be okay, Marylyn. I tried to pay the Vowdun her price, but she refused," Wilfred had stated. Marylyn then gasped.

"A PRICE?" Marylyn had blurted. She then refused to hear Wilfred explain anything.

Andrew and Gary had glared at those red eyes, which were accompanied by an ever-growing shadow that seemed to make the oncoming road even darker.

Lashing shadows awaited the vehicle.

"WHAT PRICE?" Marylyn had been consumed with anger; she'd easily detected the blankness of Wilfred's mind. Wilfred had been at a loss of words. Even he had no knowledge of what the Vowdun had expected from him; that was the very thought that had frightened Wilfred to the core.

The car then moved at seventy miles per hour! The saddened mother of two had finally turned away from her husband's stare. At that moment, Marylyn couldn't bare Wilfred's presence. When her sight fell on the oncoming road, Marylyn screamed out loudly in terror. Wilfred then instinctively turned forward to see what frightened her. His mouth had fallen ajar at the sight of the nightmarish form ahead of him. Filled with panic,

Wilfred tried to turn the steering wheel to avoid crashing. It was too late.

The sudden impact of the collision had caused the car to explode into immense flames, flames that roared to the night sky. The evil creature that caused it had gone, leaving behind its chaotic destruction; and the reason for it.

Out of the flickering flames and screeching metal had come a small boy, who held his baby brother carefully in his fragile arms. An illuminating blue sphere then surrounded their forms, which kept Andrew and Gary, unscathed from the fires, and jagged metal of the wreckage. Incredibly, they were both physically unharmed. Andrew then walked away from the crash in a sentinel manner. In the middle of his forehead was a large, newly formed third eye, which stared out bizarrely. Not until Andrew had been far enough away did he sit down, the blue orb then vanished.

Gary looked up at Andrew, speaking baby talk to get his attention. Andrew had ignored Gary. He was staring at the flaming vehicle as his parent's flesh had burned horridly, causing a foul stench that polluted the air. Through glassy eyes, Andrew's vision didn't waver; the child was beyond mourning.

Finally, Andrew had he gazed down at the precious baby he'd embraced. Gary then smiled, assured, unfazed by the tragic event. With his tiny arms, Gary tried to reach upwards, trying to touch the strange, silver eye on his brother's forehead, playfully. The new organ amused Gary, as any brand-new toy would've had.

"Mommy and daddy are gone now," Andrew then sobbed, as streams of tears rolled down his young face. He was trying his best to explain his sorrow. "I'll never leave you, Gary, I promise," Andrew had cried. Gary then giggled, still trying to reach Andrew's eye as best he could.

For the price of the Vowdun to bestow her gifts from her dark powers to the children, Wilfred Romulus had paid the ultimate price—the life of he and his wife. Their children were given gifts, far beyond their father's imagination, and for this, Andrew and Gary were also cursed with fates, not of their choosing.

The future held in store, untold suffering. They were no longer innocent. No longer the children of Wilfred and Marylyn Romulus. They were now and forever, *Sonz of Darkness.*

An excerpt from ***LONDON REIGN*** by
A. C. BRITT
A GHETTOHEAT® PRODUCTION

Back in *Detroit,* Mercedes is bragging to her sisters about how great the sex is with London. She's truly falling in love with "him", and wants to do something really special for London.

Tonight, Mercedes goes over to the *Lawrence House*, and convinces the landlord to let her into London's room. Mercedes has all kinds of decorations and gifts for "him", wanting to surprise London when "he" comes home.

"I can't *believe* you're going through all this," Saiel says before she starts blowing up balloons.

"I know. I can't believe I'm *feeling* this *nigga* this hard. I think I'm just whipped!" Mercedes replies.

"From what? You and London *only* did it once."

"But London can eat the *fuck* out of some *pussy* though! That *nigga* stay having me climbing the wall. You know…I have never been in here when London wasn't home. I wonder what he got *going* on around here that he doesn't want me to see," Mercedes says, as she begins to go through London's things.

"Mercedes! Don't go through the man's *shit!* You might *find* something you *don't* want to see—and then what?" Saiel spits.

"…This *nigga,* London keeps talking about how there's *shit* I don't know about him anyway, so I *might* as well play detective. He's taking *too* damn long to tell me." Mercedes then picks up a pile of papers out of a file cabinet and starts flipping through them. "Pay stubs...bills...bills...more bills," Mercedes says to herself.

"Mercedes, you *really* need to stop."

"Perhaps you're right, Saiel," Mercedes answers, as she puts London's papers back and opens the closet door. Saiel then looks in the closet.

"Mercedes, why you leave so many *tampons* over here? That's weird."

"…Yeah, it is...because those *ain't* mine." Mercedes pulls the box of tampons out the closet, and looks in it to see how many are missing. "I don't even *use* this kind, must belong to some other *bitch.*" Mercedes then put the tampons back where she found them, yet, Saiel now picks up a stack of medical papers that had fallen when Mercedes opened the closet.

Saiel reads the contents of the paper, and her mouth practically *drops* to the floor. Mercedes notices her sister's reaction, so she immediately walks over to Saiel.

"What, Saiel? …What is that? What does it say?"

"U-m-m-m...doctors' papers."

"What? London ain't got no *disease,* do he? Because I don't even know if London used a condom," Mercedes confesses. Saiel looks at Mercedes again and shakes her head.

"Naw…no disease…and whether London used a condom or not, doesn't matter," Saiel answers worriedly, having a traumatized look upon her face. "Mercedes…I think you better sit down."

"Why? What that *shit* say?" Mercedes asks anxiously.

"London ain't...Mercedes, this nigga…damn! Mercedes. W-O-W! London *ain't* no dude!" Saiel says emotionally, completely shocked.

"WHAT?" Mercedes asks with much confusion.

"London...Mercedes, London is a girl!"

Mercedes can tell by the look in her sister's eyes that Saiel isn't kidding. Mercedes immediately snatches the papers out of Saiel's hand, and reads everything from the name of the patient, to the diagnosis of a urinary tract infection.

"A girl? ...But I *fucking*...I *fucked* him! Her...it! We had *sex,* Saiel, how the *fuck* is London a girl?" Mercedes now being hurt, quickly turns into anger: "THAT'S WHY THAT *MUTHAFUCKA* NEVER WANTED ME TO TOUCH DOWN THERE! AND WHY HE…I MEAN SHE, *WHATEVER,* DIDN'T REALLY WANT TO HAVE SEX WITH ME!

"I am so *fucking* stupid! He made me…*FUCK!* She made me wear a blindfold. Said she wanted to try something new…. I don't understand Saiel, I've seen London's chest, and she *ain't* got no breasts. I mean, there are nubs, but I ain't think nothing of it," Mercedes explains as she begins to cry.

"Mercedes...sweetie, she had us *all* fooled! London don't *look* like no girl! She doesn't *sound* like no girl, and London *sure-as-hell*, doesn't *act* like no girl! We had no reason to think otherwise. Sweetie, just leave this *shit* alone and let's go!" Saiel instructs, taking the papers out of her sister's hands while ushering Mercedes to the door.

An excerpt from ***AND GOD CREATED WOMAN*** by
MIKA MILLER
A GHETTOHEAT® PRODUCTION

Some people call me a *hoe* because I strip for *niggas* and hustle for cash.

Yeah, I turn tricks!

I tell niggas: "If the price is right, then the deal is real." My momma used to say, *"As long as you got a pussy, you sittin' on a goldmine. Never give your shit away for free."*

If that means I'm a *hoe,* so *be* it!

None of these *bitches* pays my bills or puts food on my mutha...*fuckin'* table, so *fuck* 'em!

GOD didn't give me the type of brains where I can understand all that "technical" book *shit.* In elementary school, I was never good at math and, to tell the truth, I was never that good at readin' either.

It's not like I didn't try.

It's just that, when it came to school, nothin' really registered. In high school, I tried to learn the secretarial trade. I figured that if I had some sort of technical skill, that I could at least get a halfway decent gig after I graduated. Well, it turns out that typin' and shorthand was just another thing that I failed at.

So bein' somebody's secretary was *out* of the question.

With no real education or skill, I had to settle for minimum wage jobs. My first job was workin' as a maid at a five-star hotel. After about two weeks, I got tired of cleanin' after rich *bitches* that *shitted* all over the toilet seats, and hid bloody tampons all over the *goddamn* place!

And I wasn't 'bout to work in *nobody's* fast-food restaurant. So I had to come up with a new plan. And that's when I met this f-i-n-e-ass, *Puerto Rican muthafucka* by the name of Ricky.

Ricky was a straight-up thug—tattoos all across his chest and stomach like *Tupac* and *shit.* When I met Ricky, I had two kids. I was single, workin' my *ass* off as a hostess in a restaurant and braidin' hair on the side.

I was finally maintainin', you know, gettin' money. But I was always workin', so I didn't have no time to enjoy my kids or my money.

Ricky came on the scene and promised me all kinds of *shit.* He was like, *"Baby, you ain't gotta work that hard, why don't you lemme take care o' you and nem kids."*

Ricky had my head gassed up, for real!

Plus he was layin' the pipe on the regular. *Fuckin'* me *real* good wit' his fine *ass.* So one night, after Ricky got finished eatin' my cooch, he was like, *"Baby, I'ma take you to* Philadelphia *wit' me. You an' the kids can come wit' me, and I'll hook ya'll up wit' errythang."*

Me, bein' naive, I followed his fine *ass* all the way to *Philly* and *shit,* and the *nigga* started trippin'! Beatin' me up, knockin' me all upside my head, accusin' me of cheatin'...which I wasn't. Ricky started kickin' my *ass* to the point that I was too ashamed to go to work with black eyes and busted lips, and I eventually got fired.

Long story short, after a while, I finally had enough. I packed me and my kids up and went to a shelter. I didn't know no *fuckin'* body, I didn't know shit about *Philadelphia*—all I knew that I was broke and I needed a place to stay for me and my kids.

So I went to the welfare office....

I tried to work within the system. Well, welfare was draggin' they feet, and in the meantime, I needed to make some cash, fast.

That's when Marilyn popped up on the scene. Marilyn was basically a po' *White* trash version of myself. She was stayin' wit' me at the shelter.

Marilyn told me between puffs of her *Marlboro* cigarette: *"Mekka, why don't you strip? You got a beautiful body, and I know you would make plenty of money 'cause you tall, you got them big, perky titties, and you high yellow. You could make some good money and be outta here in no time; you perky-titty bitch!"*

I figured what I lacked in the brains department I'd make up for with the "gifts" that GOD did give me: my pretty face, this small waist, and these big ole *titties!*

So I took Marilyn's advice. I rolled around wit' her, and she took me to some strip clubs. That's how I got this gig where I'm at now. Strippin' at a hole-in-the-wall called *Dutch Gardens. Dutch Gardens* is where "Mekka" was born, but I gotta finish this story another time, I think I hear them callin' my name.

"Hey Mekka, you go on in five!" Trish hollers from the entrance of the locker room. Trish is a white bitch who *swears* she's *Black!*

Only fucks *Black* men….

And she can get away wit' it 'cause, Trish got a ghetto-booty and a body like a sista. And some *niggas* think that *"White-*is-right", but they'll be alright. Trish is kinda cool though, as far as white girls go.

"Hey hoe; Mekka, you hear me?" Trish calls again.

"*Bitch* wait! I heard your *muthafuckin'* ass!"

I check my face in my magnetic mirror hung on the inside of my locker, spray on a hint of *Bulgari* "Omnia Eau de Toilette" body mist, adjust my g-string and tighten the laces on my thigh-high boots. Other bitches wear them tall shoes, but I'm gettin' old, and my old-*ass* feet and ankles need a lil' mo' support.

Plus, it's easier to slide them dollar bills in your boots and keep it movin'.

I slam my locker shut and take inventory of my surroundings. There's a room full of beautiful *bitches* all *hatin'* on me!

They wanna know how I *make-it-do-what-it-do!* How I make all dat dough in the course of three hours, and they been in here all night lettin' *niggas* suck on they *titties* and finger their coochies...and still comin' up broke?

FUCK BITCHES!

Like I always say: "Money over *niggas; bitches,* stick to the script!"

An excerpt from **GHOST TOWN HUSTLERS** by CASTILLO
A GHETTOHEAT® PRODUCTION

It's early in the morning, and I hear someone knocking on the door, calling my name. I sit up and reach for my watch that I placed on top of the nightstand.

It's seventy-thirty.

"WHO IS IT?"

"Senor! Lo estan esperando pa desallunar! (Sir! They're waiting for you to come have breakfast!) I hear the voice of Maria yell from behind the door.

"Dame unos cuanto minutos!" (Give me a couple of minutes!)

I hear footsteps going away. I get out of bed, walk over to a table on the far left corner of the room, where a vase full of fresh water has been set. Once downstairs, I see the boys sitting down at the table along with Emilio. I sit next to Pedrito.

"Where's Martha?" I ask.

"She didn't want to eat," Pedrito says while shrugging his shoulders.

Minutes later after we ate, Pedrito and I get up and walk out onto the porch, sit down and light up our cigarettes. Emilio sparks up a cigar, like the one Don Avila used to smoke.

Pedrito says he wants to show me something, so we stand up and walk away from the house. He explains to me that the two men that were sent to pick Don Avila up from the airport has betrayed them, and that Emilio has all of his men looking throughout *Medellin;* having his connections search the rest of *Colombia* for any signs of them. So far, no one is able to find anything.

We notice that the house is barely visible, so we decide to go back. When we reach the house, the boys are inside, and Emilio is waiting for Pedrito with three men by his side.

"Come," Emilio says, gesturing with his hand to Pedrito. "I want to show you something I found." Emilio has a smile on his face, but I notice that it's very different than any other smiles he'd given before. It's as if Emilio is smiling to himself and not at Pedrito.

"Can Raul come, too?" I hear Pedrito ask. I stop midway up the stairs, proceeding to go into the house. I look back and see Emilio staring at me, almost as if he's thinking about what to answer.

"Sure," Emilio replies shortly. "He can come." Emilio begins walking towards the back of the house, where there are three smaller houses, ones that's not visible from the front of the main house; one of the smaller houses is guarded by two men. One man is holding a rifle; the other guard has a gun tucked inside the waist of his pants.

"Donde estan esos hijo-eh-putas?" (Where are those sons-of-bitches?) Emilio asks once he, Pedrito and I are before the guards.

"Hai dentro patron!" the guardsman with the gun at his waist answers as he opens the door for us.

We walk into an unfurnished room, yet it's well lit. In the center of the room, there are two men on the floor on their knees with their arms raised above their heads; tied up with rope that has been thrown over a beam and secured to a pole. They're shirtless, and it seems as if someone has been beating them badly with a whip—the two men having cuts on their chest and faces.

They're bleeding profusely from their wounds.

"These are the ones that sold out your father," Emilio says, pointing to the two men who are still on their knees. "They're responsible for the death of your father. That's Angel, and that's Miguel."

Pedrito walks up to the two badly beaten men: "Who *killed* my father?"

Neither of the two beaten men answers Pedrito.

Pedrito then forcefully kicks Angel in his stomach. "QUIEN?" (WHO?) Pedrito shouts.

"Pedrito," I say while taking a step forward. I immediately stop when I feel a hand rest upon my shoulder firmly. I look back to see that it's Emilio.

"Leave him," Emilio commands. I turn to look at Pedrito, who's now violently shaking Miguel's head, grabbing him by his hair as he continues to yell loudly.

"QUIEN FUE? DIME!" (WHO WAS IT? TELL ME) Pedrito asks and shouts. Moments later, Pedrito looks around, still holding Miguel by his hair. He then let's go of Miguel and walks toward Emilio and I.

The guardsman who let us inside is now standing next to Emilio. Pedrito walks up to him and snatches the gun from his waist, cocks it, and runs back to where Angel and Miguel are. I see that Angel and Miguel's eyes are dilated before Pedrito blocks my view of the two men, now standing in front of them.

"Por f-f-f-avor no-no-no-no me maates!" (P-l-e-a-s-e don't kill me!) Angel begs for his life. "Yo no fui quien le mato." (It wasn't me who killed him.)

"Entonce fuiste tu, eh?" Pedrito says, turning the gun to Miguel.

"N-O-O-O-O-O-O-O!" Miguel screams.

An excerpt from ***GAMES WOMEN PLAY*** by
TONY COLLINS
A GHETTOHEAT® PRODUCTION

A woman always sees a man before he sees her. Then, in a blink of an eye, she completely checks out everything him about him from head-to-toe—without him even knowing what the woman is doing. Even faster than her lightening quick assessment of him, she studies very swiftly, all of his surroundings; including any other woman who is interested in him.

Yes, a woman notices every little personal detail about a man. That's right, not one thing about him escapes her laser-like focus. So, as she studies him, at the same time, the woman makes a complete mental list of the number of turn-ons and turn-offs regarding any or all of his personal details. These turn-ons or turn-off may include: details about his personality, his looks, a man's level of personal grooming and cleanliness, body type, clothing, shoes and accessories, financial status, a man's relationship status, and so on.

However, a woman doesn't just stop at this point, the level of merely making a "check list" of superficial observations about a man. She doesn't stop her analysis of a man at the point that most men would end their analysis of a woman. A woman looks beyond the surface of a man's visible details, when she considers whether or not to pursue him. A woman analysis of a man is more complex.

Not only does a woman make a mental check list of all the personal details that a man possess, but also, she notices how well he maintains his personal details. Yet, a woman doesn't stop even at this point in her study of him. She is still not done putting him under her mental microscope. She takes her analysis of him to an even deeper level.

A woman notices if any of his personal details lacking, and she observes which personal details a man should have, but are completely missing. Why does a woman go through all these levels of observation regarding a man's personal details? Well, a woman makes such an in depth study, because she knows that by analyzing the presence, and/or the absence, and/or the condition of a man's personal details, that these three factors raises questions in her mind about him, making the woman go "Hmmm,

I wonder why that is?"

Once she begins to ponder, then her naturally-analytical mind, kicks right into high gear. Instantly, a woman starts trying to figure out what's the most probable answer to each of the questions raised in her mind—from studying a man's personal details; putting two-and-two together.

By taking this approach, and backed by a lifetime of observing men, combined with her training from the "Female Mafia", a woman knows that what she can come up with quite a lot of accurate information about a man. Although she may not always be exactly correct with all of her on-the-spot analysis, and "guesstimates" about him, usually a woman is very accurate with most of her breakdown regarding him.

Even more amazing, and usually to a man's complete bewilderment, a woman's reading of him, using his personal details, can be so on point, that she even figures out things about a man that he was purposely trying to conceal.

So, from studying the presence, the absence, or the condition of a man's personal details, and then "guesstimating" the most probable answers to the questions raised by studying them, a woman gets not only a superficial understanding of him, but also, she gets a deeper insight into who this man really is, and what he is really about; at the core of his being, beyond the image that he is presenting to the world.

Therefore, given this scenario, let's follow along as she studies, analyzes, questions, and then figures out, everything about a man without him even knowing what she is doing; all of this taking place in a blink of an eye.

An excerpt from ***SKATE ON!*** by
HICKSON
A GHETTOHEAT® PRODUCTION

Quickly exiting the *155th Street* train station on *Eighth Avenue,* Shani, purposely walking with her head held down low, decides to cross the street and walk parallel to the *Polo Grounds;* not chancing bumping into her parents. As she approaches the corner, Shani contemplates crossing over to *Blimpie's* before walking down the block to the skating rink. She craves for a *Blimpie Burger* with cheese hero, but immediately changes her mind, fearing of ruining the outfit Keisha gave her.

Shani then heads towards *The Rooftop*, feeling overly anxious to meet with her two friends. As she carefully walks down the dark and eerie block, Mo-Mo creeps up behind Shani and proceeds to put her in a headlock; throwing Shani off-guard.

"GET OFF OF ME!" Shani desperately pleads as she squirms, trying to break free. Already holding Shani with a firm grip, Mo-Mo applies more pressure around her neck.

Trying to defend herself the best way she knows how, Shani reaches behind for Mo-Mo's eyes and attempts to scratch her face. Mo-Mo immediately pushes her forward and laughs.

"Yeah, *bitch,* whachu gon' do?" Mo-Mo teases. "SIKE!" Startled, Shani turns around with a surprised expression on her face.

"Mo-Mo, why are you always *playing* so much? You almost scared me half-to-death!" Shani whines while panting heavily, trying hard to catch her breath.

Mo-Mo continues to laugh loudly, "Yo, I had ya heart! You almost *shitted* on yaself! I could've put ya ass to sleep, bee!"

"Mo-Mo, please stop *swearing* so much," Shani replies, as she smiles and reaches out to hug Mo-Mo. Mo-Mo then teasingly tugs at the plunging neckline of Shani's snug-fitting leotard, pulling it down to reveal more of Shani's cleavage.

"Since when you started dressin' like a lil' *hoe?*"

Shani, quickly removing Mo-Mo's hand from her breasts, becomes self-conscious of what she's wearing.

"I *knew* I shouldn't have put this on. Keisha made me wear this. Do I *really* look sleazy, Mo-Mo?"

Mo-Mo frowns. "Whah? Shani, stop *buggin'!* You look

aiiight. I'm just not used to seein' you dressin' all *sexy* and *shit.*"

Shani soon looks towards *Eighth Avenue* to see if Keisha is nearby.

"Mo-Mo, where's Keisha? I thought you two were coming to *The Rooftop* together."

Mo-Mo rudely points across the street, as she loudly chews and pops on her apple flavored *Super Bubble* gum.

"Yo, see that black *Toyota Corolla* double-parked by *The Rucker?* She in there talkin' to some Dominican *nigga* named, Diego we met earlier on *145th Street.* We made that *fool* take us to *Ling Fung Chinese Restaurant* on Broadway. Keisha jerked him for a plate of Lobster Cantonese—I got chicken wings and pork-fried rice."

Shani shakes her head and chuckles, "You two are always scheming on some *guy.*"

"AND YOU *KNOW* IT! A *BITCH* GOTTA EAT, RIGHT?" Mo-Mo asks, before blowing a huge bubble with her gum, and playfully plucking Shani on her forehead.

Mo-Mo is a belligerent, lowly-educated, hardcore ghetto-girl who's extremely violent and wild. Known for her southpaw boxing skill and powerful knockout punches, Mo-Mo often amuses herself by fighting other peoples' battles on the block for sport. That's how she met Shani.

Last January, Sheneeda and Jaiwockateema tried to rob Shani of her *Bonsoir* "B" bag near Building 1 of the *Polo Grounds.* Mo-Mo observed what was happening and rescued Shani, feverishly pounding both girls over their heads with her glass *Kabangers.*

Mo-Mo didn't even know Shani at the time, but fought for her as if they were childhood cronies. Since then, the two have become close friends—Mo-Mo admiring Shani's intelligence, innocence and sincerity.

In addition to her volatile temper, ill manners and street-*bitch* antics, Mo-Mo is rough around the edges—literally and figuratively. Eighteen-years-old and having dark, rich, coffee-colored skin, Mo-Mo's complexion is beautiful, even with suffering from the mild case of eczema on her hands—and with her face, full of blemishes and bumps from the excessive fighting, cheap, greasy junk food, and sodas Mo-Mo habitually drinks.

Bearing a small scar on her left cheek from being sliced with a box cutter, Mo-Mo proudly endured her battle mark. *"The*

Deceptinettes", a female gang who jumped Mo-Mo inside of *Park West High School's* girls' locker room last year, physically attacked her. Mo-Mo boldly took on the dangerous crew of girls all by herself, winning the brutal brawl, due to her knowing how to fight hard and dirty.

With deep brown eyes, full lips and high cheekbones, Mo-Mo highly resembles an *African* queen. She isn't bad-looking, Mo-Mo just doesn't take care of herself; nor was she ever taught how to. Because of this, Mo-Mo is often forsaken for her ignorance by most.

Awkwardly standing knock-kneed and pigeon-toed at five-foot-seven, big boned with an hourglass figure, Mo-Mo is a brick house! Thick and curvaceous with a body that doesn't quit, she has ample sized forty-two D breasts, shifting wide hips, big legs, with well-toned thighs.

Having the largest ass in *Harlem,* Mo-Mo's behind is humongous—nicely rounded and firm. It automatically becomes a sideshow attraction whenever she appears, as everyone, young and old, stares in disbelief; amazed at the shape, fullness and size of Mo-Mo's butt. A man once joked about "spanking" Mo-Mo's rear, claiming that when he'd knocked it…her ass knocked him back!

Mo-Mo's hair length is short, in which she wears individual box braids, braiding it herself; having real, human hair extensions. Often, her braids are sloppy and unkempt, having naps and a fuzzy hairline. Mo-Mo's coarse, natural hair grain never matches the soft, silky texture of her extensions, but she always soaks the ends in a pot of scalding, hot water to achieve a wet-and-wavy look.

Mo-Mo never polishes her nails or keeps them clean, having dirt underneath them regularly. Rarely shaving the hair from under her armpits or bikini line causes Mo-Mo to have a rank, body odor. Someone even left a package at her apartment door one day, filled with a large can of *Right Guard, Nair* and a bottle of *FDS Feminine Deodorant Spray,* with a typewritten note attached. It read: *"Aye, Funkbox, clean ya stank pussy and stop puttin' Buckwheat in a headlock—you nasty bitch!"* Mo-Mo assumed it was either a prank from Sheneeda and Jaiwockateema, or Oscardo—still sulking over Mo-Mo kicking his ass six years ago.

She now lives alone in the *Polo Grounds,* due to her mother's untimely death six months ago—dying of sclerosis of the liver from her excessive drinking of beer and hard liquor. Just days after Mo-Mo's mother's death, she received a letter from *Social Services,* stating that they were aware of her mother's passing, Mo-Mo's only legal guardian, and that she would receive a visit from a social worker; one who would be instructed to place Mo-Mo in an all-girls group home in *East Harlem.*

Mo-Mo begged her other family members to allow her to live with them, but they refused, not wanting to deal with her nasty disposition, constant fighting and barbaric lifestyle. Nor did they wish to support Mo-Mo emotionally or financially, resulting her to rely on public assistance from the welfare office. At that point, Mo-Mo hadn't any relatives whom she can depend upon—she was on her own and had to grow up, fast.

Luckily Mo-Mo's eighteenth birthday arrived a day before she was accosted in front of her building, by a male social worker, having the rude investigator from *Social Services* antagonize her with legal documents; indicating that she was to temporarily be in his custody, and taken immediately to the group home.

"SUCK A FAT BABY'S ASS!" was what Mo-Mo yelled at the social worker before walking inside the lobby, defiantly slamming the door in the man's face.

Failing most of her classes, Mo-Mo barely attends high school. She's in the tenth grade, but belongs in the twelfth. Mo-Mo is still a special education student, now having a six-grader's reading and writing level. Her former teachers passed her in school, being totally unconcerned with Mo-Mo's learning disability.

Their goal was to pass as many students as possible, in order to avoid being reprimanded by superiors for failing a large number of students. The school system still has quotas to meet, and doesn't receive the needed funds from the government for the following term—if a large amount of students are held back.

Along with other personal issues, Mo-Mo is hot-in-the-ass, fast and promiscuous, having the temperament of a low-class whore. She's a big-time freak, a sultry sex fiend with an insatiable appetite for men with huge dicks—becoming "weak at the knees" at the sight of a protruding bulge.

Mo-Mo's self esteem and subsidized income is low, but her sex drive is extremely high, having sex with men for cash while soothing her inner pain. Mo-Mo doesn't sell her body for money due to desperation and destitute—she does it for the fun of it. Mo-Mo *l-o-v-e-s* dick, and decided to earn money while doing what she enjoys the most—getting *fucked!* Mo-Mo's going to have frivolous sex regardless, *"SO WHY NOT GET PAID FOR IT?"* she often reasons.

Academically, Mo-Mo's slow, but she's *nobody's* fool; being street-smart with thick skin. A true survivor, one who perseveres, by hook-or-crook, Mo-Mo is determined to sustain—by all means necessary.

"AYE, YO, KEISHA, HURRY THE *FUCK* UP!" Mo-Mo beckons.

"Hold up! I'm comin'!" Keisha squeakily replies with irritation in her voice; concluding her conversation with Diego, "My friends are waitin' for me—I gotta go."

"Can I *see* you again and get ya digits, mommy?" Diego begs, talking extremely fast with his raspy voice.

"Maybe! And *no* you can't get my number—gimme yours!" Keisha audaciously snaps.

Diego immediately becomes attracted to Keisha's beauty, snootiness, nonchalant attitude and bold behavior. He smiles, writing his beeper number on the flyer he received an hour ago for an upcoming party at *Broadway International*—while exiting the Chinese restaurant with Keisha and Mo-Mo.

Now handing Keisha the flyer, Diego attempts to wish her goodnight, but Keisha immediately interjects: "Can I get three hundred dollars?" she says, looking straight into Diego's eyes.

"Damn, mommy, what's up? I just met you an *hour* ago, and you *askin'* me for money already?"

Keisha pauses for emphasis, "...Are you gon' give it to me or *not?*" Keisha coldly asks, still piercing into Diego's eyes—not once she ever blinks.

"Whachu need three hundred for, mommy?"

"First-and-foremost, my name is *Keisha,* not mommy! And I don't *n-e-e-e-e-e-e-d* three hundred dollars—I want it!"

Diego sits silently...simultaneously bewildered and turned on by Keisha's brashness.

"Diego, don't you want me to look cute the next time you *see* me?" Keisha insincerely asks in an innocent manner while batting her eyelashes, deceiving Diego with her fake, light-hearted disposition.

"So I'm gonna see you again, huh, mommy?" Diego nervously asks, smiling, as he pulls out a wad of cash from his pocket. The teenager's large bankroll, wrapped in jade-green rubber bands causes Keisha's eyes to widen.

"Uh-huh," she effortlessly replies while staring hard at Diego's money, now loudly turning up the volume on his *Benzi* box; Diego's playing his *DJ Love-Bug Starski* mixed tape.

Keisha bobs her head, rhythmically rocks shoulders from side-to-side, rubs her thumb swiftly against her middle and index finger, while singing to *Money: Dollar Bill, Y'all* by Jimmy Spicer; *"Dollar-dollar-dollar-dollar-dollar bill, y'all!"*

Diego observes Keisha with his right eyebrow raised, peeling off money from his bundle. He hands the dirty bills to Keisha, hopelessly gazing into her eyes.

Keisha, becoming annoyed with Diego for showing too much of an interest in her so soon, rolls her eyes and retorts harshly, "Gotta…go," as she attempts to reach for the car handle. Before grabbing it, Keisha quickly pulls out a napkin from her brand-new, blue and white *Gucci* bag with the signature "G's", wipes her fingerprints off the console and opens the car door with the napkin in her hand.

"Yo, Keisha, why you wipe down my car like that?"

Keisha ignores Diego's question and beckons to Shani and Mo-Mo, signaling them by waving her fabulous five-carat, diamond-adorned right hand in the air, now quickly bringing it down hard to slap her right thigh.

"Yo, I'm ready, y'all—let's go!"

Keisha walks around the front of Diego's car and proceeds to cross the street, eager to enter *The Rooftop*. Shaking his head in disbelief, chuckling, Diego can't *believe* Keisha's sassiness.

"YO, WHEN YOU GON' CALL ME, MOMMY?" Diego yells out to Keisha from his car window.

Keisha immediately stops in the middle of the street, causing the flow of traffic to halt. She flings her long, silky, straight hair, looks over her shoulder and tauntingly replies, "As soon as you step-up ya whip, *nigga.* Do I *look* like the type of girl who be *bouncin'* 'round in a dusty-ass 'one-point-eight'?"

Diego freezes as Keisha continues to speak.

"You don't even take ya *whip* to the *car* wash. And *stop* callin' me 'mommy'!" Keisha concludes, flinging her hair again by sharply turning her head. She then sticks her butt out and switches while crossing the street.

Diego stares long and hard at Keisha's rump, as she walks

away, noticing how good the young girl's behind looks in her skin-tight jeans. He immediately drives towards *Eighth Avenue,* repeatedly hearing Keisha's last comments over in his head.

Keisha soon stands near the front entrance of the skating rink and notices the huge crowd lined-up outside as, Shani and Mo-Mo greets her.

"It's about damn time!" Mo-Mo snaps. Keisha disregards her and reaches out to hug Shani.

"What's up, college gurrrl?" Keisha playfully asks.

"Hey Keisha! I'm fine. I'm *chilling*-like-a-villain." Shani replies awkwardly, not use to using slang in her daily dialect.

"Shani, it's *'chillin''* not 'chill-i-n-g'! Why you be always talkin' so *damn* proper anyway? I wonder sometimes, yo, if you *really* from the hood!" Mo-Mo barks.

Shani attempts to politely respond back to Mo-Mo, but Keisha rudely interjects: "So, Shani, how's D.C.?" Keisha asks, cleverly examining Shani's outfit from head-to-toe without her realizing what Keisha is doing.

"I like D.C. so far. I'm very excited about attending *Howard University.* I just need to learn my way around campus," Shani answers. "I—"

Feeling jealous and left out of the conversation, Mo-Mo interrupts.

"Can you two *bitches* learn y'all *muthafuckin'* way inside this skatin' rink?" Mo-Mo snaps before entering *The Rooftop,* skipping everyone standing on line.

"Mo-Mo be illin'! She *betta* watch her mouth 'cause I'm-not-the-*one!*" Keisha retorts while rocking her neck and waving her right hand in the air, flashing her diamond ring for all to see.

Shani, experiencing bad cramps from her period, and the stress from sneaking off from *Washington, D.C* to *New York City* for the grand opening of *The Rooftop*, tightly shrugs her shoulders to relieve the tension she's feeling.

Shani inhales a breath of fresh air…slowly exhales, and quickly adjusts the plunging neckline of her scoop-neck leotard to conceal her cleavage—as she and Keisha follows inside.

An excerpt from ***SOME SEXY, ORGASM 1*** by
DRU NOBLE
A GHETTOHEAT® PRODUCTION

BIG BONED

"I need you, Melissa; oh I *love* your body! Let me taste you, mmmph, let me *love* you—just give me some sexy!" Jezebel begged while still squeezing the woman's luscious crescents. Melissa had no hope of resisting this sudden passionate impulse that flooded her.

She felt Jezebel's grip tighten on her, then a finger slowly traced between her curvaceous legs. The unexpected jolt of excitable pleasure caused Melissa to rise on her side, throwing Jezebel off of her. She palmed between her own thighs, trying to silence the rest of the roaring waves threatening to overcome her preciousness.

Jezebel couldn't take her eyes off of Melissa, as she breathed erratically, while Melissa couldn't help but to stare back with conflicting desperation. Melissa's hand reached out and grasped the back of the Native-American woman's neck, as she pulled Jezebel towards her forcefully.

Their lips touch, melded, then opened. Jezebel's tongue dove into Melissa's mouth, finding the versatile muscle was eager to wrestle her own. A groan vibrated down Melissa's throat. Her hand came up, and two fingers strung like guitar strings on Jezebel's upturned beady nipple—first playing with it, then catching Jezebel's hardened nipple between her index and middle fingers; closing it within tight confines.

Jezebel then straddled Melissa, the two women's hands meeting, immediately intertwining before their kissing ended.

"I wanted you since I *first* saw you; I've been wet ever since that moment. You're so *fucking* sexy, Melissa. I *need* you, can I have some sexy? Give it to me," Jezebel said in a low, hushed voice.

The twinkle in her beautiful brown eyes affected Melissa like an intoxicating elixir. Melissa watched on, as Jezebel took her captured hand and began to suck on two fingers with her hot, steamy mouth. Jezebel's checked hollowed, as she continued to close in on Melissa's dainty fingers.

Melissa, voluptuous and womanly, petals became slick, and damp—natural juices now running down towards her rounded rear end.

"I want you, too Jezebel, come get some sexy!" she pledged. Jezebel smiled as Melissa's fingers slid from her mouth, leading them down her body. With her lead, Melissa allowed her hand to enter into Jezebel's bikini. A glimpse of her fine, black pubic hair came into view, as Melissa then felt the lovely grace of Jezebel's vagina.

A soothing hiss breathed out of Jezebel. The moistness of her internal lake coated the fingers that ventures to its intimate space. Melissa then bent her hand so the bikini could come down, and she was grand the delightful vision of where her fingers ventured.

Jezebel's outer labia had opened, as Melissa's fingers split between her middle, like tickling a blooming rose. She tipped her hand up, and used her thumb to peel back the protective skin over Jezebel's engorged clitoris. The pink button revealed itself exclusively, and Melissa used her thumb to caress it; stirring up Jezebel's burning desire.

Melissa had never seen or touched another woman's pearl, but found that she'd loved it completely. Two of her fingers then slipped within Jezebel's hot, oily insides, and the Native-American woman had thrust her hips forward to take all Melissa had to offer.

"You're so *hot* inside; burning up my fingers, baby."

"Just don't stop; *please* don't stop what you're doing," Jezebel instructed. Her hips began to undulate, rocking herself to a sweet bliss. Jezebel rode Melissa's fingers like she would her fiancé's long, pleasure-inducing dick.

Melissa then curled her wet fingers back slightly, as she would if she were touching herself, searching inside for that magical area most women long to discover—the G-spot.

Melissa felt Jezebel's tunnel pulsate, and a shock ran through the humping woman, giving Melissa total satisfaction that she'd found Jezebel's spot; now also realizing that, by her being a woman, she had full advantage to knowing another woman's body, better than any man could.

An excerpt from ***TATTOOED TEARS*** by
BLUE
A GHETTOHEAT® PRODUCTION

INTRO

When I began brainstorming for what I consider, will be the perfect novel to reach the desired audience (everybody), I didn't know that *TATTOOED TEARS* would come pouring out of my state-issued pen, and onto state-issued writing paper. I didn't know if I would have the motivation and drive needed to put it together. Now that it's done, I can honestly say that, I didn't know I had the stomach to do something like this.

The reason: being that our youth, children, younger generation, or whatever else you choose to call our leaders of tomorrow, mean so much to me. So much in fact, I didn't want to do them an injustice by not telling it like it is, for our kids.

Our children go through so much at such a young age, I myself sometimes wonder, how it is that some are capable of making a future for themselves; a future without gangs, a future without violence, a future without hate and ignorance, a future that doesn't involve dealing directly with the hypocrisies, of this system of so-called justice we live under in America.

Despite what our news broadcasts, newspapers, politicians, jails and institutional statistics may lead you to believe, along with our juvenile detention centers, we as a society must realize that not all of our youth are going to crumble under the pressure.

TATTOOED TEARS, however, is about those who suffer through more trials and tribulations than your average convict on Death Row. And they're not even old enough to drive, yet they find the strength and willpower in themselves, to overcome those obstacles and trying times that are laid before them, in order to succeed in their own little worlds.

My father used to tell me, *"Boy, listen to me and listen good. I done already been down the road you on..."* I'm sure that 90% of our up-and-coming generation has heard this at least once in their lives. But did my father *really* understand what I was going through?

Had he really gone down the same roads that I've been

on? I mean, my father didn't go to school with me, didn't get locked up with me, nor did he didn't drink alcohol with me, or smoke or sell marijuana with me. My father also didn't get into the fights I got into, or get shot at with me. Do you understand the point I'm trying to get across to you?

Now, we as adults can do what we can, to detour our children from doing the things we did, or from getting into certain types of situations we got into, but the fact remains that, they will make their own decisions, with or without our guidance. In a way it's scary—frightening even, but what can we do?

All we can do is hope and pray that they make the best choices possible with the hands they're dealt. All the advice in the world—given to any random child, means nothing if the child it's directed to, doesn't grasp the true meaning of what he or she has been told. And if that kid *does* understand the concept of what's been taught to them, it now becomes a new weight on their shoulders; a new "pressure" to deal with—a new rebuttal to what they were probably originally thinking, contemplating or anticipating.

We want our youth to be responsible, and become right-minded enough to act on the positive voices in their heads, opposed to the negative ones. With peer pressure coming in all forms from sex, drugs, gangs, and guns, battling the anxiety of getting good grades, going to college, carrying a team to the state championship, and holding a job all at the same time, a kid can really become a victim in his or her own world, which can result in becoming, his or her own worst enemy.

That, in itself, is what I feel is the biggest problem facing our children today, and has been in years past. It's the stress they feel, the depression they suffer, and the grueling temptations they need to avoid, yet seem to fall prey to it every time.

I guess what I am trying to ask in writing *TATTOOED TEARS* is...why? *Why* must they go through it? If we as adults claim to have been down that road of suffering, and of every problem in the book that these kids can endure for the benefit of them, so they wouldn't have to undergo it themselves, *why* does it still happen? *Why* are more kids carrying guns? *Why* are more children having sex? *Why* are more-and-more kids joining gangs, or even associating or affiliating themselves with these groups?

WHY? WHY? WHY?

If these *same* children are our future—truly 'our' future—

why aren't their lives being molded today, for the betterment of that future?

There are a million answers to these questions, along with some potentially powerful debates that can be brought forth for a much needed discussion on this topic. However, to make sure our youth are going to be the productive citizens in society, we should be hoping them to be, we have to do more than just *talk* about it. We, as the leaders of today, must take the initiative to *do something* about it.

NOW!!!

Granted, there are issues that are a part of a young person's life that we cannot understand because the fact remains: this is a new generation coming up—a new breed. That means new problems, new barriers to get around, new hindrances, that are affecting their everyday living.

With that said, maybe we—the role models, heroes and saviors in our children's lives, should just fathom that, we can't save the world. We can't do it all! We can't be there for our kids twenty-four hours a day, seven days a week, because it's just not physically possible. We can't be at school in class with them, and we can't be at their jobs.

We just can't do it all!

Yes, as I said before, it's scary. But *they* are *our* children—*our* future—so what can we do? We can love them, share with our youth, and listen to our kids. We can occupy their lives with an unconditional amount of appreciation, showing we value their existence, showing that they're wanted, and needed.

In *TATTOOED TEARS*, Amir struggles with his own issues and demons—the types of things that most kids experience at one time or another in their young lives. But will Amir make it pass the temptations, struggles, and everyday battles that all kids encounter as part of just doing the one thing nature asks of him, growing up?

As a writer, I am *desperately* asking you, the reader, to pay attention to this story carefully. Even though it's a complete work of fiction, I need you to understand that these things really do happen to our children on an everyday basis. Not to *all* kids, but to our youth in general. The problem is that, they constantly feel as if they're alone in the process, and that no one is expecting them to succeed in the first place.

What is also disturbing to me is that, a lot of children are labeled as having certain disorders, after they've made a 'cry for help'. Labels that many, in my opinion—and I stress my opinion, are wrong in various cases—'misdiagnosed' for lack of a better term.

Ritalin is *not* always the answer!

I know from having more than eighteen years of experience, living with a kid that was 'diagnosed' with Attention Deficit Disorder (ADD), Attention Deficit Hyperactive Disorder (ADHD), and admitted to classes designed to meet the 'special needs' of the Behavior-Emotionally Handicapped (BEH).

He took Ritalin for many of those years. I'm not in any way trying to talk down the prescription drug, as it has worked for some, yet Ritalin just didn't always prove to very effective in our household.

Once again, I say that *all* of our children are in danger of failing in life, or taking the wrong path. I say that all of our children are potentially at risk of doing so, because 'growing up', simply isn't the same as it once was.

We can, however, help our youth get through it, be there for them, do what we can for the kids, without robbing them of a childhood.

This is *TATTOOED TEARS*...

Shed some if you'd like.

An excerpt from ***DIRTY WINDOWS*** by
JOI MOORE
A GHETTOHEAT® PRODUCTION

The windows were all painted black…

That was the picture so deeply imbedded in her psyche.

Heat from bodies stacked upon bodies.

Moist vapors of breath and smothering sweat.

A tightly, perfected puzzle…

Put together by the grim reaper himself.

The rank smell of old urine reeked throughout the cramped, narrow space. She wanted so desperately to cry but, knew that there was limited oxygen.

The massive weight on top of her was painful and intense.

The woman drifted in-and-out of consciousness hearing voices and last wishing pleas of dying partygoers—one, the cries of a young man who was trapped two bodies below her, praying for one last time to see his mothers face.

She heard the crushing of bones as many scuffled, trying desperately to free themselves from being squashed alive; their faces, pressed against the locked glassed door at the base of the stairs.

The red light of the exit sign blinked on and off. The only source of light, and a bleak reminder of the deceptiveness of its reasoning that night. Yet through it all, the lady managed to hold tight to the man's dying hand.

The touch of his skin was wet and sticky, covered with fresh blood from his wound. In the mist of all the drama surrounding the two, their love was undeniable.

Faint screams rang out from above and beneath him.

He smiled at her, ignoring the ghastly language.

The wells of the woman's eyes filled with tears, as she managed to lip-sync the words, "I love you" and "I'm sorry". She slowly watched her man's eyes fixate upon hers. It was as if he was tuning out of the lady's life and staring into *Heaven.*

Her heart burned…she no longer cared about the screeching sounds of the rescue sirens, beyond the painted black door. The purple strobe lights were dimming. Repetitive beats of a hot house music mix had played its last number at "Triple Platinum Nightclub", that cold wintry night.

An excerpt from ***SWORDFIGHT*** by
WALTER VICKERIE
A GHETTOHEAT® PRODUCTION

Midway through my last drink, I feel my body growing intensely warm, as Vaughn and I continue our conversation. Although he's short on words, when Vaughn speaks, I can't help but pay attention to everything he says. Turns out that Vaughn has been separated a year from his now ex-boyfriend of four years.

Same old story…

Boy meets boy.

Boy falls in love with boy.

Boy gets bored with boy.

Boy cheats on boy.

Boy breaks up with boy.

Vaughn—being the boy that got his heart broken.

Immediately I empathize with his story. I'm personally not on the market to date seriously, and have resorted to bed-hopping, since most brothers I meet are more talk than substance. So stories of love on the rocks are of particular interest to me because, in my mind, it confirms that relationships are fleeting and ultimately a waste of time.

"So what are you looking for now?" I ask Vaughn, attempting to lighten the mood and get a feel if he's 'substance' or simply sexual sustenance.

"To be honest…I just want to have fun. I spent four years of my life worrying about being a perfect boyfriend, and that didn't work out too well for me. Now I just want to enjoy my life."

"And you should—here's to the New Year!" I say, certain that Vaughn's attainable. We raise our glasses and clink them against one another.

"What are we toasting to?" interrupts Luis.

"To having a good time in *New York!"* Vaughn states, as he squeezes my thigh with his free hand.

"Cheers!" Gabe joins in.

The alluring rhythm of reggae music encourage the four of us onto the crowded dance floor, and I feel as if there's a traveling strobe light overhead. Perhaps it's just in my head, but it seems like we're on display for everyone to gaze and gawk. I love the attention, but keep focus on my current conquest that has me conjuring up thoughts, of how intense the sex with Vaughn and I would be.

Vaughn and Luis dance together, while Gabe and I sandwich them in an intense foursome on the dance floor. I love reggae because it sways the body to give into its wanton desires and leave all inhibitions behind.

The alcohol definitely has me feeling more aggressively flirtatious towards Vaughn. I find my hands traveling along his body like an animal on the prowl. Vaughn's lean and tight swimmer's build feels smooth as hardened clay, as I press up closely against him.

I rest my chin against the rear part of his shoulder while Vaughn cocks his head next to mine. It feels good being this close and connected to another. My eyes are shut, and I can only feel the beat of my heart along with Vaughn's, as they both race towards what seems like a distant finish line.

"You feel so good," I whisper in his ear.

"You feel even better," Vaughn whispers back.

"Gentlemen, we're almost down to the last ten seconds of the year! Grab the one you're with…the one you want to be with…or the one you want to be getting with, and count down with me as we bring in the New Year! TEN…NINE…EIGHT…SEVEN…" announces the DJ.

This is one of those moments that I *don't* want to end. If I could bottle and cork up the feeling, and save it for another day I would. I open my eyes just to make sure Vaughn is real, and not just a figment of my intoxicated imagination. I can see, smell, and touch him so it has to be real. However, the entire room around me has become blurry.

"SIX…FIVE…"

I hear a thunderous chant of voices murmuring something indescribable. I see Gabe and Luis in front of us, but even they seem hazed and distant. The music's tempo has slowed down, and the lyrics are slurred beyond recognition.

I feel flush…feverishly cold…

And agitatedly hot at the same time.

My body feels twice as heavy—something isn't right with me. My grip on Vaughn is weakening, I feel him slipping out of my hands. I'm officially drunk.

"FOUR…THREE…TWO…ONE: *HAPPY NEW YEAR!*" I hear from everyone around us.

An excerpt from ***FOR THE LOVE OF HONEY*** by
RALL
A GHETTOHEAT® PRODUCTION

As Honey quickly makes her way down the back stairway, she's rudely greeted by the rank smell of old, stale urine and trash, which is predominant in the air; many drug deals, sex acts and other foul activities that people normally couldn't do in public, goes on in this area.

Honey, being in the projects for so long, isn't bothered by the harsh stench, as she smiles, skipping down the concrete stairs, having her mind fixed on a plan to get Jahfeak's attention. Suddenly, Honey is completely caught off-guard by the hit man, Ray, as he quietly steps out of the shadows of the dimly lit stairway, grabbing a handful of Honey's hair from behind and snatching her off of her feet, pulling the young girl backwards.

Honey immediately gasps, as the forceful pain being applied to her scalp and neck instantly registers, shocking her thought process into the moment.

Honeys backward motion abruptly stops, as she slams into Ray's torso, her back momentarily resting against his muscular chest. The teenager's fresh scent of baby lotion and powder fills the hit man's nostrils, and Honey's plump, rounded rump, presses against Ray's manhood, which causes him to become instantly aroused. Soon after, Ray lets Honey's hair go, and swiftly places her in a chokehold.

With one arm tightly wrapped around the teen's neck, Ray uses his free hand to fondle Honey's young perky breast, all the while, grinding his bulge against on her backside. The hit man is suddenly overwhelmed with lust and perversion, as Ray now decides to get his freak on, and have a little taste of Honey.

Realizing that she's about to become a victim of one of the many predators within her project, Honey struggles hard to relax, instantly plotting to use her sexuality correctly, in order gain the upper hand in this situation, which is now way out of Honey's control.

Ray—now turned on by the young girl's vulnerability, forcefully slams Honey's face hard into the grimy, tiled wall, instantly bruising and swelling up her face. Instantly, Honey is dazed, struggling to remain conscious, as Ray rapidly runs his free hand up her pink summer dress and violently rips off Honey's white cotton panties.

Fearing that she's in terrible danger of being raped, Honey thinks fast on her feet, hatching a plan to change her position in the situation.

"O-o-o-h, son, you like it rough, huh?" Honey cunningly asks in a seductive whisper.

Now Ray is caught off-guard.

He smiles, thinking of the many ways to violate sweet Honey, his "little project hoe".

"You like this *shit,* don't you? You lil' *bitch,*" Ray replies and smacks her ass.

"That's all you got *nigga?* Slap it harder."

Ray, now squeezing and smacking Honey's smooth, firm behind, isn't holding Honey with the strong grip as he had before, when Ray first forced her face into the wall. Yet and still, he has a hold on Honey, but she's now the one who is in control.

And knows it.

"You like my fat *ass,* don't you? ...I'm *so* hot right now," Honey murmurs through her teeth.

Ray loses all the power as Honey talks tauntingly. Caught in the moment, he somewhat forgets his mission, as Ray releases the pressure off of Honey's neck, slowly turning her around and ripping the front of the young teen's dress wide open; exposing Honey's full bosom. The hit man's only thought now is to put one her bouncing breasts, in his mouth.

Honey—frightfully scared, with face swollen and bruised, manages a smile, knowing that she has Ray right where she wants him.

"C'mon, yo, suck on my titties," Honey insists. Ray then leans forward and licks her young, tender breasts, before gently nibbling on Honey's nipples.

Honey, pretending as if she's enjoying it, passionately tosses her head back before moaning. Honey opens her mouth slowly, carefully slides her tongue to the side, and out comes a small, shiny, double-edged razor that cleverly rested underneath.

An excerpt from ***CLUB AVENUE*** by
JAY BEY
A GHETTOHEAT® PRODUCTION

This is the comprehensive story of Rizzo: a man torn between friends and foes, love and destruction, viewed by the public as a gangster and a social outcast; belonging to a dysfunctional street-crime family. His physical description resembles a "Class A" thug—the *Washington, D.C.* native standing at six feet, dressed today in a black oversized *Enyce* sweater with multi-colored lettering on the front, and a twenty-two-inch platinum necklace with a *Nothing To Lose* pendant hanging, accents Rizzo's attire.

Black cargo pants with deep pockets appear to hold heavy objects, and his feet, snug inside the thick thermal tube socks he wears, are secured in three-quarter length black *Timberland* boots. The outfit Rizzo wears on this particular day is immaculate, in which his black leather *Roca Wear* coat, keeps the "suspected gangster" warm. Usually, on Rizzo's two-week-old cornrows, he sports a ball cap that coordinates with his attire—not this evening. The son of an ex-pimp woke up today, feeling the need to dress up.

Rizzo's haggard face depicts years of hardship: a receding hairline, heavy bags under his eyes from lack of sleep, and scars on Rizzo's rich caramel profile, shows the battle, time has placed upon him. You can tell the man has the age of wisdom in his soul, but barely a few strings on Rizzo's face; he presents an aura of young innocence.

A broad nose with full lips reveals his bloodline, and the truth behind the conquering of the *Carthaginian* general, *Hannibal*—Rizzo's mother is *Italian,* his father of *Moorish* descent.

On this cold, windy fall evening, Rizzo carefully positions himself across the dimly lit street corner, in contemplation of a destiny that's waiting to be fulfilled—in a matter of moments. He takes two more inhales of a personally rolled "cigar", tosses it to the ground, and begins to walk across the cracked asphalt to enter the tavern called "Club Avenue".

Once inside, Rizzo smoothly strolls through the bar, making sure not to draw any attention to himself. Precisely and delicately, he takes the initiative to scan the entire establishment, reason being—he's looking for five individual figures: Joseph Britt, Stanley Pralow, James Heights, Delante Thomas, and Mario Trenton.

As Rizzo moves deeper and stealthily inside "Club Avenue", he calls remembrance to his aid. Out of the multitude of faces, Rizzo sees three that appears familiar, giving reason to why he clutches intently, with the strength of ten men, two silver/black *Smith & Wesson,* 40 caliber semi-automatic pistols.

An excerpt from ***UGLY/BEAUTIFUL: ME*** by
GOD MATH
A GHETTOHEAT® PRODUCTION

My father didn't love us in the correct way.

I don't' think he knew how.

Pops went to the grave like that, leaving us looking for love in all the wrong places.

I still loved him…

My mother tried to teach me how to be a man in a world that seemed to *hate* the sight of me. I must've died a million times under the conditions the world offered me in its embrace.

Lived in the streets.

Grew up in the streets.

I was in love with a "thing" that couldn't love me back in return. I picked up the gun when I found that the fights out there would no longer be fair.

I felt…in control…

Went to war with some of the most *dangerous* cats out there and survived. Fought anyone and *everyone* who threatened my safety, from the streets, to the police, cats at *Rikers Island, Sing-Sing, Auburn, Elmira,* and then some.

I fought to stay alive.

Mayor Koch stood on *City Hall's* steps and called me an animal. That was before I went to trial. He's never been shot four times, beaten by school teachers, hungry, called names by adults when he was a child, handcuffed *naked* in a chicken coop, and literally locked in a basement of a jail.

I sleep next to a toilet…and have done so for twenty-two years now. I guess *Mayor* finally got his wish—I've been caged longer then any animal in a public zoo.

I'm not bitter though.

I don't *hate* anyone.

What I've gone through made me a better and stronger man.

This is "Me" today, verses the "Me" of yesterday—the story of a boy who became a man, under the silent lash of his conditions.

This is *Ugly/Beautiful: Me.*

ghettoheat

GHETTOHEAT® MOVEMENT

GHETTOHEAT® MOVEMENT is a college scholarship fund geared towards young adults within the inner city, pursuing education and careers in Journalism and Literary Arts.

At GHETTOHEAT®, our mission is to promote literacy worldwide. To learn more about GHETTOHEAT® MOVEMENT, or to see how you can get involved, send all inquires to: MOVEMENT@GHETTOHEAT.COM, or log on to GHETTOHEAT.COM

To send comments to CHARLES D. ELLISON, send all mail to:

GHETTOHEAT®, LLC
P.O. BOX 2746
NEW YORK, NY 10027

Attention: CHARLES D. ELLISON

Or e-mail him at: ELLISON@GHETTOHEAT.COM

Artists interested in having their works reviewed for possible consideration at GHETTOHEAT®, send all materials in full with snapshot photo included to:

ghettoheat
P.O. BOX 2746
NEW YORK, NY 10027

Attention: HICKSON, CEO of GHETTOHEAT®

GHETTOHEAT®: THE HOTNESS IN THE STREETS!!!™

ghettoheat

ORDER FORM

Name____

Registration #______________________________(If incarcerated)

Address____

City_________________ State__________ Zip code_________

Phone____________________ E-mail_____________________

Friends/Family E-mail_________________________________

Friends/Family E-mail_________________________________

Books are $15.00 each. Send me the following number of copies of:

__ CONVICT'S CANDY	__ GHETTOHEAT®
__ AND GOD CREATED WOMAN	__ HARDER
__ AND GOD CREATED WOMAN 2	__ HARDER 2
__ GHOST TOWN HUSTLERS	__ TANTRUM
__ GHOST TOWN HUSTLERS 2	__ TANTRUM 2
__ SONZ OF DARKNESS	__ LONDON REIGN
__ SONZ OF DARKNESS 2	__ SKATE ON!
__ SONZ OF DARKNESS 3	__ SKATE ON! 2
__ GAMES WOMEN PLAY	__ CLUB AVENUE
__ DIRTY WINDOWS	__ TATTOOED TEARS
__ DIRTY WINDOWS 2	__ SOME SEXY
__ DIRTY WINDOWS 3	__ SOME SEXY 2
__ FOR THE LOVE OF HONEY	__ SOME SEXY 3

__FOR THE LOVE OF HONEY 2

__UGLY/BEAUTIFUL: ME

__SWORDFIGHT

__TOUGH

ghettoheat

Please send $4.50 to cover shipping and handling. Add a dollar for each additional book ordered. ***Free shipping for convicts.***

Total Enclosed = _________

Please make checks or money orders payable to GHETTOHEAT®. Send all payments to:

GHETTOHEAT®, P.O. BOX 2746, NEW YORK, NY 10027

To order large quantities of books at wholesale prices, contact: HENRI NDOMBO, International Sales Director: 646.281.6108

Or e-mail him at: HENRI@GHETTOHEAT.COM

GHETTOHEAT®: THE HOTNESS IN THE STREETS!!!™

3 1901 04585 8125